PARIS
AT FIRST
LIGHT

BOOKS BY AMANDA LEES

WW2 RESISTANCE SERIES

The Silence Before Dawn

AMANDA LEES

PARIS AT FIRST LIGHT

bookouture

Published by Bookouture in 2022

An imprint of Storyfire Ltd.
Carmelite House
50 Victoria Embankment
London EC4Y 0DZ

www.bookouture.com

ISBN: 978-1-80314-685-0
eBook ISBN: 978-1-80314-684-3

This book is a work of fiction. Whilst some characters and circumstances portrayed by the author are based on real people and historical fact, references to real people, events, establishments, organizations or locales are intended only to provide a sense of authenticity and are used fictitiously. All other characters and all incidents and dialogue are drawn from the author's imagination and are not to be construed as real.

For Julia and Phil

PROLOGUE

5 DECEMBER 1944, HIGHGATE CEMETERY, LONDON

She gazed down at the gravestone, waiting. He was late. Of course he was. Arrogant, like all the rest.

'*Pas de problème*. We have time, don't we, Karl?'

She thought she heard an answering sigh. A freezing blast whistling through the bare branches maybe. Or Marx whispering to her from his grave.

It was exposed up here on the hill, the December wind stroking her face with its icy fingers. Her palms, though, were hot, burning to get hold of those names. She pulled her coat tighter around her. Red. A deliberate choice, along with the blue-and-white scarf knotted around her throat. The colours of the tricolour. Of France. Although he didn't need that clue to spot her.

She was quite alone in the cemetery, a slender figure standing erect, her shoulders squared, just as she had learned to do through the long years of leading her men alone. It was a signal, one that she hoped he would read and understand. She wanted no fuss. This had to be quick and clean.

A crack from her right. She spun round to see him emerge from behind a tombstone.

'How long have you been there?'

He smiled. 'Long enough.'

She didn't rise to it. She had no time for his petty games.

'Did you bring it?'

'Yes.'

'Show me.'

His eyes narrowed in avarice. 'You first.'

She fixed him with a stare that was icier than any gust. 'You're the one selling. I need to see the goods.'

He tried to glare at her down his patrician nose, but he was no match for her froideur. Lucien, that was his name. An old gambling buddy of her husband's. The last time she'd seen him, he'd been smirking as Philippe ordered her to serve wine to his cronies at the card table, her head still exploding from his last onslaught. She remembered his snigger as she inadvertently spilled some and Philippe snarled over her stupidity. Who was the stupid one now?

She tapped her fingers impatiently against her thigh. 'Well?'

He withdrew an envelope from his inside pocket and held it inches from her grasp.

'Oh for God's sake.'

She reached out and snatched it from him, at the same time slamming her other hand down on his wrist, a chop that sent the knife he'd pulled clattering from his fingers to spin across the gravestone.

'That was stupid,' she snarled.

He shrugged. 'You have quite a reputation.'

'So do you. As a cheat and a thief, among other things. A

man who would sell his own mother for a few more francs to waste on the turn of a roulette wheel.'

His smile was still wide. Confident. 'We all have our weaknesses. You have your children, for instance.'

She felt the blood drain from her face, her heart, her entire body, seeping into the cold earth that lay under her feet. Her eyes blazed at him, glittering green shards of hatred.

'How dare you talk about my children,' she hissed.

He cocked his head. 'Sore subject?' he sneered.

She threw the bag at his feet. 'It's all in there. Count it.'

He let out a grunt of satisfaction as he stooped to retrieve it. It would be the last sound he ever made. She took a step forward as he once more stood erect and pressed her pistol into his heart. The sound of the shot was muffled by the folds of his coat, which flew wide as he fell backward onto the gravestone and sprawled, staring sightlessly at the sky. Here was one man who would never snigger at her again.

She picked up the bag that lay unopened and tucked the envelope into her purse.

'*Au revoir*, Karl,' she murmured.

Poetic justice. Her favourite kind. She could think of no finer place for the execution of a fascist collaborator than the grave of a celebrated German communist. Not that she cared one way or the other. She had seen enough of war to know that evil was everywhere.

She glanced at her watch. Better hurry. The car would be waiting.

Sure enough, it was parked discreetly just beyond the gates, an anonymous black Daimler, its engine purring.

'Everything all right?' enquired the driver as she hopped in.

'Everything is perfect,' she responded.

As they swooped down the hill and headed out of London, her fingers reached for the envelope, stroking it as if she could somehow absorb its secrets. She must not open it until she got there. Those were her orders. And much as she was used to defying orders, she knew this was one she had to obey.

She would find out soon enough. The names. Perhaps one name in particular. It was one thing to suspect, quite another to know for certain. Then again, maybe she had always known. It was why she had done the things she'd done. Why she would continue to do them until her dying breath.

ONE

An hour and a half outside London, the roads grew narrower and the hedges higher until, at last, we turned up a tree-lined drive that led to a Georgian mansion. We drew to a halt in a swirl of gravel, and the driver leaped out to open the door for me. I could see someone standing on the steps under the pillared portico, waiting to greet me, tall and resplendent in his uniform. As I emerged from the car, our eyes caught and held for a fraction too long. I looked away first, my heart beating against my chest like a trapped baby sparrow.

'Lieutenant Diaz.'

He snapped to attention and saluted me. 'At your service, ma'am. Or should I say madame? And it's captain now.'

'Juliette will do. Congratulations, Captain.'

He grinned, white teeth bared in what I'm sure he thought was a devastating smile. 'Come on in. We've been waiting for you.'

I had almost forgotten his American swagger. There was so much I wanted to say. So much I had to hold back.

'Am I the last?'

'You are, but I understand you had an appointment to keep.'

'I did.'

'And how did that go?'

'Perfectly.'

There was a hint of puzzlement in his eyes as he held my gaze for a second, perhaps finally hearing the note in my voice, the one that told him not to push his luck.

'Excellent. Follow me. May I take your coat?'

I shrugged it off and handed it to him, thankful for the slacks I'd chosen to wear along with a sensible sweater. It was hardly my most alluring outfit, and that was a good thing as far as Diaz was concerned.

He led me into the drawing room, where French windows framed the lawn beyond, heavy silk curtains in keeping with the old, but expensive, furniture and the oil paintings that adorned the walls. Seated on the sofa and in the various armchairs that dotted the room were Christine, Marianne and Jack, among a group of familiar faces. The old crowd were all here.

'Now that we're all present and correct,' said Diaz. 'You can meet our new boss.'

I exchanged looks with the others. Their faces were as carefully composed as mine must be. All except Jack, who nudged Marianne and dropped her a wink.

Then the door opened and a slender figure entered. I stared, incredulous. *Mon Dieu.* Surely not.

She glided across the room and took her place beside the fireplace, where a pile of files sat on a low coffee table.

'Suzanne.'

I wasn't even sure if I had spoken aloud.

She smiled, encompassing us all with her gaze, lingering

as she looked at Christine. An unspoken accord passed between the two of them. Of course. Suzanne had trained Christine at Beaulieu, although I always wondered what exactly that training involved.

'It is wonderful to see you all again,' she said.

'Ladies and gentlemen, meet your new director,' said Diaz. 'Suzanne was one of our finest agents in the field, as I'm sure you realise. She's the perfect person to lead our new organisation.'

She inclined her head at him. 'Thank you for that introduction.'

I sat straighter. There was no trace now of a French accent. And hers was perfect. She was good, whoever she really was.

'As you know,' Suzanne went on, 'the Resistance has been officially disbanded. General de Gaulle has made it clear SOE is no longer welcome in France. The same goes for any other foreign service. He wants to pretend that we never existed and that resistance was entirely down to the French.'

'*Putain*,' I muttered under my breath. De Gaulle was the man to lead France right now, but his ingratitude was embarrassing.

She looked at me. 'Which means this is the perfect time to commence operations as a new clandestine service independent of any other. You will operate outside of your former organisations, although we will, of course, work with them when necessary.'

A murmur ran through the room, a collective rumble of excitement.

'And what is the name of our new organisation if we are no longer SOE or the Resistance?' I asked.

Suzanne smiled. 'We thought,' she said, 'that it would be

a fitting tribute to our brothers and sisters in the Resistance, as well as to the fine work you did, to give you the most simple but obvious name.'

'What is that?'

'The Network.'

TWO

I felt another frisson ripple through the room. Not a rumble this time but an electric current. We had a name, a purpose. Now all we needed was a mission.

'Let me get straight down to business,' said Suzanne. 'We know from intercepted messages that German fighter forces along the Western Front have quadrupled in recent weeks. We also know that road and rail movements have increased, which indicates an imminent attack, and we believe they intend to try to separate the British and Allied armies from the American troops. Divide and conquer, if you will. Most significantly, two days ago, we received intelligence of a plot by Hitler.'

She paused as if weighing up her words. 'He plans to murder Churchill and Eisenhower simultaneously in two carefully planned assassinations.'

This time, the hush that fell was laden with shock. After five years of war, nothing should have surprised us. That Hitler was insane was evident, but this was beyond belief.

Suzanne bent and picked up the files, distributing them among us.

'His plans are complex and involve committed fascists here in Britain as well as 250,000 German prisoners of war they're going to liberate from their prison camps to march on London. We know that a number of those fascists, some of whom are ex-detainees, are planning a "social" gathering in London on the sixteenth of December. We think that's the day they're going to carry out Hitler's plans.'

'That's less than two weeks away,' said Marianne.

'Indeed. You will find details of our chief suspects here in your file as well as double agents and collaborators who are still at large in France, more specifically in Paris. We have heard that they're using German soldiers dressed in US Army uniforms to infiltrate the troops stationed there as well as on the front line.'

'Surely the US troops will pick them up?' said Marianne.

'These men were specially chosen and trained by a man called Otto Skorzeny, Hitler's pet commando and the man he sent to rescue Mussolini. They speak perfect English and even learned American slang by associating with US prisoners of war.'

'Our troops are challenging anyone they consider suspicious,' added Diaz. 'They ask them all kinds of trivia questions only a real American would know. But it's a huge task. We have hundreds of thousands of soldiers out there.'

'That's why we need to attack the Germans from the inside,' said Suzanne. 'Get to them through their agents and collaborators so we stop Hitler in his tracks.'

She looked at me. 'Juliette, I believe you have something for me?'

'I do.'

My mind flashed back to earlier this morning, to an image of that man, Lucien, lying sprawled on the grave, staring up at a sky he would never see again. Was he still there? Perhaps. But even on a bitter day like this, someone was sure to visit the cemetery and discover him. No matter. I had been careful to leave no clues.

I withdrew the envelope from my purse and handed it to Suzanne. She sliced it open with her thumb and pulled out a single, folded sheet of paper, her brow puckering as she studied it before once more addressing the room.

'This is a list of the names of collaborators we believe are aiding the Germans in their plans to assassinate General Eisenhower in Paris on the same day they attack Churchill and take London,' said Suzanne. 'We know there's another list of members of the Right Club here in Britain, recorded in a ledger referred to as the Red Book.'

'The Right Club?' asked Marianne.

'Fascists and Nazi supporters, some of whom we believe are involved in the plot to kill Churchill. You'll find details of the ones we have already identified in your files, but if we can get hold of the Right Club list, that will really help.'

I flipped through my file, taking in the faces staring haughtily out at me. One name immediately rang a bell.

'Colonel Buckman. Isn't he...?'

'The traitor we discussed back at the chateau,' said Diaz. 'Inserted into SOE to keep tabs on us all except that we, along with MI5, have been keeping tabs on him.'

I glanced at Marianne. 'The man who ran Marcus and Guy.'

Her face was set, her eyes dulling at the memory of her brother, another traitor. Stupid boy. He'd died for an ideal that didn't exist and, in doing so, broke his sister's heart.

Marianne, as ever, tilted her chin in defiance, but I could see the pain etched across every feature.

'The same,' said Suzanne, 'but we effectively neutralised him some time ago. It's the unknowns we need to worry about. The names that are not in that file but in the Red Book.'

She looked at Christine, sinuously coiled in one corner of the silk upholstered sofa. 'It's your job to find that book or at least some of the names in it. The police took it from the flat of a man named Tyler Kent, a cipher clerk at the American Embassy who was a member of the Right Club and is currently serving time at His Majesty's pleasure. We think the intelligence services have the original, but we know there were copies made.'

Christine took a sip from her tea. Somehow, she managed to make even that look seductive.

'Let me guess. Those names include members of the Establishment?'

'That's what we believe.'

Christine's lips curled in the smile that wilted grown men in seconds. 'I'll get straight on it.'

Suzanne looked at Marianne and Jack, sitting inches apart, the air between them intertwining even though they were not.

'The names in the book are the ringleaders, but we know they have foot soldiers, quite literally. German and Italian prisoners of war as well as internees, all of them prepared to do anything for the Fatherland. I need you two to infiltrate their camps and find out what they're planning.'

'Delighted to,' said Jack.

'As for you,' said Suzanne, turning the beam of her gaze

on me, 'you will be handling the Paris operation along with Diaz here.'

I stared at her, feeling darts of alarm shoot along my spine. Not Diaz. He was too dangerous. Too distracting. Too damn unreliable.

'Why Diaz? I mean, I'm sure he knows what he's doing, but I am Parisian. I still have friends and contacts there. I can handle this alone. Or you could come with me. Your French is perfect.'

'Thanks for the vote of confidence,' said Diaz.

I ignored him. He had already betrayed any confidence I might have had in him. The man certainly did not deserve a second chance.

'Captain Diaz also speaks perfect French and is crucial to this operation,' said Suzanne. 'You'll understand why when I give you your orders. I cannot risk being embedded in Paris for that length of time. After all, I ran a brothel that serviced half the Gestapo along with most of the Vichy government. I could be arrested as a collaborator.'

I didn't quite buy her explanation, but I had no other choice. She looked at us all, tiny as a ballerina and yet standing taller than any man. Her girls at the brothel had drugged those clients as well as infecting them with venereal disease, all in the name of the Resistance. I could only hope they had been spared the vengeful attacks on women who had slept with the enemy. There were so many like them, silent heroines, punished for keeping their secrets still.

Suzanne inclined her head once more, signalling that we were dismissed. 'Now I will meet with each of you individually or in your pairs. It's important that you don't know the details of each separate mission so you cannot be compromised.'

I stared at my hands, feeling that itch in my palm again. I needed to know. I had to hear that they were safe.

'I want to go first,' I said. 'I have to. Please.'

I could hear my voice rising, feel the glances of the others in the room, but I didn't care.

'I understand.' Suzanne's voice was low, her tone soothing. She knew. 'Follow me.'

I got to my feet, twisting my hands together so that no one could see them tremble. These were my friends. My comrades in arms.

Yet in this, I was alone.

THREE

'Where are they?'

I was barely through the door when the words came bursting out of me.

'They're safe. Why don't you sit down?'

'I don't want to sit down. I want to know where they are.'

I fixed my eyes on her as she moved to a couch by the window. This room was smaller than the other, a desk taking up one corner along with a filing cabinet and bookshelves that lined the walls. It felt far more like an office. Or the nerve centre of an organisation.

'I can't tell you where they are, for your safety as well as theirs.'

Of course. I was about to head into the field again. The less I knew, the better.

'Then at least tell me they are in England.'

'They are in England, in a safe house. Your mother is with them.'

'Oh thank God.'

I felt my knees go, took a step and sank onto the couch beside her. A cool hand covered mine.

'Nothing will happen to them, I promise you. I need you to focus on this mission.'

'Is that all I am to you? A weapon to be used against the enemy?'

'You know that's not true. I want you to be safe too. Or as safe as possible. If you are distracted, you are vulnerable. You have to stay strong, Juliette, for yourself and your children.'

Strong. I knew all about that. It was how I had been for years, at least outwardly. I had only let my guard slip once and that was in front of Marianne. She knew. She understood what it was like to be a woman on her own, leading the kind of men who would do the things we did.

A rap on the door signalled that my private audience was over. Suzanne squeezed my hand before releasing it.

'That will be Diaz,' she said. 'I have to brief you both. You leave tonight for Paris.'

'So soon?'

Although I knew I couldn't see my children, something twisted inside me, a wrench at the thought of leaving them once more. My precious Nicolas and Natalie, looking so grown up now compared to when I last saw them, although they were still only eight and six. After four years apart, I had spent just a few glorious hours with them in Paris a couple of weeks ago, before I had to return to London. They followed three days later with my mother, going straight to their safe house. I hadn't seen them since.

'Juliette, are you sure you can handle this? If not, say so and I'll send someone else.'

I stared at her and felt the fight flood back through me. 'I can handle this. I want to handle this.'

'Good.'

She opened the door. 'Captain Diaz. Come on in.'

He filled the room even before he entered it. But that was Diaz. His bravado preceded him.

'I was just telling Juliette that you leave tonight for Paris. There is no time to waste.'

His eyes swept lazily over me. Nothing and no one hurried that man.

'Don't forget to pack your dancing shoes.'

'What do you mean?'

'I hear Paris is once more the party town,' he drawled.

'You seem to forget that restrictions are still in force. People queue for bread every day, and many are starving. I heard that Josephine Baker sold her jewels to help feed those people. I hardly think that calls for a party.'

'Actually, Juliette, he's right, in a way. Captain Diaz has been seconded to the public relations division of the Supreme Headquarters Allied Expeditionary Force now that Paris is liberated and the Germans are on the run in Belgium and the Netherlands. Your cover story is that you're a journalist who has spent the war in London. This gives you the perfect opportunity to liaise with Diaz. More than liaise, in fact. You will make it appear as if you have started a relationship. Specifically, you will dine together regularly at the Ritz.'

I stared at her. This couldn't be happening.

'Why?'

'To enable you to spend time together without attracting attention. The staff at the Ritz were active members of the Resistance. The barman, Monsieur Meier, ran a kind of postbox, receiving and passing on messages right under the noses of the Germans. They requisitioned the hotel for the

Luftwaffe. Apparently Goering favoured the Imperial Suite.'

'Didn't a number of collaborators stay there too?' asked Diaz.

'Exactly. Some are still there, pretending their friendships with the Nazis never happened. There are also several correspondents passing through, including Mr Hemingway. All very useful to this mission. You are to make contact with Monsieur Meier, who will act as a conduit for information.'

'The Ritz,' I said, still trying to absorb my orders. 'I haven't been there since before the war. Monsieur Meier makes the most perfect martini.'

'I'll be sure to order you one,' said Diaz.

'I can order my own, thank you.'

Suzanne pinned me down with a look I'd seen before – one that brooked no argument. 'Juliette, it's imperative for this mission that you and Diaz appear to be a couple. It will help protect you. We also want you to offer to work with your former boss. He's started a new paper, *La Vie*.'

'You want me to work with Jean Levesque?'

The man who had taught me everything I knew about journalism and who was connected to everyone worth knowing in Paris.

'He's another way into the circles where many of those who collaborated mix. Some have already reinvented themselves as supporters of the Resistance. People like Pierre Taittinger, who now pretend to have been secretly working against the Nazis all along.'

'Taittinger as in the champagne?' asked Diaz.

'The very same. That's another good reason for you two to appear to be a couple. You can cosy up to these people without fear of consequences.'

'You think my having a lover would stop some of them?' I snorted. 'I can handle those idiots.'

'I'm sure you can. Captain Diaz, you will be stationed in the Hotel Scribe along with the rest of the public relations department and war correspondents. That puts you in a perfect position to keep your ear to the ground as well as tapping into their sources. You will also be visiting the SHAEF headquarters at Versailles where Eisenhower is based, and we already have a man in place by the name of Dick Ward.'

'Sounds good to me.'

'Juliette, we thought you would fit right back into the Left Bank circles you frequented before the war so we have an apartment for you in Saint-Germain. We use it precisely because there is no concierge, so you can come and go as you please.'

'Sounds way more fun than my billet,' drawled Diaz. 'I had no idea you were so bohemian.'

'I'm not.'

He still had that way of getting right under my skin. Damn him.

'When I was working as a journalist in Paris, that was where all the writers and artists gathered, so naturally, I was there too.'

'I had you down as the kind of woman who lived in some genteel neighbourhood and mixed in high society.'

I arched an eyebrow. 'That was a long time ago.'

Before I left my husband and the life that kept me chained to him.

'There's another reason we have chosen that particular building for you. A man named Harry King. He's British, a former double agent and conman who worked for the SS in

Paris. When they left, he went into hiding, sometimes staying with one of his women who lives two floors below your new apartment.'

'You want me to get to know him?'

Suzanne shook her head. 'Far too dangerous. He's a nasty piece of work but bright. He may well rumble you and compromise the mission. Instead, we want you to keep tabs on him. Bug the apartment where he's staying. Follow him and find out who he's meeting. We believe he's a key part of this. On no account try to stop him. We need him to lead us to the top dogs, the people who are actually running the show.'

'I'll do my best.'

'I know you will.'

Suzanne pulled the envelope from her pocket, the one for which I had killed a man only that morning.

She handed it to me. 'I think it's time you had a look at this.'

Such an ordinary piece of paper, thin and smooth under my fingers. I scanned the neatly typed names, Harry King among them. One or two others were familiar. And then I saw it, leaping out at me as if it was typed in red ink rather than black. A name. His name.

'*Mon Dieu,*' I gasped.

Although I was half-expecting it, it was still a shock to see it there, cemented in type.

'What is it?'

Diaz reached for the list, but I snatched it away.

'He has to know, Juliette,' Suzanne murmured. 'He's part of this mission too.'

I handed it to him, my eyes averted, hating the way the paper shook as my hand trembled.

'I don't understand,' said Diaz.

'Here, look. This name.' I stabbed at it with my finger. 'Philippe de Brignac. My husband.'

'You're married?'

'I was. I left him.'

'Because he's a collaborator?'

'I left him before the war but yes, his political inclinations were one reason.'

'And now he's on this list.'

'We believe he's the ringleader,' said Suzanne. 'He's proving a difficult man to pin down. We've had agents trying to track him with no luck. But with you there, he won't be able to resist. That's why you must make it known that you're back by calling on the right people as well as working with Levesque. Specifically, your aunt, who is, I understand, friends with his mother. We need you to flush him out. Act as bait.'

I closed my eyes for a brief moment, then forced them open. I had to face this. Had to do it.

'And then?'

Suzanne looked straight at me. 'You find out what he's up to before you stop him in his tracks.'

'How?'

'By killing him.'

I thought of my children, of my son who looked so like his father. My voice when it came out was barely a whisper.

'It will be a pleasure.'

FOUR

17 AUGUST 1944, THE CHATEAU, PROVENCE

I turned away from the window, blinking back tears. It was both heartbreaking and wonderful to see Marianne's brother driven away to safety. By tonight Edward would be in a hospital in England, the torture wounds Klaus Barbie had inflicted upon him tended by skilled doctors and nurses. Hopefully he would recover physically in time, although the wounds inflicted on his mind and spirit might take longer to heal.

'A penny for them.'

I hadn't seen Diaz standing there, framed by the doorway.

'What do you mean?'

'Oh nothing. Just a saying. Why are you crying?'

'I'm not crying.'

'You are. Your cheeks are wet.'

The man could be so obtuse.

'I know what you're thinking,' he added. 'Why the hell doesn't the damn Yank give it a rest?'

At that, I laughed.

'There you go. That's better.'

He pulled a handkerchief from his pocket and handed it to me. 'Rough day?'

'Not at all. Well, no rougher than any other. It was just... I was just...'

'Watching Edward leave? I know. I was out there. One of the bravest men I've ever seen. Between you and me, I had a lump in my throat too.'

'You did?'

Surely not. Diaz always struck me as irrepressibly upbeat. Or maybe just irrepressible. It was something to do with that way he had of looking at you, as if he knew all kinds of amazing secrets he wanted to share.

'Of course. I know you think I'm an insensitive bastard, but I can cry just like the next man. Or woman.'

'I don't think you're insensitive.'

'No?'

Why had I never noticed his eyes before? Or at least, never noticed how they liquified, like molten caramel, when you really looked into them.

'Want to go for a walk?'

'I'm sorry?'

'A walk. With me. We could go up to that plateau. You look like you could do with some fresh air.'

I stalled, trying to think of an excuse. There was none. Maybe, for once, I could do something just for pleasure. 'I'd love to.'

'Great. Come on then.'

We slipped out the back door and made our way up the hill behind the chateau, to the plateau where Diaz and the others had first parachuted in what felt like months ago but was, in fact, only weeks. I could smell the lavender before we crested the ridge, wafting towards us from the rows we'd planted to disguise the landing strip.

'That scent always reminds me of France,' said Diaz.

'It's evocative, isn't it? My mother sprayed lavender water on all our linens at home so it reminds me of childhood. Of home.'

I could feel him glance at me as we stood, staring down at the fields far below, purple and gold swathes of yet more lavender and sunflowers, the imperial ribbons that decorated Provence in high summer.

'Where is home?'

'Paris.'

'Do you miss it?'

A sudden flash of my children nestling up to their grandma as she read them a story. 'I miss my family.'

He smiled, a different, gentler smile, his eyes wistful. 'So do I.'

I gestured to the rock behind us. 'Shall we sit here? You can tell me about them.'

A haze was settling over the valley below, the breeze picking up here on the plateau as the sky deepened from azure to a soft violet. Soon the sun would start to slide down to the horizon and the cicadas to sing, sending it to sleep with a lullaby. We perched on a rock, Diaz dusting it down for me before I took my place.

'You're quite the gentleman,' I teased.

'For a barbarian, you mean?'

'You know I didn't mean that and I don't think it.'

He half-turned towards me, tilting my face with his fingers, his touch featherlight. Even so, it sent electric shocks thrilling through me.

'You remind me of someone,' he murmured.

'Someone good, I hope.'

For some reason, I was having trouble getting my words out, never mind breathing.

'Very good. Like you. You have integrity, Juliette. I've seen that so many times. You're kind and courageous and just so damn beautiful.'

'I...'

He cut off whatever I was about to say with a kiss that seemed to last forever yet was still over far too soon. If it had felt like an electric shock when he touched me, this was even more intense, heat pulsating through me in waves that kept on crashing, my body begging for more even as my mind tried to work out what the hell was happening. When at last he drew back, I was still trying to make sense of it.

'I've been wanting to do that for a very long time,' he said.

'You have?'

'Since the moment I first laid eyes on you.'

For once, I was speechless.

'We'll all be leaving here soon. I'm being sent back home for a couple of months. May I write to you while I'm away?'

'If you would like to.'

He raised my hand to his lips and kissed that too. 'I'd like that very much.'

My mind was still whirling, my body stunned. This was Diaz, who I had alternately despised and secretly rather liked. I thought I had been imagining those moments throughout these past months when our eyes met and connected or when he annoyed me far too much over something trivial. I should have known then that I was overreacting. And the reason I was overreacting was because, somehow, he got right under my skin.

'I'm going from here to Paris and then on to London. There's a post office box address I can give you.'

He looked at me, his eyes searching. Then he took my hand and raised it to his lips. 'I'll see you in London, but until then, I'll write as often as I can. I want to get to know you better, Juliette. I want you to know me. The real me. Not the one you've gotten to know here.'

I could feel the warmth from him flooding through my skin. It was as if the sun had broken through the clouds of my own doubt and I was seeing him clearly for the first time.

'I would love that,' I said. 'Maybe we should start now?'

And so we talked on and on, of everything and nothing but mostly of our hopes and dreams, until the cicadas were in full-throated chorus and the sun had all but disappeared beneath the horizon, the breeze sending wafts of lavender our way. I could smell it still every time I checked the post in the weeks and months that followed only to find nothing from him. Eventually, I gave up. Back there, on that ridge, it was perfumed with promise. It was only later it became the scent of betrayal.

FIVE

The apartment was tiny but perfect. I flung open the windows overlooking a courtyard below and breathed in the Paris air. It felt heavier than before, redolent with all that its inhabitants had suffered during the years of occupation. I had passed a queue of men and women on the street, waiting patiently outside a bakery for their rations. They seemed weary, their chatter muted and their faces resigned. Paris may have been liberated, but its people were still enslaved by their memories.

It was time to get to work. First things first, I needed to sweep the place. The SS, in particular, were adept at bugging locations and phone lines, as we had learned to our cost. They might have physically left Paris, but they were still capable of listening in from afar. There were also those they had left behind, the collaborators and agents who had gone underground to escape the vengeance of the people and were all the more dangerous for it, like rats in sewers, unseen but very much there. People like Harry King.

I unscrewed light fittings and doorknobs, stripped apart

the telephone, searching under furniture and behind pictures for tell-tale wires or tiny devices. When I flung open the wardrobe door in my bijou bedroom it was to find outfits for all occasions hanging, ready for me. I pulled out a black evening dress, its shoulders embroidered with silver thread, a chiffon tie at the neck. Nina Ricci. The fabric felt whisper soft under my fingers; the cut was sublime. And it was exactly the right size for me.

'Suzanne,' I murmured.

This bore all her hallmarks. In the same way she'd kept clothes for fugitive agents in her Lyon apartments, she'd made sure I was outfitted correctly for Paris. The woman was brilliant at what she did.

I pulled open the drawers. They, too, were stuffed with underwear, nightwear, sweaters and tops. I swooped on the contents of one drawer, pulling out silk stockings with cries of delight. Perched on a hatstand, a fedora and a little veiled number for evening. On the dressing table, an array of lipsticks and powders, perfume and face creams. I picked up the perfume and sprayed myself with it. Femme de Rochas – my favourite. She had thought of everything, including the fact that Parisian women had made a point of looking their very best throughout the occupation as an act of defiance. I would have to follow suit if I was to fit back in.

Now I understood why Suzanne insisted I travel light, not that I had too much to bring after my years with the Maquis.

I unpacked my sparse wardrobe within minutes. My equipment took rather longer as I retrieved my pistols, knives and ammunition from the concealed bottom of my suitcase. France wasn't quite free of the Germans, and there were dangers everywhere, even among our own.

There was a safe within the apartment, hidden at the back of a cupboard in the kitchenette. It took some rummaging between old jars of jam and packets of flour left behind by previous occupants, but I finally located the correct point to press, feeling the wood give and slide back to reveal a dial set into the safe door. I recited the combination in my head as I turned it to and fro, my fingers sensitive to the slightest change, until I heard that all-important click.

The safe door swung open, and I stashed the larger Welrod pistol inside along with my jackknife and spare ammunition. Then I snapped my pistol belt around my waist and slotted the smaller Colt into it, tugging my sweater down to conceal it. Thank God it was winter. It would be much harder to hide the bulge under a light summer dress.

I chose my outfit with care. A sensible skirt that would allow me to run if necessary paired with a caramel cashmere sweater. My mother's pearls. The silk scarf at my throat that I had worn to kill only yesterday. My aunt wouldn't get the message either, but it made me feel good to show my colours one way or another. The colours of France. The true France. The country my brave men had defended to the last and which was now free of the enemy. I would do everything in my power to keep it that way.

It took me just over an hour to walk from my apartment in the 6th arrondissement to my aunt's home in the 16th. I wanted to reacquaint myself with Paris rather than take a bus or a vélo-taxi, and many metro stations were still closed. On foot, I could once more absorb the sounds, the smells and the sights that had accompanied me through childhood and beyond. I loved the way the neighbourhoods changed as I passed through the different arrondissements, the bohemian 6th giving way to the more formal 7th as the Eiffel Tower rose above the chic boutiques and gardens of Faubourg Saint-Germain, the Seine moving inexorably beneath the Bir-Hakeim bridge I crossed.

Everywhere there were still signs of the aftermath of the occupation. Shops were stocked with meagre rations and the people looked emaciated, especially in the poorer districts. Even the roads were far quieter than I remembered as fuel was still so scarce. Now and then a military vehicle roared past adorned with the stars of the US Army, and I sent out a silent cheer coupled with a jolt of trepidation. Were there Germans even now among those US soldiers, infiltrating them, their accents so good they were undetectable unless challenged by someone in the know?

As I approached my aunt's street, I saw the sign for Avenue Foch where the Gestapo had been headquartered, the neighbours kept awake night after night by the agonised screams that emitted from the building. So many had been tortured there before being sent to Fresnes Prison and the camps after that. I only knew some of their names, brave men and women of the Resistance and SOE along with ordinary citizens who had the misfortune to be Jewish, communist or in some other way a target for Nazi brutality. My old comrade in arms from Lyon, Antoine, still didn't know if his Jewish family were alive or even where they had been taken.

How my aunt could countenance even being civil to the Germans while this was happening was beyond me. I had to take a deep breath before announcing myself to the concierge at her building.

She was typical of her profession, an elderly woman whose sharp eyes saw too much and whose mouth remained shut only when she chose. Some concierges had been stalwart supporters of the Resistance, warning of raids and hiding Jewish families. Others had denounced them instead, pocketing their thirty pieces of silver as a reward for their betrayal. I wondered into which camp this one fell.

She glanced at the scarf around my throat and then admitted me with nothing more than a nod before shutting the door to her own tiny apartment once more, a lodge that no doubt was furnished in stark contrast to the good antique furniture and Persian carpets that greeted me as my aunt's maid opened the door.

'Juliette. This is a surprise.'

My aunt did not rise from her armchair but extended a hand, indicating I should sit on the couch opposite under a portrait of my uncle, long since deceased, no doubt worn out by her demands. She was still a handsome woman, some years older than my papa. Or older than Papa would have been. She was slim, as fashion dictated, but in a healthy way, unlike those poor, starving souls I'd seen en route. But then, the wealthy had thrived during the occupation while many others barely survived. It was yet another divide in a city already fractured by the war.

I remembered why I was here and attempted a smile. 'It's good to see you again, Tante Lucie.'

'Is it?'

She rang the bell beside her and, when the maid reappeared, ordered coffee without asking what I would prefer.

'To what do we owe this pleasure, after all these years?' she said, spitting the word out as if it physically hurt her.

'I have just arrived back in Paris. Naturally, the first person I wanted to see was you.'

My aunt peered at me over her spectacles. They were about her only adornment. Otherwise, she still favoured widow's weeds in the form of a black dress – Chanel if I wasn't mistaken – along with the enormous diamond ring that my uncle had given her to mark their engagement. I suspected she continued to wear mourning clothes long after his death only because black suited her so well.

'Very good of you,' she said, her words dripping with vinegar. 'You will forgive me if I'm a little surprised you have the nerve to visit me after what happened to your poor father.'

I stared at her. 'I have no idea what you mean.'

'Really? You have no idea that he died refusing to reveal your whereabouts?'

I felt something try to burst its way up from deep within me, not so much a scream as a roar of disbelief.

'No,' I whispered. 'I had no idea. Maman told me Papa was arrested, but she didn't know what happened to him after that.'

My aunt snorted. 'Is that what she said? Silly woman. Always trying to protect you. The truth is, my dear, that your poor papa, my brother, was tortured to death by the Gestapo because they wanted him to tell them where they could find you. He refused to and so they killed him.'

I buried my face in my hands. My sweet, gentle papa subjected to the inhuman cruelty meted out by our conquerors. The Gestapo were especially vicious, employing all kinds of implements to inflict maximum pain.

'No point crying now,' said my aunt. 'What's done is done.'

I raised my head, swiping the tears from my cheeks with a shaking hand.

'And you blame me,' I said. 'You blame me for what those Nazi bastards did to him. Those German brutes you cosied up to while my papa remained a true patriot.'

'Patriot? Is that what you call it? The man was a fool. He died defending someone who did not even stay here in Paris but fled as soon as it fell.'

I looked at her, at this woman with her turkey neck that gobbled with indignation, eyes glassy with self-pity and stupidity.

'Where do you think I *fled*, as you put it?'

She shrugged, staring straight ahead as if pretending I was no longer present.

'I'll tell you where I went,' I said, my voice rising to match the anger that threatened to spill over into hot tears once more, catching myself just in time. I had to stick to my cover story come what may, even if it cost me the satisfaction of seeing her face on hearing the truth. 'I went to London,' I said. 'To work with de Gaulle's Free France and as a journalist, serving my country. Exposing the truth of what was happening to people like my poor papa, even though I didn't know it then.'

I could hear myself choking on my words now, but I didn't care. She sat, still as a statue, barely flinching when I slammed my fist down on her precious coffee table, sending cups rattling and silver scattering.

'My papa was a hero. A true Frenchman. Do you not think it kills me too to know that he died defending me? As for you insulting my mother, how dare you? She is twice the woman you will ever be.'

She blinked then, a slow blink that only emphasised the malevolence of her tone.

'I don't care how you feel, Juliette. It has nothing to do with me. You are as gullible and foolish as that son of mine who calls himself a communist. And now, if you will excuse me, I have better things to do than sit here and entertain you.'

'Like call on your fascist friends maybe?'

It slipped out before I could stop myself.

She reached for her bell again.

'My niece will be leaving now,' she said to the maid.

I rose, looking down at her for a moment. 'No wonder Papa always hated you,' I said. 'Guillaume too, no doubt.'

She twisted her mouth in a sour little smile. 'Goodbye, Juliette.'

'*Au revoir,* Tante Lucie.'

I wanted to leave her wondering when she might see me again. If she would ever see me again. I fully intended that she would once I knew the truth of her dealings with the Germans. Then there was my husband's mother. I refused to think of her as my mother-in-law. No doubt Tante Lucie would be scurrying over to see Pauline to share the news of her vile niece who was back in Paris. The niece who had taken her husband's children away from him. I was surprised she hadn't prodded me about them as well. No doubt she would have, given time. Still, at least I'd accomplished what I came to do. Now all I had to do was wait for the news to reach Philippe's ears. In the meantime, I would mourn my papa all over again in the only way I knew how – by continuing the fight and completing our mission.

I had my hand on the street door when the concierge called out to me.

'Leaving so soon?'

I turned. Her gaze was less beady now, although she was still scrutinising me from top to bottom.

'You don't remember me, do you?' she said.

'I'm sorry. I don't.'

'My husband was the caretaker here before he died, the useless wretch. Drank himself into an early grave. I used to see you come and go with your parents when you were a little girl.'

'Of course. I didn't recognise you, madame. It's been a while.'

She came closer, pressing a piece of paper into my hand. 'This is your cousin's address,' she said.

'Guillaume doesn't live here anymore?'

She shook her head and pressed a finger to her lips. 'He lives in Saint-Germain now. He's studying art, or so he says.'

She sniffed, her eyes rolling in disbelief.

'I see. Thank you. I will contact him.'

'Your parents were always very gracious to me. I was sorry to hear about your father.'

It was my turn to study her, to try to make an educated guess which side of the fence she fell on.

'He was a great man,' I murmured, the words seizing my throat. 'I'm only sorry I didn't see him before... I went to London, you see. To work for Free France and cover the war as a journalist from there.'

'He was and he would have been proud of you.'

The tears welled then. 'Thank you.'

I turned away, not wanting her to see me cry.

'May God go with you,' she called out after me. 'Give my regards to your cousin. He's on the side of the people too.'

I pocketed the piece of paper she'd given me and waved in response. My cousin Guillaume. I hadn't seen him since he was a sulky teenager. My aunt always referred to him as her mistake, the baby who miraculously appeared when she was past forty and past caring, although my uncle had doted on him. When he died, my aunt blamed her son. It was no wonder Guillaume had left home as soon as he could.

I would drop a message at his residence. He could be a

useful contact, especially if, as the concierge implied, he was some kind of activist.

I glanced up at my aunt's apartment as I reached the end of her street, wondering if she was already on the telephone to her friend Pauline, my husband's mother. I hoped so.

The trap was set. Now all I needed was for the rat to appear.

SIX

It was getting dark by the time I returned to the apartment, having dropped off a note at the scruffy hotel where my cousin Guillaume apparently lived. Soon it would be time for an aperitif. I knew just the place. Café de Flore was a five-minute walk away, on the corner of Boulevard Saint-Germain and Rue Saint-Benoît. I had no idea who made up the usual crowd now, but it was time to find out. I stuffed my notebooks and pens into the large canvas bag I'd purchased expressly for the purpose. It was exactly the kind of bag I'd used when I worked for Levesque at the paper, practical but still chic enough to pass muster.

The lights were twinkling in the streets below and beyond, more threadbare than it had been before the war but still a carpet of stars that spread out across the city. My city. The city where I was born and where I grew up, although I was barely a woman when I married Philippe. Of course, I didn't realise it at the time, deaf as I was to my mother's entreaties that I wait a while and my father's silence on the subject, which spoke louder than anything my mother could say.

Perhaps they genuinely thought I was too young, although other girls of my age and class were getting married. More likely they spotted something in Philippe that I did not, blinded as I was by what I thought was love. It didn't take me long to realise that lust and love are two very different things. Just as long as it took to reel back from the first attack. But by then I was pregnant and there was no escape – or so I thought.

He was always so charming in public. When he wrapped his hands around my throat, it was with his open palms so as not to bruise me with his fingers. The clumps he pulled out as he dragged me across the floor by my hair were covered up by my chignon. After all, who would believe me? Philippe was a pillar of Parisian society, a man from a good family and even better connections. Worst of all were the insults he rained down on me, abuse that left me feeling filthy from the inside out.

Little by little, his words eroded my soul, sapping any confidence I'd once possessed. Soon I stopped leaving the house except to take the children to the park. Even then, I had to beg him for a few francs to buy them an ice cream or a drink. He loved that, loved the fact I was dependent on him, that I was so broken. Until the day I found a tiny fragment of fight that was still intact, walked out the door with my children and never went back.

Now I would know what to do. I could kill him with a blow deadlier than any he rained upon me. Back then, I had been afraid. Worse than that, ashamed. But my years with the Resistance had taught me well. I wasn't ashamed of anything I had done or anything I would do in the name of France. Part of me was desperate to see Philippe again so he would know that. Another, deeper part, still quaked at the thought, no matter how much I tried to pretend it didn't.

A slam from the street below brought me back from a place I thought I'd left behind. I moved to the window and saw a man striding away from the apartment building, his hands in his pockets and his shoulders hunched, hat pulled low over his forehead. There was something about the way he walked that caught my attention. His gait was uneven, perhaps a slight limp. The set of his shoulders odd. Six foot. Skinny. Red hair. King – it had to be. He fitted the description. I would bet my life he was my target. It was a bet I'd made many times and I hadn't lost it yet.

Quite apart from Harry King, the choice of building was no coincidence. The apartment had been a safe house throughout the occupation, selected for its proximity to the Hotel Lutetia where Abwehr officers were billeted. The intelligence arm of the German forces was merged with the SS early in 1944. It felt good to have operated under their noses. But we weren't the only ones who had chosen lodgings close to the Nazi occupiers, even though they were gone, at least for now. This war wasn't over yet, not by a long way. And someone like King would be in constant touch with his SS masters.

Paris might be free, but fighting was still fierce in Alsace and on the borders with Belgium. The Nazis genuinely believed they could still retake our city, which was why they had left so many spies behind. Spies and collaborators who would aid the plot to infiltrate US forces and murder Eisenhower, among them my husband.

I shrugged on my coat and locked the apartment door behind me, plucking a hair from my head and inserting it into the tiny gap. It was time to get to work.

I glanced in the direction King had taken as I emerged into the street. No sign of him. I looked again at the intersection with the Boulevard Saint-Germain, but he appeared to have vanished into thin air.

The lights of the Café de Flore beckoned to me even as I approached. It had been a long time. Too long. Which was exactly what Monsieur Boubal, the owner, said as I walked through the door.

I smiled. 'I've been away.'

'It's good to see you back.'

He summoned a waiter to take my coat and lead me up to my usual corner table on the first floor, from which I could observe the room, absorbing the welcome heat from the big stove in the centre of it that permeated the entire café. So many other times I'd sat here before the war while my mother looked after the children, eking out a coffee, as did all the other writers, luxuriating in that warmth, notebook and pen at hand as I watched the artists and philosophers who also loved this place.

Sartre, de Beauvoir, Picasso, Camus... they all came to the Café de Flore. It was our home from home as well as office, which was useful when I was living once more with my mother, determined to forge a future for my family without Philippe. I could see a table of what looked like writers now, heads huddled together in earnest conversation. I thought I recognised the slender, dark woman, hair pulled into a chignon, her eyes fixed on the bespectacled man alongside her, tapping his pipe for emphasis as he talked. Simone and Jean-Paul. They were still here. It was as if they, none of us, had ever left.

'Your martini, madame.'

Another welcome memory. A martini, just the one, at the Flore before dinner.

I raised it to my lips, inhaling the merest hint of vermouth, feeling it slide ice cold onto my tongue.

'Juliette? Is it you?'

He pulled out the chair opposite without asking and sat, raking his fingers through his hair in that characteristic way of his, staring at me as if he'd seen a ghost.

'Yes, Guillaume, it's me.'

The smoke from his cigarette curled between us.

'I got your note. So you're here. In Paris.'

'Very astute.'

He threw back his head and laughed. 'You haven't changed. That's good.'

'Nor have you.'

His clothes were as rumpled as ever, his hair, now that he'd raked it, sticking up in spikes. But his eyes were sharp, alive with intelligence, the rings under them more pronounced. Guillaume had changed in the time I'd been away. He was older of course. A man now. But there was something else, an air or maybe an edge. I wasn't sure I liked it.

'So how have you been?' he asked.

'Oh, you know...'

'Yes. I do. Perhaps more than you think.'

I looked at him more intently. 'What do you mean by that?'

'Nothing.'

'Really?' I smiled into his eyes. They were grey. Sizing me up. His blink slow and steady.

'You don't believe me?'

'No.'

'Fair enough. The concierge at my mother's building told me that someone had come by asking for you. They said they thought you were already back in Paris. She sent them packing, telling them that you might be in Paris but you certainly were not in my mother's apartment.'

'I see.'

I regarded him coolly, this young man I had known since he was a babe in arms and I was a shy ten-year-old. He was full of himself even then, demanding to be fed on the hour, although I had a soft spot for him. He was all impulse and emotion. That bubbled through the silence I left hanging in the air, something I knew would be unbearable for him.

'Juliette, I'm sorry about what happened between you and Philippe,' he finally blurted out. 'I hate his beliefs. As for the rest, I wasn't there, but I can well believe it.'

'It's a shame your mother doesn't feel the same.'

'My mother is old-fashioned. She is also a great friend of Philippe's mother, precisely because she is a bourgeois snob, as well as a fascist.'

'I realise that. It still doesn't make it right.'

He tapped out his last cigarette from the packet, which he crumpled and dropped in the ashtray before lighting up.

'Juliette, what are you doing here? You're obviously up to something, coming back all of a sudden like this.'

'Don't be ridiculous, Guillaume. Paris is my home. It's where I was born and grew up. I missed it, that's all.'

'If you missed Paris so much, why didn't you bring your children back with you to live? And Tante Claudine?'

I could feel my face tightening as I forced another smile. 'My mother prefers it where she is, as do the children.'

'Far away from Philippe, you mean?'

'Something like that. Although it is none of your business.'

'What about your father? Is that none of my business too?'

'How dare you mention my father. You know what happened.'

I could feel myself quivering in anger now, on the edge of losing control.

Guillaume pushed his chair back.

'It was good to see you again,' he said as he rose and made his way back to the table across the room where his friends were waiting, pretending not to look.

I plucked the packet from the ashtray with a shaking hand and smoothed it out so I could read the brief message scrawled on it in green ink.

'l'Eglise de Saint-Sulpice. One hour.'

The church was a five-minute walk from here. Seven at best.

I took another sip of my martini and then delved into my bag for my pen, pretending to make notes with it. The charge of tear gas it contained was sufficient for one shot. Enough to blind someone while I made my escape. Or pulled my pistol from my belt. Hopefully it wouldn't come to that. The last thing I wanted was to draw attention to myself.

I glanced at the page I'd been scribbling on as I thought, seeing the words I'd slashed across the page.

'Vivre libre ou mourir.'

Live free or die.
The motto of the Resistance.

SEVEN

I stood just inside the church colonnade with its two white turrets soaring above me, concealed by a pillar, the lights that illuminated the square in front casting long shadows that made me think of prison bars. Not a good thought. I pressed my forehead against the cold stone to steady myself, keeping my eyes on the square, scrutinising any lone passer-by in case it was Guillaume. I assumed he would approach from the Café de Flore, just as I had done. He was still there when I left, not even glancing my way as I wove through the tables to the staircase, apparently engrossed in conversation.

I heard the bells chime seven o'clock. One hour and five minutes precisely since he'd dropped his cigarette packet in the ashtray. The night air was seeping through my bones, turning them to icicles in spite of my coat. I buried my cheeks in my gloved hands, rubbing them to bring life back to my face, my fingers.

'Are you cold?'

A match flared. I looked up to see Guillaume's eyes glinting at me over his Gauloise.

'Where did you come from?'

Stupid question. Somehow he'd managed to sneak up on me. I hated that, hated him for doing that.

'Shall we walk?' he said.

I looked around. I could see a few people in the square, a couple walking arm in arm along the street ahead.

'Where to?' I asked.

'I have something to show you.'

He tried to take me by the arm. I shook him off.

'Cut out the man of mystery act, Guillaume. I'm not in the mood.'

His fingers tightened around my bicep. One more minute. That was all I would give him.

'OK. You can answer my questions here.' His tone was uglier, his expression more so. His fingers dug in, hurting me. Thirty seconds.

'I don't think so,' I said, twisting out of his grasp and slamming him against the pillar with an audible crack.

'Bitch.'

He spat blood from his mouth, then wiped it with his sleeve.

'What are you?' he sneered. 'A collabo?'

I kept him at arm's length, reaching inside my bag for my pen.

'Is that what you are, a dirty collaborator?' he repeated. 'Let me guess, you've been fucking those Nazis in Vichy. Or maybe Germany. Is that where you went, you slut?'

'Where I've been and what I've been doing is none of your business,' I snarled.

'It is when you betray your French brothers and sisters, your comrades.'

'So that's it, is it Guillaume? You're a communist now so you can say what you like?'

'And proud of it. We will run France, just you see. Not you bourgeois collabos who are now pretending the occupation never happened. You lick de Gaulle's arse while all the time you sold your soul to save yourself.'

He was panting like a dog, his eyes wild, fervent with the belief that he was right. I shook my head.

'You know nothing,' I said. 'You know nothing of war or of real sacrifice. Yes, you may have printed some leaflets and held a few meetings in cafés, but as for actually risking your life, you have no idea.'

I flicked the cap off my pen as he lunged, at the same time pulling my scarf up over my mouth and nose. Even so, my eyes began streaming as the tear gas did its work. I left him there, choking and coughing, and strode across the square, slipping into the shelter of the trees that lined it, heading for the street beyond.

'Nice work,' said a voice from the shadows. A figure detached itself from the trunk of the tree directly in front of me.

'Diaz. What the hell are you doing here? Wait... were you following me?'

He took me by the arm just as Guillaume had done, although his grip was a great deal gentler.

'Let's get out of here,' he said. 'Before your friend gets any more bright ideas.'

'He's not my friend,' I rasped, the gas still burning my throat.

'The two of you looked as if you had a lot to talk about.'

'He's my cousin, Guillaume. Last time I saw him, he was

still at school. Now it seems he has become a communist. More than that, he thinks I'm a collaborator.'

'How in the world did he get that idea?'

'I don't know, but he's looking for trouble. Which is exactly why I made sure he and a few others would know I was back in Paris. He could be useful to us.'

Diaz looked at me more closely. 'Who else?'

'I went to see my aunt, his mother, whom he despises because of her political leanings. She probably cosied up to the Germans, although I have no proof. She's still friends with my husband's mother as well as my husband. They all share the same views.'

'Sounds complicated. Do you think your cousin is working with your husband?'

'You never can tell, but I doubt it. You haven't answered my question. Were you following me?'

We were some distance along the street, far enough from the church for Diaz to pause in his stride and spin round to face me. The street light cast his face into hollows, but his teeth flashed as white as ever.

'And what if I was?'

'I'd make sure you never did it again.'

'Oh yeah? How? You didn't spot me this time.'

'So you were following me.'

The grin disappeared into the hollows. When he spoke, the timbre of his voice was deeper and far more serious.

'I was hoping to find you, yes. I needed to tell you something. I spotted you leaving the Café de Flore, but I also saw this guy hard on your heels so I hung back, wanting to get a fix on him. Turns out it was a good call.'

'I handled it.'

'You did.'

'Which means I don't need you playing bodyguard.'

'Juliette, we're supposed to be working this together.'

'Working it, yes. That does not include spying on me.'

'For the last time, I wasn't spying on you. I was bringing you some urgent information.'

'Which is?'

He glanced over his shoulder, looking up and down the street. 'Not here.'

'All right. My apartment is not far from here.'

'Not there either. In fact, you can't go back there.'

I stared at him. 'Why not?'

His lips were still forming an answer when the shot rang out.

EIGHT

It looked like any other white stucco house in South Kensington, its steps leading up to a shiny black door. Christine rapped on it three times with the lion-shaped door knocker. Interesting. It was a lion that marked the entrances to the secret passages or traboules of Lyon, although doubtless this one held a different meaning.

The maid who opened the door regarded her primly, her eyes sweeping over Christine's red coat and matching hat, a deliberate nod to the Nazi flag.

'Countess von Strassburg,' said Christine.

It was the same name she'd used when dealing with Klaus Barbie back in Lyon, the Germanic overtones chiming with her platinum-blonde hair.

'Would you tell Lady Rattray that I'm here?'

'One moment please.'

The maid left Christine alone to scrutinise the entrance hall as she waited to be announced, taking in the good portraits that hung all the way up the stairs, ancestors no doubt of Lady Rattray and her notorious husband. There were more portraits adorning the room into which the maid led Christine, but she had no time to study them, pinned down as she was by the fierce gaze of the gaunt woman who stood before her. Isobel Rattray was a good ten years older than her husband and no looker, though what she lacked in beauty, she more than made up for in animal magnetism, fuelled no doubt by the fanatical fascist beliefs she shared with her spouse.

'Countess von Strassburg, how good of you to join us.'

Her thin lips were painted an unflattering dark red, her hair dyed to match the coal-black eyebrows she'd pencilled in. The effect was somewhat vampiric, Christine noted. Which was apt considering the bloodlust with which the Rattrays pursued their cause.

'I'm delighted to be among like-minded people,' purred Christine, her eyes sweeping the assembled men and women perched on dining chairs or squeezed together on sofas and armchairs.

'We are rather more than I anticipated,' said Lady Rattray, beckoning to a man standing in the centre of the room. 'Perhaps you could find Countess von Strassburg somewhere to sit?'

Christine didn't dare look directly at him, knowing his real role in all this. Edward, in turn, acted as if he'd never met her before in his life. Instead, she gazed at his hands as he pulled out a chair for her, taking in the scars and the way his poor fingers still twisted, a legacy of Barbie's brutality back in Lyon.

'Can I get you anything else? A glass of water perhaps?'

He'd noticed her staring at his hands.

She flushed. 'Nothing, thank you,' she murmured, discreetly scanning the room. A few faces registered, ringing bells. Two Members of Parliament. A lord of the realm and one of the richest men in London. A well-known soprano and her escort, a much older man who did not at first seem familiar. Assorted women. She wouldn't dignify them as ladies. At the back, a man with hooded eyes, eyes that were inspecting her with as much interest as she was him. There he was. Her mark. Lord Maximilian Archibald Mytton.

She met his gaze, held it, refusing to blink. Finally, he did. Round one to her.

'Shall we begin?' Lady Rattray pulled her lips back from her teeth in some semblance of a smile. 'Over to you.'

'Thank you.'

Edward took up his place once more in the centre of the room. His smile was as charming as ever, disarmingly so.

'Ladies and gentlemen, welcome. Many of you will know one another from other groups which were formed before the war although certain Acts of Parliament sadly interfered with our activities.'

'Not my doing,' snorted one of the MPs. 'About time Churchill was brought to heel.'

A murmur of assent ran around the room accompanied by shouts of 'hear, hear'.

'Which brings me to the purpose of our meeting,' he said. 'We are proposing that we send parcels to prisoners of war currently incarcerated in camps across the land as well as on the Isle of Man, especially Le Marchant camp in Devizes. These will contain food and useful items.'

'Such as?' piped up one of the women present.

He chuckled. 'I'll leave that to your imagination.'

'But surely any parcels sent to prison camps are opened and inspected?'

'They are. That's why the items we intend to include are

apparently everyday things like tubes of toothpaste, bars of soap. Pens and notepads.'

He paused, waiting for his words to sink in, for realisation to dawn.

Another woman raised her hand. 'These items. Are they entirely regular?'

He smiled. 'Not entirely, no. We are fortunate to have among our number someone who works for, shall we say, a government department. These items are supplied to agents working in the field, but we have got hold of some. Judiciously distributed, they will aid our cause.'

Christine's eyes flicked to her mark again. He was apparently rapt, not for one moment giving off any hint that he might be the person intimately acquainted with a certain government department. A department that had got its hands on the notorious Red Book.

Another murmur, this time of appreciation.

'Ladies, we are asking you to assist in the packing of these parcels. Gentlemen, we need your help to distribute them. We intend to do so under the guise of a charitable enterprise.'

A few more guffaws from the room.

'If you are able to help, please make yourself known to Lady Rattray,' he added. 'And now I think it's time for tea.'

Christine stayed seated while others rose and made their way into an adjoining room. She sat, looking straight ahead, waiting. Sure enough, he took the bait.

'Are you not thirsty?' asked Lord Mytton.

She looked up and smiled into those hooded eyes. Reptilian eyes. Or perhaps serpentine. 'I am but not for tea.'

Her smile was inviting, her tone even more so.

His smile broadened. 'Then I think I know just the place. Shall we?'

As they headed for the front hallway, Christine looked over her shoulder. Edward was staring after them, brows drawn together in a frown, damaged hands twisted together in a way that made her heart lurch. She dropped him the briefest of winks and sailed on out of the room, arm in arm with her prey. The game was on. And she would outplay him, just as she had all the rest.

NINE

'You absolutely cannot go back to your apartment.'

'I absolutely have to.'

Diaz's face was set, his voice vehement. We were safely huddled under the awning of the Café de Flore, tables shielding us from the mysterious shooter. Although, if anyone did take aim, they'd probably miss again. Whoever it was had to be the lousiest shot ever. That or they meant to scare us more than anything else. 'It's far too dangerous. They've made you.'

'Who are "they" exactly? And what do you mean they've "made" me?'

He sighed. 'OK, he. King. He's been inside your apartment. He's an accomplished burglar and lockpick, among his other talents. The point is, he knows who you are or suspects it.'

'Maybe he was just looking for something to steal.'

'He left something behind.'

Diaz held up a tiny listening device from which loose wires still dangled.

'Not that accomplished then,' I said.

'I'm good at sweeping places.'

'I'd already done it. In any case, how the hell would he know who I am?'

'That man who sold you the list was a gambling buddy of King's as well as your husband. He could have alerted him before he met with you.'

'So? It's possible King knows my apartment is a safe house and therefore that I could be an agent, but I can turn that to our advantage, keep him on his toes. Maybe even leave him a bug to find as a matter of professional courtesy.'

'You'll do no such thing.'

Diaz might have a good ten inches in height over me but he had yet to learn that was no advantage. I drew myself up and stepped closer. 'I will do exactly as I please.'

'You seem to have forgotten we're working this together.'

'What the hell do you know about working together? You seem to have forgotten you said you would write to me. Begged for my address, as I recall. Don't worry – I understand. You had better things to do.'

'I did write. I wrote you almost every day.'

'Really?'

'Yes, really.'

I stared at him. 'I didn't get a single letter from you.'

'Juliette, what can I say? I wrote you all kinds of stuff, all the time. What I was doing and how I was feeling. Mostly how I was feeling, which was missing you. Although obviously you didn't miss me or you would be a little more understanding right now.'

'Understanding? You're the one who said he would write.'

'Like I said, I did.'

'So what happened to the letters?'

'I don't know. Ships go down in the Atlantic. It's wartime. Things happen. All I know is that I sent them to you. When I didn't hear back, I assumed you'd moved on. That first time I saw you again, I didn't know what to feel. All I could do was put a brave face on it.'

He sounded infinitely weary and dignified. As if he was telling the truth. I looked at him, at his guileless eyes. I could taste regret in my mouth, bitter. All that time wasted thinking he'd let me down when, in fact, he'd done nothing of the sort. Or so he said. I wasn't going to entirely let him off the hook, not until I had absolute proof.

'I believe you. Now, how do you know King was inside my apartment? The last I saw of him, he was leaving the building and that was less than a couple of hours ago, which means you must have been watching it.'

A shrug. 'So maybe I was. I got a tip-off that King might be on to you.'

'From whom?'

'One of our agents here in Paris.'

Interesting. 'So they told you and not me?'

'Yes, but only because he's working out of the Hotel Scribe too. An OSS guy who knows we're on assignment here. London asked him to keep his ear to the ground before we got here without telling him exactly why.'

'Fair enough. Do you think it was King who was shooting at us?'

'Could have been. I don't think it was your delightful cousin. If he was going to pull a gun, he'd have done so back at the church.'

Diaz's face was sombre in the sulphuric glow of the street

lamps. All his swagger seemed to have momentarily disappeared.

'Juliette, Harry King is a very dangerous man. The SS have left Paris, but they're not far away. There's no doubt they're part of Hitler's plans to sabotage our armies and assassinate General Eisenhower.'

'All the more reason to stay close to King. You say he may already have searched my apartment. Well, good. I took the precaution of hiding anything that could compromise me. I swept it for bugs when I arrived, and I will sweep it again myself. I am a professional, you know.'

At that, he laughed, the old Diaz emerging in a full-throated roar and a blinding display of teeth. This was how I remembered him from the chateau, his eyes alight with mischief. Those irresistible eyes. Damn them.

'I know you are. I was – I am – just worried about you. If he only broke into your apartment after you arrived it means it's you he's after. I don't believe in coincidences.'

'Nor do I, but you don't need to worry about me. I can take care of myself.'

A memory of his eyes turning to liquid, just as they were doing now. Shadowed pools of night water, drowning me in something. Something I thought I'd long forgotten. Something I half-remembered. I took a breath. It sounded more like a gasp.

'Can you?'

His finger traced my cheek. I swatted it away.

'Yes, I can. And now I am going back to my apartment. I'm tired and I'm hungry. I will say goodnight.'

'Not so fast. I'm coming with you.'

'You most certainly are not.'

Another dazzling smile. 'It's OK. I'm not inviting myself

in. I'm just going to walk you home. It's what my mamma taught me to do.'

Was that a twist of disappointment in my gut? No. I wanted to be alone. It was far better to be alone.

'If you must.'

'I must.'

There was so much more behind his words that I chose not to hear.

TEN

8 DECEMBER 1944, PARIS

The Hotel Scribe was aptly named, its lobby buzzing with war correspondents scribbling notes or conducting interviews as harried press officers scurried past. Glancing up from the lightwell that formed the centre of the lobby, I could see yet more journalists dressed in army shirts, cigarettes hanging from their mouths as they tapped away at their typewriters. I made my way through the throng to the reception desk.

'I am here to see Captain Diaz of the public relations division.'

'At your service, ma'am,' said a familiar voice in my ear.

I turned and held out my hand. 'Juliette Villeneuve. *London Times.*'

'Very good to meet you,' he responded with only the faintest trace of a smile.

'Likewise.'

He led me to a quiet corner where two armchairs were set next to a coffee table. 'Tea? Coffee? Breakfast?'

'Just coffee, thank you.'

'Rough night?'

'You could say that.'

I could feel eyes upon us. The other correspondents were no doubt curious about this upstart new arrival. Most of them evidently knew one another from the theatre of war, calling out greetings laced with a competitive edge as they raced out the door to be the first to scoop and file a story. Still, my cover was watertight. The editor of *The Times* was another old friend of Suzanne's, happy to help out when it came to the war effort.

'So.' I smiled, pulling my notebook from my bag and laying it on the table. 'Shall we get started?'

'No time like the present. I gather you're writing a feature on the GIs in Paris?'

The perfect excuse to visit plenty of the troops who might already have been infiltrated, accompanied by Diaz.

'I am also interested in visiting Versailles,' I said. 'To get a different angle on how officers and chiefs of staff are finding Paris after liberation. Perhaps even get a few words from General Eisenhower, if he's not too busy.'

'I'm sure that can be arranged. I'm here to help you in any way I can.'

I'll bet, I thought. Very smooth.

I'd lain awake for hours last night, remembering the touch of his finger as it caressed my cheek, as light as a moth's wing but more potent than any weapon. After all, it wasn't the bullet that had missed us both by inches that kept me from sleep or even the crazed look on my cousin's face. He swore he'd written to me. And I believed him, fool that I was.

Dangerous, that was what Daniel Diaz was. And I had long ago learned to avoid unnecessary risks. Caution had kept me alive this far. I wasn't about to lose my heart again to someone as distracting as him. Besides, we both needed to concentrate on our mission.

'Are you OK?' he asked.

'Yes, of course. Why wouldn't I be?'

'It's just I don't believe you've heard a word I said for the past few minutes.'

'Don't be ridiculous.'

'Go on then. What did I say?'

I wanted to slap him. Hard. Instead, I went for my favourite weapon: hauteur. It was something bred into us Parisians. A frosting of the eyes, a hardening of the voice accompanied by a posture that conveyed absolute disdain. It worked like a charm every time. Except on Diaz.

'You know, Juliette, you really need to loosen up.'

He caught my wrist as I raised my hand, laughed, then bent to kiss it.

I felt that kiss all the way down to the soles of my feet. All at once, I was back there, on that ridge.

My hand was still tingling as I wrenched my wrist from his grasp, crossing my legs at the knee to put some distance between us.

'I've offended you. I'm sorry.'

He didn't sound in the least bit sorry.

'May I remind you that we're here to do a job?' I struggled to keep a straight face. Just about managed it.

'I thought that's what we were doing,' he said, eyes wide in injured innocence. 'Aren't we supposed to fall for one another?'

'Not quite that fast.'

'Oh come on, Juliette. Don't you believe in love at first sight?'

'Do you?'

'When it comes to you, yes.'

I took a sip of my coffee, tasting it acrid on my tongue, feeling it cut through my confusion. I had really thought something happened between us that night on the plateau, that we had a connection. But then eager anticipation turned to disappointment and finally resignation as the weeks passed and no letters arrived. He swore he'd written, but what proof did I have of that? *Detach, Juliette. Make him work for it.*

'You're funny,' I said.

'I'm not kidding.'

There was a hint of hurt in those puppy eyes now.

'Look, I'm sure many women fall for that line, but I'm not about to be one of them.'

I had once. Never again.

'It's not a line. In fact, I've never said that to anyone before. Apart from to you, of course.'

The hurt had spread to his voice.

'Right.'

'Damn right.'

'Captain Diaz, it's ten o'clock in the morning. A little too early for this kind of thing.'

'Dan. Call me Dan. Or Danny. And I don't know about you but I've always thought morning was the perfect time for this kind of thing.'

I couldn't help it. I had to laugh. 'You're a very bad man.'

'And you are very beautiful.'

I felt the flush tinge my cheeks and bit back my instant retort.

'Thank you,' I murmured.

'You're welcome.'

The hubbub of the lobby had faded into the background.

I was only dimly aware of the melee, but something, or rather someone, caught my eye.

'Over there. Quick.'

Dan glanced in the same direction I was looking.

'It's him. Harry King.'

'Are you sure?'

'Completely sure. What's he doing here?'

'Only one way to find out.'

Dan was up and striding over before I could stop him.

I watched as he held out his hand, oozing charm, the professional PR liaison man. King was equally good, but then he was a professional conman. I bent over my coffee, averting my face as Dan led him past.

'I'll just need to see your press credentials,' I heard him say.

'Certainly, old boy.'

King's voice was plummy, pure British upper class. He was wearing plus fours, I noticed out of the corner of my eye, and sporting a clipped moustache that was a darker red than his hair. As he patted his jacket pocket, I noticed the bulge beneath.

'Careful!' I cried out just as he pulled the gun and levelled it at Dan.

A sudden hush fell over the lobby. Everyone appeared frozen, apart from one or two correspondents who hit the floor.

'No one's going to get hurt,' said King. 'I'm just going to walk out of here and you're coming with me.'

Dan raised his hands slowly, his eyes never leaving King.

King smirked. 'That's right, old chap. Nice and easy now.'

He pressed the pistol into Dan's temple. 'Let's go.'

Don't try anything, I silently begged. *Just play along.*

They were almost at the main entrance now, Dan matching King step for step. King couldn't resist a final flourish.

'Sorry to disturb you all,' he sneered, his smile at odds with his tone.

It was at that moment that Dan pounced, grabbing his arm and twisting it upwards so that King fired uselessly into the air. Then they were down, kicking and scrambling as Dan tried to get a hold.

Another shot. Now everyone was screaming and diving for cover. King was on his feet, slamming his way through the door, turning to fire one last time before disappearing into the street beyond.

'After him,' Dan yelled at the soldiers sprinting towards him.

'Oh thank God. You're alive.'

I was across the lobby and on my knees beside him in seconds, scanning his face and his body for any signs of injury or blood.

'Good to know you care,' said Dan, pushing himself upright.

There was blood oozing from a graze above his ear. I pressed my handkerchief to it. 'Looks like the bullet just nicked you.'

'Bastard's a lousy shot,' he said. 'Lucky for me.'

A couple of the men who'd raced after King burst back through the door.

'We lost him,' said one. 'Vanished into thin air.'

'Don't worry,' drawled Dan. 'He'll be back. Besides, we know where to find him. He's obviously playing some kind of game, trying to prove he can just walk in here and do what he likes, any time he likes. Terrorist tactics.'

He looked at me, at the bloodstained handkerchief in my hand.

'Now,' he said. 'Where were we?'

I looked back at him, my heart tilting in a way I believed I would never feel again. For a moment there I thought I'd lost him. A moment filled with an agony that wrenched me to the core, startling me with its intensity. This was what I'd been bottling up for months, ever since I'd last seen him. The lack of letters had only stoked my longing, in spite of all my attempts to pretend otherwise. Well, I wasn't going to lie to myself any longer. I wanted to throw my arms around him and never let him go. This brave, stupid, annoying, beautiful man.

'I have no idea,' I said.

But I knew where we were going. Eventually.

'Shall we?' I indicated the table where we'd been sitting only moments before, our coffee still cooling in its cups.

His eyes locked on to mine, teasing. 'Isn't it a little early for this kind of thing?'

'Very funny. For that, you can buy me dinner this evening at the Ritz.'

I patted his cheek and smiled. 'Gives you plenty of time to work up an appetite.'

ELEVEN

Jean Levesque swivelled in his chair and surveyed me over the top of his spectacles. The smile that played around his mouth spoke volumes. Levesque barely scraped five foot in height, but what he lacked in stature, he more than made up for in girth. His face fell in froglike folds, his eyes twinkling at me from between the creases.

'Well, well,' he said. 'Now who do we have here?'

'How are you, Jean?'

My old mentor and friend, now an unwitting accomplice in my cover story. Although Jean Levesque never missed a trick so I'd better make this good.

'Oh, you know, *comme ci, comme ça*. But you, Juliette, you look really good. Tell me, what have you been up to?'

'Oh, you know, this and that.'

He laughed and sat back in his chair, lacing his fingers behind his head in one of those theatrical gestures I remembered. The trappings, however, were far more stylish than before. His shirt was made of the finest silk, his cufflinks heavy and gold. This was not the Levesque I knew of old.

Back then, his shirts had been neatly pressed but ordinary, his suits ill-fitting. I preferred him like that, a little crumpled around the edges.

I glanced around his office. That, too, reeked of prosperity. His desk was a fine antique, Louis XV at a guess, the paintings on the walls rich oils set in gilded frames. One was of a nude, her dark hair falling over her alabaster shoulder as she gazed out over it from the frame. Her heart-shaped face looked familiar. An actress maybe. An interesting choice for the office of a newspaper editor. But then, Jean Levesque was no ordinary journalist. He owned this paper and several others too. Rumour had it that he drew a salary of 100,000 francs a month now, more than enough to pay for those fancy shirts and several mistresses besides.

'You've done well, Jean,' I said. 'Your papers must have quite a circulation.'

He dipped his head in a modest gesture. 'Plenty of people want to read what we have to say.'

'They must do.'

'Listen,' he said, leaning forward so I caught a whiff of his cologne. Expensive, like all the rest. 'I give people what they want. Right now, what they want is something to uplift them after the long days of darkness during the occupation. If that's not as serious as some newspapers, well then. Some people might call what we print salacious or gossip, but it keeps people amused.'

'I see,' I murmured.

'I'm not sure you do, Juliette. Where were you during the occupation? Certainly not here in Paris.'

'I was in London,' I said.

'Why? What were you doing there?'

'I took the children to England, along with my mother.

The Times asked me to work for them there. It was safer for us all.'

A tiny white lie, although I would have said anything if it meant convincing Levesque.

'*The Times* asked you?' He sat back, his smile widening in admiration.

'Yes, Jean. You taught me well.'

He extracted a cigar from the box on his desk, cut off the end and lit it, grinning at me through the smoke.

'I did, didn't I?' he said, flourishing his cigar like a trophy. 'And you learned well. You were an excellent student, and you are an excellent journalist. I'm not surprised they wanted you.'

'Which is why I'm here, for professional reasons. *The Times* sent me back to Paris to write features. I was thinking we might collaborate on some of those.'

His gaze sharpened. 'Really? What kind of features?'

'I'm writing about Paris now, after liberation. How people across society feel about it, the good and the bad. You've been here throughout, Jean. You can give our readers a unique perspective.'

Flattery was every man's Achilles heel. I pressed on it harder. 'You also have excellent connections within Parisian society. It would be good to hear things from their point of view. Find out what the elite think.'

He looked dubious. 'It's true. I know everyone worth knowing, but that's because I have to. *The Times*, you say?'

I nodded, noting the glint in his eye. Levesque might be my old mentor, and a good one at that, but he was never one to miss an opportunity.

'I have carte blanche to write whatever I wish. The editor is, you might say, a good friend.'

I left the implication dangling in the air.

Levesque laughed. 'You're a smart one, Juliette. Keep your friends close and your enemies closer. I really did train you well.'

'You did indeed. And look at what you've achieved here.'

'Well...' He glanced through the door at the newsroom where three journalists were at work alongside Levesque's secretary, a dark-haired woman who went by the name of Anna Léon although I knew her real name was Levy. 'We're a small outfit, but we make an impact.'

'I'm sure you do. So what do you say? Would you like to work with me on this?'

I tried not to glance at the clock above his head. Nearly five. I had a dinner reservation with Dan at seven.

Levesque sat back in his chair and I knew what was coming next.

'Why don't we discuss it over a drink?' He loved a good gossip over a drink or several. It was his way of unwinding at the end of the day.

'I'm afraid I have plans for this evening.'

'Ah. Too bad.'

No doubt he did too and probably with one of those expensive mistresses. I adored Levesque, but he was a terrible ladies' man. Lucky for him, his wife was similarly indiscriminate.

'Another time.'

I got to my feet.

'There's a gathering tomorrow evening,' he said. 'A soirée I think you might enjoy.'

'Oh really?'

'You may already know one or two of the people there. It

could be a good opportunity to reacquaint yourself with them.'

'What time and where?'

'I'll pick you up at your hotel at eight.'

'Very good,' I said. 'The Hotel Scribe. I'll meet you in the lobby.' Not even an old friend like Levesque could be trusted with the address of the apartment. Safe houses were called that for a reason. Far easier to pretend I was staying at the Scribe too.

'But of course.'

He made to rise, but I gestured to him to stay where he was, blowing him a kiss from the door.

'I can see myself out. So lovely to catch up. Until tomorrow, Jean.'

I was halfway down the stairs before I remembered where I'd seen the face of the woman in the painting before. She was younger in the picture, her features softer but unmistakable. It could have been painted anywhere, although the style, to me, looked French. But there was no doubt in my mind that the subject was Suzanne.

TWELVE

He was waiting for me in the Ritz Bar, a perfect dry martini set on the table in front of my empty place.

'You look absolutely beautiful,' he said, kissing me on each cheek.

'Thank you.'

I smoothed the Nina Ricci dress as I sat in the chair he pulled out for me, raising my glass to meet his and taking a long, appreciative sip.

'Oh that is good. How did you know I like it like this?' I asked.

'I figured you were a dry martini woman by the shade of your lipstick.'

I looked at the imprint of my lipstick on the glass and then at him in time to catch the glint of mischief in his eyes.

'Red Hot,' I murmured as I took another sip.

'You certainly are.'

'It's the name of my lipstick.'

'Suits you.'

He was staring hungrily at my lips, the air between us suddenly electric with promise.

'Madame, it is good to see you again. Is your cocktail to your satisfaction?'

I looked up at the man in the white jacket, moustache bristling above a generous mouth.

'Monsieur Meier, it is good to see you. My cocktail is perfect as always, thank you.'

He executed a tiny bow. 'If there's anything you need, anything at all, please just let me know.'

I wondered how much he knew about our mission here. Probably everything, knowing Meier, and without having to be briefed. He had the skill of the true bartender, seeing and hearing everything while remaining invisible until necessary. The ideal spy, in fact.

'Thank you. I – we – will.'

Another tiny bow, this time a fraction longer as his eyes met mine. For the merest blink of a second, I thought I saw acknowledgement there and then he was moving on to the next table, offering them the same immaculate greetings.

'Did you tell him you were meeting me?'

Dan tried and failed to look innocent. 'I may have done.'

'Lipstick colour my ass, as you Americans would say.'

He laughed, an easy sound that was infectious. 'Touché.'

'So,' I said, 'to business.'

'I thought you'd never ask.'

I slapped the hand away that was reaching for mine. 'Concentrate, Diaz.'

'It's Dan, remember? I think we've got to the first-name stage of our relationship.'

His eyes twinkled. He was enjoying this.

I leaned towards him, lowering my voice and looking up

at him through my lashes so that anyone watching would have thought us to be flirting up a storm. 'Our relationship, as you know, is strictly business. Dan.'

'That wasn't the way it looked or felt this morning.'

He had a way of speaking plainly that was at once irresistible and irritating.

I smoothed my hair. 'I'm good at what I do.'

'I'm sure you are.'

Those eyes were still dancing. He really was enjoying this far too much.

'If you think I'm simply going to fall into bed with you because I'm French, you have the wrong idea.'

'I don't think that at all. I'm not some GI out for a good time, you know.'

He sounded genuinely insulted.

'I'm sorry. That may have been a little strong. But you must admit that you Americans have a certain reputation.'

'"Oversexed, overpaid and over here." Yes, I know. And only one of them is true. Too bad about the pay.'

It was my turn to laugh. 'Very good. You have a way with words. What did you do before the war?'

'I was a member of the French Foreign Legion.'

I nearly choked on my martini. 'You? How come?'

'I was born in New York but educated here, in France. My father is French and Spanish, my mother American. I wanted an adventure after university here so I applied for the Legion. My father was furious when he found out and tried to buy me out, but I refused to leave.'

'How did you make the leap from the Legion to OSS?'

'The Legion offered me a permanent commission, but I decided to go back to the US, to Hollywood. I was working there when war broke out so I enlisted.'

'You were an actor?'

'I was a stuntman. Comes in handy for this kind of work.'

I looked at him more closely. He was certainly handsome enough to be an actor, but there was something about him, a lack of ego perhaps, that had led him in a different direction. I'd been wrong about the arrogance. Or maybe I'd chosen to believe it because it suited me to. And because I found him so annoyingly attractive.

'That is incredible,' I said.

'So are you.'

It was back, the charm and the cheek, only it no longer grated.

'Did you know,' I said, 'that in France we don't date like you Americans do.'

'Really? How do you do it?'

His fingers brushed my arm. This time I didn't swipe them away.

'We have dinner, like this. We get to know one another. We assume from the beginning that we are interested only in each other, at least until we decide whether to take things further or not.'

'I see. And when do you know if you're going to take things further?'

'That's up to the woman to decide. Maybe after two or three dinners. Maybe twenty.'

'Anything I can do to speed things up?'

'Not really.'

'Flowers? Poems? Declarations of undying love?'

'A bit clichéd.'

'OK, how about a kiss?'

Somehow, we'd moved towards one another so that our

heads were now only inches apart. It would have been so easy to close that gap. So tempting.

'Monsieur, madame, I am sorry to disturb you.'

I looked up to see Meier hovering by our table.

'There is an urgent telephone call for you, madame. From London.'

He took my elbow as I got to my feet and gestured to Dan to follow.

'This way, madame, monsieur. Don't look back. There is a man pointing a gun at you from underneath the next table.'

THIRTEEN

'It seems a lot of people want us dead.'

'They want us scared, Juliette, and to create chaos. More typical terrorist behaviour, just like King's antics this morning. I'm pretty sure it's all part of their plan to create chaos and unrest before they attempt their assassination and whatever else they have in the works. So let's scare them in return and create a little chaos of our own.'

We were in the third-floor suite where Meier had led us, overlooking the Place Vendôme.

'Well, I don't know about you,' I said, 'but I don't scare easily.'

He glanced at me, his finger on the trigger of the pistol he was pointing at the vast square below. We waited, watching the expanse in front of the hotel, listening out for the signal. The room phone rang once. Stopped. Then rang again. Seconds later, a figure strolled into the square from the hotel as if he had all the time in the world.

'There,' I whispered, pointing out the second figure who

moved from the shadows to join him. The square was all but empty on this side, its lights affording us a clear view.

The two men conferred for a moment, faces obscured by the head coverings they wore, although there was no mistaking the height of one of them.

'Harry King,' I murmured. 'He really must like us a lot. But who is his friend? The one who came out of the hotel?'

'Time to find out,' muttered Dan and raised his gun at the same time as I levelled mine. We fired in perfect unison, letting off a volley of shots aimed at their feet.

They leaped apart, looking around, scanning the square. We let off another round, and King howled in pain, grabbing at his foot, his companion taking to his heels and sprinting out of the square while King hobbled off in the opposite direction.

'Look at him dance,' said Dan. 'Too bad his partner abandoned him.'

'At least we got a good look at his face.'

It wasn't the kind of face you would forget. Where King was quintessentially British, his companion looked to be Mediterranean in appearance. He could have come straight from the streets of anywhere from Naples to Marseille. He was powerfully built, his mouth a cruel slit beneath a hooked nose, eyes glinting from under his cap. It felt as if he was looking straight at me even though I was hidden behind the curtain.

'I've seen that face before,' muttered Dan. 'But I can't remember where, goddamn it.'

'He was in the bar. The one who was about to start something until Meier spotted him.'

'Yes but somewhere else too. A while back.'

He stared into the middle distance for a few seconds.

'Got it. He's Italian. We have him on file. Another nasty piece of work. Acts as a heavy for those aristocratic types, specifically the ones who think old Adolf's a good thing.'

'Fascists you mean?'

'More than that – collaborators. The ones who are actively conspiring to help him win this war. In other words, the very same people we were sent here to hunt down.'

The phone rang again and this time Dan picked it up.

'Coast is clear,' he said. 'Meier has people following both men.'

'At least then we might find out who sent them.'

'I think we already know that.'

'Yes but it doesn't make sense. Why do King and his friends keep following us and waving their guns without actually shooting to kill? They could if they wanted to. And why us? No one else knew about our mission. Or the details. It was just you, me and Suzanne in the room when she briefed us.'

'I agree. This doesn't smell right. These guys are openly trying to scare us. If they'd wanted to kill us, they'd have done it by now. My guess is that the guy with the gun was going to start shooting to miss us just like he did in the street. It would have caused mayhem in the bar and spread more fear, which is what they want. Maybe this has nothing to do with our mission. It could be because of something else entirely.'

'Something or someone,' I said, an old, familiar fluttering starting up in the pit of my stomach, like bats swarming in a cave, their tiny claws clutching at my guts.

'You have someone in mind?'

'No. No one in particular,' I lied.

It was too soon to be sure, but this bore all his hallmarks.

The crude attempts at scaring us. The stalking. The control through fear. It was why I'd left Paris rather than stay and fight with the Resistance here. In the south, he couldn't track me down. Not out there, in the ruined chateau that was our headquarters, the rugged terrain riddled with my men – my brave, loyal Maquis. The same chateau where I'd first got to know Dan. If my husband even guessed how I really felt about him, he would make both our lives hell.

Perhaps that was why I'd been so eager to lead my own army. Why I endured the loneliness and the danger, sabotaging the Germans day after day. Of course I wanted to fight for France, for my people and freedom. But a tiny part of me also wanted to feel I could face him down too.

Now my army was scattered, some returned home to their families, others joining official factions, still more heading to the front to see the Germans off once and for all. Without them, I was once more alone, an easy target. Or so he thought. What he didn't know was how much I had changed. How I no longer feared him.

'A penny for them.'

I looked up to see Dan watching me, mouth quirked in an unspoken question.

'I was just thinking.'

'I could see that.'

I let out a long breath that was more a sob than a sigh. 'I was thinking about my husband.'

'Oh. I see.'

'No you don't. You couldn't possibly.'

'Try me.'

He reached out and tucked a stray strand of hair back into my chignon. We were so close I felt his breath caress my cheek. Another second and our lips would meet. Then all would be lost.

I turned away, feeling as if I was ripping off layers of skin as I did so. Better that than to ever suffer again in the way Philippe had hurt me. My heart was my own now. I intended to keep it that way. I had to keep it that way, for my children, if not for me.

'Juliette...'

It wasn't so much my name as the way he said it that tugged at me.

I hesitated, torn between two worlds, between the past and the present, when a discreet tap at the door made the decision for me.

'My men followed them to different addresses,' said Meier. 'One in Saint-Germain, the other in the 16th.'

'Where in the 16th?'

My voice sounded sharper than I intended.

'Passy. An apartment building on Rue Henri-Martin.'

'So it is him.'

This time I wasn't even aware I'd spoken aloud. Blindly, I reached out for something to cling on to as the room dipped and swayed around me.

'Juliette? Here. Sit down here.'

A strong arm around me, helping. Gentle words cutting through the mist.

'Take a sip of water. That's it. Deep breaths now.'

Finally, the world settled once more, the room swimming back into focus. I looked at the two men bending over me in concern, at Dan's arm still around me and Meier holding a glass.

'I'm all right,' I said. 'Thank you. I'm fine.'

I shifted slightly, not wanting to shake off Dan's arm but feeling trapped all the same.

'You don't look fine,' said Dan, releasing me with some reluctance. 'You look as if you've seen a ghost.'

'In a way, I have,' I murmured.

The ghost of a past that still haunted me. Of a bastard who once said he would never let me go. Except that he was very much alive. Now I understood just how much he'd meant it.

I heard an echo of Suzanne's voice in my mind, urging me to find him and kill him – and all the other collaborators on the list.

But even if he were dead, I would never truly be free.

FOURTEEN

Le Marchant barracks loomed above them, looking more like a gothic fortress than a prisoner-of-war camp in a sleepy Wiltshire town. Marianne glanced at Jack, dressed in his brown POW uniform, his right wrist cuffed to that of the prison guard beside him.

'You ready?' she murmured.

'As I'll ever be.'

The guard saluted another on the gate and then they were passing through, entering a reception area where yet another guard led them into a side room.

'McMahon.'

Marianne stared at the man waiting beside the desk. Behind it stood a US Army colonel who looked pointedly at the two guards, waiting until they had uncuffed Jack before snapping: 'Dismissed.'

It was only when the door had shut firmly behind them that McMahon gestured to the two chairs in front of the desk.

'Sit. We don't have much time. Word will already have

gone round that a new inmate has arrived. The camp commander has lent us his office so the prisoners will simply believe you're meeting with him.'

Aside from the insignia on his collar, you would never know that McMahon was a counter-intelligence agent. Look harder and there was a certain cynicism in his stare that gave him away. It was what had first struck Marianne about him when he'd turned up at Juliette's chateau in France. That and the self-righteousness that made her want to wipe the grin off his face every single time she saw him.

A shudder ran through her. The last time she'd seen him was forever etched on her heart. That was when he'd revealed that poor Maggie had been transported to Auschwitz. It was only a few months back and yet it felt like forever.

I will find you, she silently promised Maggie. *We will come and get you.*

Right now though, they had to focus on infiltrating the committed Nazis who were imprisoned here, all of them still ready and willing to die for the Fatherland. And McMahon was the last person she expected to see to help them do that.

'Things that tight here with the prisoners, are they?' asked Jack.

'They practice Vehmic law,' said McMahon. 'You know what that means?'

'It's a medieval system of vigilante law adopted by the Nazis,' said Jack. 'Essentially it means that a German prisoner of war is regarded as being on active duty, awaiting orders from the Führer.'

'Correct,' said McMahon. 'If they break it, they get beaten to death. And worse. Only the other week they hanged a guy in the latrine block as a warning to others. He was already dead when they strung him up, but before he died, he knew they'd go after his family back in Germany too.'

'Nice,' said Marianne, glancing at Jack. She had heard the careful note in his voice. He was wary of McMahon too and with good reason. It was McMahon who'd tried to set him up, handing Marianne the message that supposedly proved Jack was a traitor – except it was a fake.

She wondered what he was faking now. Sincerity, no doubt. She still had no proof who was behind that message, but she had her suspicions. There were too many unanswered questions in her mind about McMahon. But if there was one thing she knew, it was that she didn't trust him an inch.

'So do we know anything more other than that they're planning something?' asked Jack.

'Not yet. As you may know, prisoners of war are interrogated by both British and US officers. Two of our men were here on a familiarisation exercise when they overheard a group of prisoners talking about an arms store. The prisoners didn't know they spoke fluent German, but they shut up as soon as they saw them. Then these parcels started arriving, apparently from a charity sending comfort packages.'

The colonel reached behind him and pulled a box from a shelf, spreading the contents on the desk.

Marianne peered at them. 'Toothpaste. Carbolic soap. This all looks like the kind of things a charity might send, although I suppose there's more to it.'

'Correct again,' said the colonel. 'We sent some for analysis. The toothpaste is, in fact, aluminium powder, and the centre of the soap is red iron oxide. Combined, they make thermite, which is a highly effective explosive.'

'Bomb-making equipment. I wonder if this is part of the arms store?' said Jack.

'That's what we hope you'll find out. We've reactivated the hidden microphones in the cells in case we can pick up anything that way, and there are German interpreters listening in, but these prisoners are careful. Many of them are Waffen-SS. That's why we need you in there, picking up anything you can as well. Your cover story is that you're a British fascist detainee. At no time must you reveal that you understand German.'

'You don't say?' Jack got to his feet. 'No time like the present.'

'What about me?' asked Marianne.

'You're officially here representing the Red Cross to ensure that prisoners are being treated in line with the Geneva Convention and have everything they need. That means you'll inspect the prison, talk to the inmates and listen to their concerns.'

Marianne nodded. 'Excellent.' It also meant she could keep a weather eye on Jack.

As if reading her mind, he gently squeezed her arm. 'I can look after myself.'

'I know that.'

They knew one another better than anyone, better sometimes than they knew themselves. That squeeze of her arm was the best he could do when all either of them wanted was to throw their arms around each other and never let go.

McMahon cleared his throat. 'Are you ready?'

'I am.'

He opened the door and called for the guards, at the same time snapping one end of the cuffs around Jack's wrist once more.

Marianne stared straight ahead, not daring to look as Jack was led off to the cells. This was what they had signed up for after all. And it was more important than anything. More important even than the love that burned between them, the fires of which would never die. Not even if one of them were to perish, thought Marianne. She pushed the thought of that hangman's noose from her mind.

Jack was posing as a British prisoner. A traitor to his own country rather than the Führer. That should protect him from the fanatics and their Vehmic law with its vicious reprisals.

Even as she told herself that, Marianne knew there was no protection from the Nazis. They had both seen too much, done too much throughout this damn war to believe anything else. They were ruthless, remorseless and prepared to do anything.

Stay alive, she whispered in her heart.

'Be safe,' she muttered under her breath.

But no matter how much she bargained with the gods, Marianne knew there were no guarantees and no safety nets. Jack would live or die depending on the fates. They could be cruel or kind according to their whim.

FIFTEEN

9 DECEMBER 1944, PARIS

Levesque was late. I looked across the lobby at Dan, who held up five fingers. Fine. We would give it five minutes but no more. This was typical Levesque. He was probably embroiled in a conversation somewhere. Or possibly something a little more risqué.

With a minute to spare, he burst through the entrance, pausing theatrically to hold out his arms in an apologetic gesture, smiling and nodding at one or two correspondents he knew.

'Juliette, my dear, my apologies. I was held up in a meeting.'

I smiled my sweetest smile. 'Well, you're here now. Shall we go?'

He crooked his arm for me to take. I looped mine through his, aware that Dan was watching even though he was apparently engrossed in some paperwork.

'You look absolutely lovely tonight, by the way,' said Levesque. 'That colour suits you.'

I was wearing a burgundy Lanvin gown, the sleeves long

in line with its elegant silhouette, which plunged deeper than I would normally wear at the front. The perfect dress to get and keep the right kind of attention – which was exactly what I intended. It spoke of privilege and power, of the Paris I had left behind. The Paris I was re-entering, if only for tonight.

'Thank you,' I murmured. 'Tell me, who is our host this evening?'

Levesque tapped his nose and winked. 'All in good time.'

'Jean, you are such a tease.'

I slid into the chauffeur-driven Bentley which was waiting outside the hotel for us, inhaling the leather of the seats and the lingering scent of Levesque's cigars.

'I had it brought from England,' said Levesque. 'You like it?'

'It's very elegant,' I murmured, staring out of the window at a line of people still waiting patiently for their evening bread rations. Some were barely dressed for the harsh winter weather, their coats threadbare, fashioned from old blankets, while their feet were thrust into wooden shoes. Leather had been reserved for the German troops while material was still in short supply.

I twisted a fold of my satin gown between my fingers, feeling the weight and warmth of my wool coat on my shoulders, the guilt sitting like a solid lump in my stomach.

'Will Philippe be there this evening?'

I kept my tone as conversational as I could, but Levesque wasn't fooled for an instant.

'I believe he is out of town,' he said. 'So you can relax.'

That was the thing I loved most about Jean Levesque. He had his own moral code, one which served him well. Philanderer that he was, he was also a gentleman. He had seen the marks Philippe left on me and he didn't like them one bit.

We drew up outside an art nouveau mansion in the 16th, not too far, I noted, from my former home. Not far, either, from the former Gestapo HQ at Avenue Foch. At least now the neighbours wouldn't have to listen to the screams that rang from it night after night.

The people milling around in the grand salon we entered were also spectres arisen from my past, couturier-clad, reeking with privilege and perfumes from the finest houses, including that of Coco Chanel. There was no sign of her among the throng. Too dangerous, perhaps, to openly socialise with such a well-known collaborator now that Paris was liberated. Not that these people cared what anyone thought. They cared about their wealth, their businesses and escaping reprisals, although at least one also cared that I still lived and breathed, free of Philippe.

My eyes flicked around the room, searching, hunting him down, but he wasn't here. At least, not as far as I could see.

Relief flooded through me, mixed with disappointment. He was the big fish I was here to catch. A shame to bait the hook only to find the river was empty.

Levesque whisked me over to meet our host, a short man with a monocle and rather taller sense of his own importance.

'Louis, may I present Juliette de Brignac.'

'It's Juliette Villeneuve now,' I muttered.

Louis's hand in mine was too soft, his touch limp. But the feel of his lips on the back of my hand was like that of a slug, invasive and clinging.

'De Brignac? Any relation to Philippe?'

'I was married to him.'

A poisoned chalice but one which might gain me entry to this circle.

'Aren't you still married to him, my dear?'

'Technically, I suppose.'

I turned away, affecting boredom as I took a glass from the tray a waiter was holding out. Taittinger. Of course.

Turning back, I saw Louis was regarding me with a new interest.

'I'm surprised we haven't met before,' he said.

'I've been in London, working.'

'Working? My goodness. What is it that you do?'

'I'm a journalist, back in Paris on assignment for *The Times*.'

'How exciting. What will you be writing about? Fashion? Personalities?'

'Something like that.'

'I trained Juliette,' chimed in Levesque, beaming with fatherly pride.

Louis patted him on the arm. 'I'm sure you did. Come, let me introduce you to some people you may find amusing.'

He swaggered up to a dull-looking couple who were pointedly ignoring almost everyone in the room.

'May I present the Duc and Duchesse d'Aquitaine. I believe you know Juliette's husband, Philippe de Brignac.'

All at once their flat, bored stares sharpened.

'Former husband,' I murmured.

'Yes. Quite.'

Louis left us to it with a wave of his hand and a conspiratorial wink.

There was a pause as the pair continued to inspect me and then the *duchesse* turned to her husband. 'When is Philippe back from Berlin?'

She addressed him as if they were the only two people present.

'I thought it was today. I must have been mistaken.'

There was a stirring of the air in the room, as if someone had unleashed a wild bird. Or perhaps a predator.

'No, my dear. You were quite right.'

I followed the *duchesse*'s gaze, taking in the figure silhouetted against the entrance to the salon, his height, the breadth of his shoulders. I saw the *duchesse* raise her hand and beckon him over even as my mouth formed the word 'no'. Then he was standing there, a metre from me, not out of town after all but very much present.

'Juliette.'

'Philippe.'

I was damned if I was going to move so much as an inch. Instead, I stood my ground and stared at him, my gaze steady, my heart less so.

'Well, this is a surprise.'

He couldn't have loaded more into those words if he had tried.

'How was Berlin?' cooed the *duchesse*.

'Very productive,' said Philippe, his eyes never leaving my face.

I wanted to reach my hand up to my throat, had to fight to keep it where it was.

He can't hurt you now, Juliette. Just breathe. That's right. In and out.

The last time I'd seen him, he'd had his fingers wrapped around that same throat as he raped me. The very same night, I left him, taking the children with me. I could see from his knowing leer that he was thinking of that night too.

'Work trip?' asked Levesque, his voice tinged with dislike.

'You might say that.'

I could feel my throat closing. Tried not to gulp. I was suffocating, the room beginning to spin on its axis.

'Are you all right?' asked Philippe. 'You look a little pale.'

'I'm perfectly fine,' I snapped, hating the knowing sneer on his face.

'That's good to know.' He smiled. 'After all, our children need their mother.'

Cold rage cut through the heat that had been threatening to engulf me. I felt my mind and my heart ice over, red-hot anger replaced by clear, precise hate.

'I think I know what's best for my children,' I said. 'Now, if you will excuse me.'

Another minute and I would have pulled the tiny pistol from the top of my stocking holster and pressed it against his skull.

'Leaving so soon?'

Somehow he'd managed to get to the door before me. There was no way I could pass by him without having to get within arm's reach.

'Yes, Philippe, I am. I have work to do.'

'You? Work?'

He let out that short, derisive laugh of his that spoke volumes.

'Still scribbling are we? Writing for that idiot Levesque?'

'How about you, Philippe? Still slapping women around for fun?'

His eyes widened so that I could see the whites. I could also see the rage roiling behind them.

'Don't even think about it,' I murmured as I stepped

forward, coming up so close I could kiss him. 'I'm not the same woman you knew, Philippe. I've learned a lot since I last saw you.'

'Oh yes?' His sneer was only matched by the derision in his voice. 'Well, you always were a whore.'

'Ah but not for you, eh, Philippe?' I smiled, enjoying his fury.

'Where are my children?' he hissed.

'Safe, now that they're away from you.'

'You bitch. You have no right keeping them from me.'

'On the contrary, I have every right. I do what's best for them, and that does not include you.'

His hand shot out and grabbed my arm, his grip tightening in a way I remembered only too well. I twisted out of his grasp in a move he wasn't expecting, dealing him a sharp blow in the ribs, and took a step back.

'Like I said, I'm not the same woman you knew.'

His lips were pulled back from his teeth in a rictus grin, disbelief etched across every feature.

'Good to see you again,' I added more loudly for the benefit of those standing near. 'I'll be sure to keep an eye out for you now I'm back in Paris.'

My meaning was clear, the threat explicit. And I knew Philippe would be unable to resist.

Berlin. What the hell was he doing in Berlin? I needed answers. We needed answers. If I had to turn myself into a target then so be it. Make Philippe come after me. Blind him with his own hatred. Then I could pick him off like the vermin he was.

SIXTEEN

Max really did have the eyes of a snake, thought Christine. Unblinking. Ever watchful. And right at this moment they were watching her undress. She eased her strap over her shoulder, peeling the dress away so that he got a glimpse of what lay beneath. He blinked then, very slowly, and sucked in his breath. Any moment now, she thought. He blinked again, those eyes beginning to cloud over. Then he slid to one side and slumped on the bed, out cold.

She waited a couple of minutes to be sure before taking his pulse, which was slow but steady. Thank goodness for Suzanne and her expertise with sleeping potions. All that practice drugging the Nazi officers and Vichy government officials who'd frequented her brothel in Lyon had stood her in good stead. It had certainly worked on Klaus Barbie although, mercifully, Max Mytton wasn't in the same league. A nasty piece of fascist work certainly, but an amateur compared to the Gestapo chief.

She gave it another couple of minutes and then began to work her way through his pockets, starting with the coat he'd flung across the couch. His wallet was tucked in the interior pocket and, as she rifled through it, a couple of items caught her attention. One was a receipt from a hotel in Paris, the other a German banknote. She glanced from them to the figure sprawled on the bed, his lips quivering as he let out the occasional snore. The receipt was dated the day before. The Ritz. Of course.

There was nothing in the wallet to suggest who he'd met up with in Paris. Nothing in his trouser pockets either. She would just have to get it out of him some other way. She stood, looking down on him, at the trail of saliva trickling from one corner of his mouth.

'Where are you hiding that Red Book?' she muttered. 'And what the hell have you been up to in Paris?'

He let out another snore, a deep grunting sound that would have done a pig proud. Except that she quite liked pigs. Intelligent animals. This one was pretty sharp too. She'd have to play it carefully if he wasn't to rumble her and ruin the entire operation.

She settled down in an armchair to observe him. The moment he seemed to be coming round, she could slip off her things and whip on her robe, ready to soothe his ego and hint at the promise of another chance. Until then, she would read her book and while away the hours with a cup of tea.

She glanced at the cover – Simone de Beauvoir, *She Came to Stay*, all about a ménage à trois.

Christine wriggled off her shoes and curled her feet under her. One lover was bad enough. Two sounded exhausting. Truth be told, she wasn't too keen on the idea of anyone at all. She would much rather put a bullet between a man's eyes than have to gaze into them.

She heard Max stir and mutter something unintelligible.

He said it again, louder this time. It sounded as if he was speaking in German. Surely not.

She got to her feet and padded over to the bed, leaning over him so that she could hear what he was mumbling once more.

All of a sudden, his eyes snapped open and he let out a yell of pure rage. She gasped and staggered back, her hand reaching automatically for her gun, when she realised he was still asleep and dreaming. His eyes fluttered shut, and he fell back into a deep slumber, his moustache vibrating with each breath.

Something stirred in her memory, something Suzanne had said.

'They're using German soldiers dressed in US Army uniforms to infiltrate the troops.'

She edged towards the bed again, staring down at him, at those heavy-lidded eyes now shut tight and the wide mouth under his clipped moustache.

'Who are you?' she murmured. 'Who are you really?'

There was no reply. He was gone, out for a good while yet. It was an insane idea anyway. As if a German could pose as a well-known English lord for that long. And yet stranger things had happened. In any case, he was evidently a fascist. A dangerous one at that. She would work on him some more. Get the truth out of him one way or another, as well as finding that book. If he was what she suspected, those might be the last words he ever uttered.

Christine smiled at the thought.

SEVENTEEN

10 DECEMBER 1944, PARIS

'I love this place.'

'You do?'

Resplendent in his uniform, Dan was a fish out of water among the bohemians who'd flocked back to the Café de Flore and yet there was something about him that belonged.

'Is that who I think it is?' he asked in a conspiratorial whisper.

I followed his gaze across the room, my eyes alighting on a man sporting thick spectacles bent over the papers spread in front of him, a couple of glasses of cognac at his elbow.

'That's Jean-Paul Sartre,' I said, watching out of the corner of my eye as he relit his pipe before continuing to write.

'Cognac for breakfast. Impressive.'

'Not as impressive as his work. You know it?'

'I've read *Being and Nothingness*.'

'You read in French?'

'In Spanish, Italian, Arabic and German too.'

'How many languages do you speak?'

'Ten.'

I did a double take.

He laughed. 'I know what you're thinking. Dumb Yank couldn't possibly speak all those languages. You didn't even believe I could speak French. Come on now, admit it.'

'That's not what I was thinking.'

He took his napkin and dabbed at my cheek. 'You want to watch that choking on your coffee. Could be dangerous.'

I felt the brush of his fingertips on my face, looked up into his eyes and was lost. It wasn't coffee that was dangerous.

'I'll bear that in mind,' I said.

'You do that. And while you're at it, bear this in mind too.'

He was kissing me before I could draw breath, his lips soft, warm and searching against mine.

'If he can have cognac for breakfast, we can have kisses,' he said as he sat back and took a bite from his brioche.

'Did I say you could kiss me?'

'Do people give you permission before you shoot them?'

I bit off my retort at the sight of my cousin threading his way through the tables towards us.

'Guillaume. Just the man I wanted to see.'

He was bristling with hostility, his hair alive with indignation.

'I got your message.'

'So I see. Guillaume, this is Captain Diaz of the US Army. Won't you join us.'

Dan rose and held out his hand. 'Call me Dan.'

Guillaume ignored him. 'What do you want, Juliette?'

I gestured towards the empty seat between us. 'Sit down and I'll tell you.'

He flung himself into the chair, folding his arms in the way he'd done since he was six. 'I'm listening.'

'Good, because what I have to tell you is important. I need your help, Guillaume. Yours and that of your friends. There is something we need to do to make sure the Germans cannot succeed with certain plans.'

He sat up, more alert. 'The Germans have left.'

'They may have left Paris, but they are still there on the Belgian border, and they are planning something which could change the entire course of this war. It might even mean they retake France.'

Now I had him.

'How do you know all this?'

I took a breath, calculating the risk. From what I had seen, Guillaume and his mother were now further apart than ever. Still, it was a risk, but one I knew I had to take if I was to get him onside.

'Guillaume, what do you think I've been doing all this time? I've been working with the Resistance, and I can tell you that this intelligence comes from an impeccable source. Hitler's got people helping him with those plans right now, right here in Paris.'

'Fucking fascist bastards,' he snarled, slamming his fist on the table. 'Collabo pigs.'

'Guillaume, keep your voice down.'

'Why? We're all of one mind in here. We all hate the Germans.'

'Maybe not everyone,' I said. 'It pays to be cautious.'

His eyes flicked from right to left. 'You think there are spies in here?'

'There could be. There are spies everywhere. And that is what I want you and your friends to find out. My job here is to flush out these former collabos, as you call them, along with anyone who still considers themselves on the side of the Germans. Including Philippe.'

His name dropped like a bomb in the centre of the table.

'*Salop*. That bastard husband of yours is the worst of the lot.'

'I agree. Which is why I am going to end this marriage one way or another.'

'You don't mean...?'

He gaped at me, an incredulous grin spreading across his face. I waited him out. Let him think what he liked.

'OK. I'm in. My friends are in. You worked with the Resistance? Bravo, Juliette. I'm sorry about all the collabo stuff, but I had to be sure, you know. What do you need us to do?'

'Find out his day-to-day movements. Follow him. Your mother is friendly with him. See what you can find out from her.'

Guillaume rolled his eyes. 'If I must. I try not to spend too much time with my mother. You understand.'

'I do, but this is important, Guillaume. You are doing vital work to keep the fascists at bay.'

'Just you wait,' he said, 'until we communists run France.'

'I sincerely hope that never happens,' said Dan.

'What the hell do you mean by that?'

Dan jumped to his feet a fraction of a second before Guillaume, grabbed him by the shoulders and smiled.

'I mean that this should help remind you of your priorities,' he said, stuffing a wad of notes into Guillaume's pocket. 'Now run along, son, before I change my mind and have you arrested for assaulting Juliette the other day.'

Guillaume fingered the wad of notes and then thrust it deeper in his pocket.

'I didn't assault you,' he said. 'I just wanted to find out if you were a traitor or not. Now I know that you're not, I apologise.'

'Apology accepted. Guillaume, I am more of a patriot than almost anyone in this room. As much a patriot as my papa was. You remember my papa?'

He looked at me for a second and then his eyes dropped. The bravado was gone, replaced by what looked remarkably like shame. I'd got to him. Maybe even Guillaume had grown up at last.

'I'll be in touch,' he muttered, already sidling towards the stairs.

'You had better be,' I said. 'Or it won't just be my husband who gets it.'

Beside me, Dan snorted. 'I love you for that. Actually, I just love you.'

The world juddered to a halt, his words slamming down a gate in my heart even as I bit back the words I so wanted to say. I looked at him, at that mouth I longed to trace with my fingertip, into the topaz eyes that met mine with something I dared not name. I wanted him so badly. An ache deep within me told me I needed him. And yet another, deeper pain warned me not to go there.

'Another coffee?' I said.

EIGHTEEN

Harry King's apartment was pristine. I'd watched his mistress leave a half hour after he did with a basket over her arm and the determined air of a woman going in search of her rations. King might be connected, but there were some things you could no longer buy on the black market without your Nazi friends around. Luxury food, for instance. That was where I would start. The kitchen, as neat as the rest of it. But not all that clean once I'd inserted the listening device into the light socket and screwed the bulb back in.

I did the same in the bedroom and living area, this time concealing the bugs in the mattress through a tiny slash I made with my utility knife and in one leg of the coffee table in front of the couch. The telephone was the trickiest, the receiver stiff and resistant to being unscrewed.

I was working at it, trying to loosen it, when I heard a key in the lock.

I looked over my shoulder. The balcony. It was barely a metre wide, but it was all I had.

I just managed to get through the French doors and pull

them shut after me before I heard someone enter the room I'd just left and start to bang heavy objects around.

The minutes ticked by. The banging ceased, but now there were other sounds, metal scraping upon metal. I risked crawling from the corner where I'd crouched to peer into the room through the crack I'd left in the lace curtains. I could see Harry King bent over a pile of weapons on the table, cleaning and checking each one before loading them with ammunition and stacking them in a wine crate at his side. From what I could see, there was an assortment of machine guns and pistols, as well as grenades. He handled them like a man who knew what he was doing.

I wonder what you're going to do with those, my friend, I murmured in my mind.

As if reading it, he looked up and straight at me, or so it seemed. I scuttled back to the corner and held my breath, every muscle screaming, ready to dive over the balcony, but he didn't appear.

I peered through the bars at the street below. Two floors. I could make it if I landed well. I pressed my ear to the edge of the French doors, listening hard.

No sounds now. Had he finished? Or was he simply waiting me out, playing a cat-and-mouse game?

A slam of the street door beneath and to my right. I risked another look. There was King and another man, hauling the crate between them to a van parked opposite. I tried to make out the letters painted on it. Could see only a white line that could be anything. Then the engine fired and the van pulled out. It was now or never. I jumped to my feet.

FFI.

My God. He was using a van belonging to the Fifis, the French Forces of the Interior, aka the Resistance. Hated by the Germans and feared by de Gaulle as a threat, many of its members, notably the communists, were resisting his demand that they amalgamate with the regular French army. King and his friends must be using this van deliberately to stir up more unrest.

As I stared down, I saw King striding along the street, hat pulled low and hands in his pockets as ever. He and the van were headed in opposite directions. Curiouser and curiouser. It was time to get out of there and find out exactly what he was up to. Less than a week to go until the planned gathering of fascists in London and we knew the attacks were supposed to be simultaneous. It looked as if King was preparing in anticipation of that.

As I raced down the stairs, I passed his mistress coming up, her basket now full, although you wouldn't know it from the expression on her face. I nodded a greeting in passing, but she looked straight through me. Either King was a lousy companion or she had something else on her mind. No point in attempting to strike up a friendship. The woman gave off an air that would have kept a lapdog at bay. Besides, she was simply his latest billet, a convenient place to lay his head and whatever else he chose until he moved on to his next mark. I almost felt sorry for her. Women had to make tough choices in this war, and no doubt he had conned her too with his pretty words and promises. But there were some choices that were no choice at all.

I was fifty metres from the Hotel Scribe when I saw the same van parked right outside. I glanced around. No sign of King. I ducked into a doorway just in time to see another van draw up alongside it, this time unmarked, and park as well.

A man jumped out, went round the back and threw open the rear doors. Four other men spilled out and stood in a huddle as the driver of the first van emerged and unloaded his crate. They immediately piled in, seizing weapons, a machine gun and pistol for every man as well as the grenades they stuffed in their jackets, each one adorned with an FFI armband, although I would have sworn these men were nothing to do with the Resistance.

They looked to be too professional, their hair cut short in military style, their stance that of trained soldiers rather than the enthusiastic amateurs who made up much of the FFI. Trained soldiers and they were yards from the hotel, full of US military and war correspondents, Dan among them. There was no way I could reach the front door without running straight through them. But I had to do something. I couldn't let Dan and the others be picked off like sitting ducks. And it was obvious that was what they were planning. The incident with King must have been a rehearsal for this.

I looked up and down the street, frantically searching for some way round. There was none. The only way was through. So that was what I had to do.

I started running.

NINETEEN

'Help me!' I shouted as I ran full tilt into the huddle of men. 'Help. He's right behind me.'

They spun round, staring at me in confusion. I had thirty seconds to play on that, maybe a minute at best. I staggered towards the one who looked like the ringleader, my arms reaching for him, at the last second snatching his machine gun instead, ripping it out of his grasp as I kicked hard at the inside of his knee so he buckled, turning on his men and spraying them with bullets.

The nearest one fell without a sound, his eyes wide with shock, and I grabbed the grenades that rolled from his grasp, pulling out a pin as I raced towards the hotel, lobbing one back at them even as they finally managed to return fire, their bullets ricocheting off the ground all around me. I saw King emerge from between the US Army vehicles parked in rows in front of me, obviously wondering what the hell was going on. He clocked me running towards him, firing furiously all the while, and dived back between the trucks.

More shouts, then the hotel doors flew open and soldiers

spilled out, pistols at the ready, taking in the carnage before them. I saw one stagger back, a red stain bursting across his chest as one of King's men scored a direct hit. That was when I turned and lobbed the other grenade, watching as it landed a couple of feet from their van, hearing the roar as it exploded, catching the petrol tank that blew, flames shooting in a kaleidoscope of fire and shrapnel, the screams of King's men ripping through the smoke that belched black across the square.

'Juliette!'

Dan's voice, calling my name.

I whipped round. Felt something slam into my chest. Spun back the other way. More shouts and then other arms guiding me, half-carrying me into the hotel.

'Juliette.'

His voice again, softer now.

'You're hit. Lean on me. That's it. Medic! We need a medic over here!'

'King. He's here. Where is he?' I croaked.

'He got away, slippery sonofabitch.'

'The others. What about the others?'

'You took care of them, darling.'

'What, all of them?'

'Well, you left a couple alive. We'll interrogate them once we've made sure they'll live too. Now let's get that dressed. It looks nasty.'

I looked down at my chest, oozing blood, and at the medic tending to it. My coat was shredded where the shrapnel had struck, its thick folds protecting me from further injury. The medic carefully cut and peeled my blouse from the wound to expose my flesh beneath. Dan tactfully averted his eyes, focusing instead on my face.

'It's nothing,' I said. 'Just a scratch. I'm fine really.'

The medic extracted a piece of shrapnel the size of a two-franc coin and I saw my blood spurt from the wound before he pressed down on it with a dressing.

'You were lucky,' he said. 'Could have been a lot worse.'

Once it was clean and bandaged, I tried to stand up.

Dan pushed me back gently in my chair. 'You're not going anywhere.'

I looked around the small room off the lobby where he'd taken me, full of military paraphernalia. There were jerrycans and ration packs stacked beside the medical equipment. This was more a headquarters than a hotel, the hub not just of the US military but of the international press who'd descended to cover everything that happened in the chaos that was post-liberation Paris.

'No wonder they targeted this place,' I said. 'Anything happens here and it will be headlines around the world, especially if the Germans claim it as their victory.'

Dan took my hand. 'You're right. And thanks to you, they failed. But they're still out there, Juliette, and now they know it was you who took them down. We can't risk you showing your face right now, not while they might still be at large.'

'How many bodies were there?' I asked.

'Four.'

'How many did you arrest?'

'Two.'

'Then the only people still out there are King and his fellow conspirator. The rest were just hired hands, and there were only six of them.'

'Even so, I don't want you going out there until we've secured the area.'

For once, I was happy to let him have his way.

TWENTY

She looked tired, thought Suzanne. As beautiful as ever, of course, but there were shadows under those lovely eyes.

'You think he's German?'

'I do,' said Christine. 'He has a perfect English accent. Very upper crust. But when he was babbling away in German, that was perfect too. Hard to fake something like that when you're dreaming.'

'Indeed. Even so, it proves nothing. He may simply have learned it at school or have family there whom he visited for the holidays.'

'He had a German banknote in his wallet. It was printed this year. He also had a receipt from the Ritz in Paris, dated three days ago.'

'I see.'

Suzanne stared out the window for a moment. It gave Christine a chance to study her profile, that tip-tilted nose she knew all too well. A nose that had never yet failed Suzanne when it came to the truth.

'Get closer to him,' she said. 'Make him fall in love with

you. Do whatever it takes, but make sure you win his trust as well as his heart. You have to find that Red Book, and we know he has a copy. He refused to hand it over to the security services, for God's sake.'

Christine rose, hooking her handbag over her arm, feeling the weight of the Welrod within it. 'Understood.'

'I realise it's a tall order,' added Suzanne. 'We have so little time. But you need to move fast on this. Remember what I taught you. Find out what he needs and play it back to him. Mirror everything he wants. Become his perfect woman so he trusts you enough to let you into his home. I'm pretty sure that's where he's hidden the book. We've already searched his office.'

'He wants what all men want. Validation. The sense that someone understands him completely and that he matters.'

Suzanne chuckled. 'You listened in class. Well done.'

'I listened and then I learned, mostly out in the field. I will listen to him too. Every word. You can count on it.'

'Thank you. I don't need to tell you how much is resting on this.'

An image tore through Christine's mind like a tornado, one she always hoped she would never see again. Her stepfather, his face twisted, lunging at her in blind lust. Men. That was the other thing they wanted. The real thing. And she would give it to this one too, right before she watched him die just as her stepfather had done, his eyes wide in astonishment that a woman could kill as well as any man.

TWENTY-ONE

11 DECEMBER 1944, PARIS

Jean Levesque was adamant.

'I cannot help you with a piece like this. It would be social and business suicide for me.'

I pouted as best I could. Another thing that didn't come naturally anymore.

'On the contrary, it would make your name internationally. Just think, Jean, your byline on the article that gives a voice to those who feel that they are the true patriots, that they were in fact fighting for France when they apparently collaborated with the Germans. They will love you for it.'

He sucked on his cigar, cheeks puffing in and out in rhythm. 'You may have a point.'

'I do have a point. Jean, these people need to speak their truth too. They should be heard along with everyone else.'

He looked at me keenly. Levesque knew me too well. 'Since when have you been interested in giving a voice to the people you openly despise?'

'Since I became a journalist, in case you hadn't noticed.

They have their stories. I want to share them. The story is everything – that's what you taught me.'

He grunted in satisfaction, sounding like an avuncular professor faced with his star pupil. 'So I did.'

I pressed home my advantage. 'You'll do it then? Write the piece with me? I need you on this, Jean.'

He sat back, lacing his hands behind his head in that characteristic gesture. 'For *The Times*, you say?'

'Absolutely. A front-page feature.'

Which Suzanne would run over with a fine-tooth comb before it got anywhere near the editor of *The Times*, although she didn't need to tell him that. It was another tasty morsel of bait, a lure she hoped Philippe could not resist. If there was one thing my husband possessed, it was an oversized ego. Too bad the rest of him didn't match up.

'So where shall we start?'

She had him hooked. Levesque might be well known here in Paris, but, to the rest of the world, he was a nonentity, a footnote in a war that had given fame and notoriety to far bigger fish than he, and she knew how he quietly resented it. At heart, Levesque was a man who cared deeply what others thought.

'With Philippe.'

'Your husband? An interesting choice.'

'Isn't that the other thing you taught me, that conflict makes for a great story? I admit things are not good between us, and that's why I need you there. We didn't part on good terms at the party, let alone before that. You'll have to be the one to set this up and sell it to him as a great opportunity. I doubt he would say anything at all if it was just me.'

'He may not want to say anything even to me. Your

husband does not court publicity. In fact, he is a man who positively avoids it.'

'Don't you ever wonder why?'

The genial smile vanished. Levesque's face as he spoke was deadly serious.

'Listen to me, Juliette, and listen well. I don't like your husband. I never did. You know that, and you know why. But there are things that are too dangerous to explore right now, here in Paris. Things you must have seen for yourself. Some people have already fled to Germany. Others are desperately trying to recast themselves as secret heroes of the Resistance. Then there are those who are doing everything they can to help the Germans return.'

I looked at him and for once saw the man beneath the bonhomie. Levesque would do what it took to make sure he came out on top, whoever ultimately won this war. But there was something that beat at the heart of him, a solid sense of decency, that also made him the man who'd employed a Jewish secretary throughout the occupation, protecting her from the Nazis while making sure her family were safe too.

'Whose side are you on, Jean?'

He laughed. 'On the side of the truth of course. Whatever that might be. As you should be too. You're a journalist, remember.'

'Of course. Which is why we need to start on this piece as soon as possible. You can do it. Appeal to his ego. Do you think you can get hold of Philippe today?'

We had less than a week until that supposed social gathering in London. Less than a week until the attempted assassinations of Eisenhower and Churchill, along with a quarter of a million Nazi prisoners of war marching on London.

'I can try. I'll call a friend of his and suggest that we all meet, but I won't tell him exactly why, just that I have a proposition for him. We have more chance of him turning up that way.'

'Whatever you think but be sure to mention that I'll be there.'

'You can be sure that I will. He could never resist you, Juliette.'

For all the wrong reasons.

'Thank you,' I said.

'I just have one question.'

'Go on.'

'Does this have anything to do with your father?'

How much did he know?

'No. Why do you ask?'

'Because rumour has it that it was Philippe who denounced your father to the Gestapo. He told them that you were a vital part of the Resistance and that if anyone knew where you were, it would be him.'

I felt my guts twist and start to burn.

'Where did you hear this rumour?'

'That I cannot tell you.'

'I see.'

'That's the problem, Juliette. You don't see. You don't understand how Paris works now. How the world works now. Go back to London before someone gets hurt or even killed. I worry about you.'

'People have already been hurt and killed, my papa for one. Philippe would do anything to find me, even betray his own father-in-law, so it's far better I control this and go to meet him openly.'

'And what do you hope to achieve by all this?'

'The same thing I have been fighting for throughout this war. Peace.'

'You'll only get that from Philippe when he's dead.'

'Then so be it.'

TWENTY-TWO

'It's all set up. Levesque and I are meeting Philippe tomorrow, along with his friend.'

'Your husband?'

'Yes.'

'He agreed to this?'

'I know it seems unlikely, but Jean can be very persuasive. There's also the fact that I'll be there. It's an irresistible opportunity for Philippe. Another chance to get at me and perhaps find out more about the children.'

Dan raked his fingers through his hair, as he did whenever he became agitated. 'Where are you meeting him?'

We were once more at what was fast becoming 'our' table at the Ritz, only this time there was no thug pointing a gun at us from under a table. Instead, there was only a woman with cut-glass cheekbones who drifted past looking far too like Marlene Dietrich to be anyone else and Meier prowling his domain, more watchful now than ever.

'The Jockey Club. Its members were very supportive of

the Vichy government, I understand, so no wonder Philippe and his friends favour it.'

'I'll make sure you have backup.'

'Will that include you?'

I hadn't meant that to slip out the way it did, the undercurrent of vulnerability ringing through. If truth be told, I wanted him there as I faced down Philippe, even if only in the background. Another dangerous truth. I had long ago learned not to rely on anyone.

'You bet.'

His eyes softened as he looked at me across the table, the candles bringing out the gold lights in them. If there was any man on this earth I could trust, it would be Dan.

'That makes me happy,' I whispered.

'I want to make you happy. That's all I want.'

I smiled at him as I raised my glass to my lips. 'Not quite all, if I remember right.'

'You do. But in your own time, Juliette. I kind of like this French idea of dating. So we go at your pace.'

'What if my pace is faster than yours?'

He threw back his head and laughed. 'Touché.'

I was wearing a dress with a higher neck tonight, my bandaged wound under it healing well, only aching now and then. Not as much as my heart ached to hold this man and be held by him, to feel his flesh upon mine, human against human, hearts beating together, an affirmation of life. But there was something I needed to know first.

'Have you ever been in love before?' I asked.

The instant the words left my lips, I regretted them. I could see the answer written on his face, in his eyes. It was one of pure agony, the kind of pain you only experience when you've lost someone you love deeply.

'I have.'

Something in me drove me on. I had to know. 'And?'

He swallowed, his eyes focused somewhere else, somewhere far from this room, this city. From me. He was looking back, down the months and years, to a time when she, whoever she was, had still been a part of him. Perhaps she still was, at least in his heart.

'And she died.'

'Oh my dear. I am so sorry.'

I grabbed his hand instinctively, but he pulled it away, withdrawing into himself at the memory. I let the silence extend between us, an invitation. Finally, painfully, he accepted it.

'In a plane crash,' he said. 'Back home. Nothing to do with the war. It was just one of those things.'

'When did this happen?'

'Right before I enlisted. But that wasn't why I joined up. I would have done it anyway. You remind me of her, you know. Not in the way you look or anything, but in your spirit. You have the same sweetness as my Elizabeth did.'

Elizabeth. I rolled her name around my mind, picturing a wholesome girl with apple cheeks and a perfect smile, just like this.

'I'm not sweet.'

'Yes you are. You just hide it well. So did she. She also had guts, like you. She was an aeronautics engineer and had to work mostly with men, be one of the guys. Ironic the way she died. She absolutely loved planes and flying them.'

An engineer who could fly planes. I mentally crossed off the apple cheeks.

'I think I would have liked her,' I said.

'I'm sure you would, and she would have liked you. Although it might have gotten a bit complicated.'

I was relieved to see him smiling.

'Oh I'm sure we could have worked something out,' I teased.

'You'd probably have ganged up on me.'

'Probably. You miss her a great deal?'

'I do but in a different way now, since I met you.'

'Met me or got to know me?'

'Both. When I first met you, it was up on that plateau. I'd just jumped out of a plane and there you were. It was there I got to know you better too. I loved our evening up there. I don't recall exactly what we talked about, but it felt like everything. At least, all the important stuff. Hopes, dreams, that kind of thing. I guess we're still filling in the details.'

'And so here we are.'

'Here we are.'

I twined my fingers through his, tightening them a little. 'Let's go,' I murmured.

His fingers curled around mine in return. 'What, now? Are you sure?'

'I have never been more sure of anything in my life.'

He smiled. 'Me either.'

As if by magic, Meier appeared at our table.

'I thought you might like to know we have a suite available this evening. At very short notice. Of course, there would be no charge. Shall I lead the way?'

I glanced at Dan and then him. 'That would be very kind.'

He gave us his customary bow and ushered us discreetly through the bar to the doorway, where a bellboy stood waiting.

'The Imperial Suite,' said Meier, handing him the key.

The bellboy in turn bowed and led us to a private lift set around the corner from the public ones. Once we were safely inside, he pressed the button for us, pulled the gates and retreated back through the doors with another bow. They'd scarcely closed when Dan pulled me into his arms, his mouth descending hungrily on mine, hands already exploring the places we both wanted him to go.

By the time the doors opened again, we were half-dressed, tearing at one another's clothes as if we were starving. I don't remember stumbling out of the lift and into the bedroom where we tumbled onto the silken sheets. All I knew was that I had a hunger that was crying out for this man, an appetite that was only matched by his and would not be sated for many hours yet. Hours that I would remember for the rest of my days.

He was shy at first, his touch tender, handling me as if I might break into a million pieces.

I took his hand firmly in mine and moved it. 'Here,' I said. 'Like that.'

My gasps of pleasure ignited something in him. It was as if I'd lit a touchpaper that set the fires burning until they consumed us both, skin melding into skin, the heat building as we moved in perfect rhythm, calling out each other's names, caressing and kissing, then a rush of pleasure as I arched up, crying out, begging him not to stop. White hot now, stars exploding in my head, every muscle rigid in ecstasy. The flames receding, dying down as I sank too, deep into his embrace, feeling his mouth featherlight on my forehead, my brow. Deep, deep peace.

'Did I hurt you?'

'What? No. I'm hardly a virgin.'

He traced the bandage on my chest with his fingertips. 'I meant here.'

'That? It's nothing.'

Another kiss, this time on my lips.

'You know what? You're really something.'

Our noses touching, breath intermingling, so close now I could feel the brush of his lashes, butterfly light.

'So are you,' I murmured.

'You sure about that?'

'Absolutely.'

'Really, really sure?'

His smile was a challenge I couldn't resist.

'Maybe you need to convince me some more.'

'I was hoping you'd say that.'

'You were? Go on then. Convince me.'

'It will be my pleasure.'

'And mine.'

I could feel him growing hard again against my stomach, his hands once more roaming my body.

'You French women sure know what you want.'

'We do. And I want you.'

'You've got me for as long as you want me.'

Forever, I whispered in my head, even as a bolt of fear shot through my heart.

TWENTY-THREE

12 DECEMBER 1944, PARIS

The Jockey Club hummed with the haute bourgeoisie along with a sprinkling of British and American officers. The management considered it wise to offer them free membership now that the Germans had left and the Vichy government was history. Women were not permitted to be among those members, although they were tolerated in the restaurant. It was the kind of club my husband loved and I loathed.

The place reeked of privilege along with the smells that permeated all gentlemen's clubs – the heady aroma of cigars overlaid with expensive cologne and fine wine, tempered by the faintest whiff of decay.

I glanced at the faces of those seated in the bar as we passed through, many with cheeks or noses as red as the carpet beneath their feet. I suspected they'd spent the entire war like this, among their own kind, refusing to acknowledge that anything outside these walls had changed.

Levesque nodded to one or two, affecting an air of belonging. No matter how much money he now raked in, he couldn't hope to aspire to membership. British and American officers were one thing. They represented a useful connection to the new regime. Someone like Levesque, though, was beneath the pale, possessed of neither the correct lineage nor a suitable title. My husband was fortunate enough to have both, which only demonstrated how breeding was no guarantee of decency. A minor aristocrat he might be, but it was sufficient for the Jockey Club.

He was already seated at a table with his friend, a man I would have instantly forgotten were it not for the fact he was with Philippe and sporting a deep scowl. The scowl remained in place through the introductions and while we were being seated.

As soon as the sommelier had departed to fetch us a bottle of the finest burgundy, he coughed and then addressed the air somewhere to the right of my ear. 'Philippe tells me you are a journalist.'

'That's right.'

I took a sip from my water glass, keeping my hand rock steady. If these two thought they could rattle me with their attitude, they could think again.

'I trained Juliette,' said Levesque. 'I publish *La Vie*.'

'Ah yes. I have heard of it.'

'I now work for the London *Times*,' I said. 'That's why I'm here, on assignment.'

I could feel Philippe's eyes upon me, mocking. He had always sneered at my writing, at what he called my 'playing at being a journalist'. Well, I wasn't playing now, and if he thought this was a game, I would make damn sure I won.

'My editors would like to hear all sides of the story here in Paris. They want to know how people like, ah, you feel about the occupation, especially now that the Germans have departed.'

'People like us?'

Philippe barely spoke above a whisper, his voice sibilant, his eyes like flint.

'Yes. The aristocracy. The privileged. After all, you had an entirely different experience of the war to, shall we say, the common folk. There is the same divide in England – some of the upper classes sympathise with the German point of view.'

I was treading as carefully as I could, but they weren't fooled for an instant.

'If you mean you would like to talk to people who want to see France and the rest of Europe free of these damn communists then, yes, I have plenty to say on the subject,' growled Philippe.

'That is one aspect,' I said as sweetly as I could, all the while fighting back the bile that rose in my throat.

This man had sold out my father to the Nazis above and beyond everything else he'd done to me. I hadn't thought it possible to hate him more than I already did, but sitting there, across the table from him, I would have happily stabbed him through the eye with my fork. Instead, I made great play of pulling out my notebook and pen to hide my reaction. Only a week until the planned assassinations. I had to get information out of them and fast.

'Is that why you collaborated with the Germans?' I asked. 'Because you hate the communists?'

I heard Levesque let out a low groan beside me. Philippe's eyes flashed, but he composed himself, as ever. He was good at that. At doling out punishment in a frighteningly controlled way.

'I have no idea what you're talking about,' he said.

'Oh but I think you do, Philippe. You're quite a fan of the Führer from what I hear.'

His friend scowled even deeper, but Philippe raised a hand before he could say anything. 'My wife has always been, shall we say, a fantasist. Haven't you, my dear?'

Not so much flint now as eyes that were devoid of light, deep wells of darkness that regarded me dispassionately – as he might a particularly troublesome pest.

'If I am a fantasist, what does that make you, Philippe? Aside from the abusive bastard you have always been.'

Levesque was stock-still in his chair alongside me now, tensed for whatever might be coming next. I knew what was coming next so I was as relaxed as I could be in the face of the onslaught I could see Philippe about to unleash. Good. This was exactly what I wanted. Then I saw his friend place a firm hand on Philippe's arm.

'This meeting is over,' he said.

'Quite. Absolutely. Well, thank you for your time, gentlemen.'

Levesque couldn't get to his feet fast enough. I remained seated, my gaze never shifting from Philippe's face.

'I'll be seeing you,' he said, the threat filtering through the reasonable tone he adopted whenever he was about to do his worst, as he intended it to.

'I look forward to it,' I said and smiled, finally taking my leave.

It was only when we reached the front door that Levesque exhaled. 'What the hell was all that about?' he asked. 'I thought you wanted to interview him?'

'I just did.'

'You barely got two words out of Philippe before you

annoyed him sufficiently to ensure he never speaks to you again.'

We were out in the fresh air now, my heartbeat falling back to its normal rhythm with every step.

'On the contrary, I got exactly what I wanted.'

'Which was?'

'Philippe is now burning to have the last word, one way or another. To shut me up once and for all.'

But first, he wanted to know where my children were. I refused to think of them as his too.

Levesque shook his head. 'You're playing a dangerous game, Juliette.'

'Maybe. Maybe not.'

All I knew was that the hook was well and truly baited now. Philippe wouldn't rest until he'd swallowed me whole and spat me out just the way he wanted. To do that, he would have to come after me. The chase was on.

TWENTY-FOUR

12 DECEMBER 1944, LONDON

Christine inspected herself in the mirror, making sure every detail was just right. Her silver dress, alluring yet elegant, her lips red with promise, platinum-blonde hair artfully falling around her face à la Veronica Lake. The effect was pure Aryan perfection and should prove irresistible to Max, provided the man stayed sober long enough. She inserted a cigarette carefully between her lips so as not to smudge them and lit it, watching the smoke curl around her reflection. If she were more fanciful, she would think it a metaphor for her life, a game of smoke and mirrors. But she was a pragmatist to her polished fingertips, and she had work to do.

Downstairs in the drawing room, Max was waiting, elegant in tails, studying one of the paintings on the walls of her borrowed house, a rather dull rendition of the English countryside complete with a herd of cows.

'Is this a Constable?' he asked as she made her entrance.

'Well of course,' she purred as he looked her up and down.

'You are quite simply stunning, my dear.'

'Why, thank you.' She leaned away from his tongue nuzzling her ear, pretending to adjust a diamond earring as she did so. 'We'd better be getting along. Don't want to miss the welcoming speeches, do we?'

'I didn't know you were so keen on hearing the same old remarks,' he said. 'I really don't mind turning up fashionably late.'

He cupped her breast with his right hand and squeezed, rotating it slightly in that way men of his type somehow thought seductive.

'I'm not,' she said. 'But I understand from Lady Rattray that there is to be a very special announcement. I don't think we should miss that.'

She was already moving towards the door, throwing a smile back at him.

'Besides, we have all the time in the world later.'

Time she would spend listening to him snore once more. He really was easy to fool, being far too dependent on alcohol to get him through an evening. All she had to do was keep him drinking and then ensure the final glass was doctored in the right way. It seemed almost a relief to him that he fell unconscious rather than having to perform. Impotent, probably, and hiding it with his crass displays outside of the bedroom.

She was more than happy to let him paw at her if it meant she could keep him at arm's length without angering him. She really needed to get inside his house in Mayfair, then she could have a good snoop round and try to find where he'd hidden that Red Book.

Then there was the question of his true nationality. She needed more time to get to the bottom of that too. For now, it was clear he was a fascist, at least in name. He was evidently more interested in the social side of the gatherings than any real activism.

Take the soirée this evening, one she knew in her bones was a precursor to the main event next week. Although nothing concrete had been said, Lady Rattray had made it clear it was imperative that everyone attend on time. She wondered who exactly was giving the welcoming speeches. She would find out soon enough.

The venue for this evening was a rather larger mansion in Kensington, a gloved butler waiting on the steps to greet arrivals and usher them towards the footmen bearing trays of drinks just inside the entrance.

Christine took a sip from her glass of champagne. Taittinger, if she wasn't mistaken.

As they entered the ballroom, she took in the raised dais set at one end, the chairs grouped around tables adorned by vases of cornflowers, a name card in front of each place. She reached out and felt the petals. Silk of course. Not even this lot could conjure up cornflowers in December. What was more concerning was their symbolism. The cornflower had once been used as a secret signal by which Nazis could identify one another. Now these people had appropriated it too. They were certainly not afraid to pin their allegiances to their chests.

There were some splendid chests in the room, spilling from tailcoats and billowing above necklines, all of them proudly displayed, the upper classes on show. Not all the people in the room were so entitled. She noticed a couple of the women from the other meeting, their dresses noticeably cheaper, their expressions less confident, although the exact same fervour burned in their eyes. The master of ceremonies tapped a gavel on the lectern to indicate people should take their seats.

She looked at his misshapen fingers curled around the handle, the cornflower attached to his lapel, cufflinks gleaming gold at his wrists. Suzanne had chosen them for him from a selection obtained from German officers kept in some luxury in a secluded country mansion rather than a prisoner-of-war camp. Each was shaped as an eagle, another symbol beloved of the Third Reich. Wires ran up the inside of his sleeves from each cufflink. She only hoped the receiver taped to his side was sensitive enough to capture everything that was said tonight. Suzanne had promised they would be listening nearby in case anything turned ugly, although with any luck, Edward's cover would hold.

'Ladies and gentlemen, it is my honour to welcome you here this evening to the newly formed Cornflower Club. Heil Hitler.'

It felt so wrong to give the Nazi salute and yet she knew she had to pull it off, arm thrust out straight, the words cried aloud with suitable passion, joining the chorus of voices that resounded off the walls of the ballroom, sending the chandeliers rattling as they sat down once more.

She stole a look at the others at her table. There was a large woman seated opposite who looked familiar from the photos on file. The man to her right belched, emitting a sulphurous odour that was a perfectly satanic summary of the atmosphere all around her, smiles masking sentiments too horrible to think about, each and every one of them a traitor to their fingertips.

She turned her attention back to Edward, who was holding an envelope.

'Under your plates, you will find your orders in an envelope like this one,' he said.

Sure enough, under the plate set in front of her, she found one and slit it open with a manicured nail.

'Each of you must be at your appointed place at exactly the time indicated,' continued Edward. 'You will receive further instructions once you arrive.'

On her instructions, there were three lines containing an address in Westminster with the time given as 11 a.m. on 16 December. She glanced at the man to her right. There was a different address on the piece of vellum in his hand, neatly typed as it was with hers. He caught her look and she quickly bestowed her best smile on him.

'I can't wait,' she murmured.

He leered back at her. 'Indeed.'

His wife peered disapprovingly at her from his other side. At least, she assumed it was his wife. Far too plain to be a mistress but still protective of her catch. If he'd been Christine's, she would have thrown him back.

'And now,' Edward was saying, 'please welcome our guest speaker this evening.'

Christine stiffened. McMahon. What the hell was he doing here, all dressed up in white tie? She would scarcely have recognised him but for the cynical little smile that she could cheerfully slap from his face.

She watched him take the stand, turning that same smile on Edward. Did Edward know who he was? Was McMahon in on this op or was he working his own?

'Ladies and gentlemen, it's my pleasure to report that your parcels were delivered safely to the respective camps and prisons. We intercepted some, of course, to make it seem as if we were doing our job, but you can rest assured that sufficient got through.'

A ripple of laughter ran through the room along with a smattering of applause.

'Less than one week today,' McMahon went on, 'we will unleash Hitler's armies on this country and in Paris, as well as on the front lines. Our targets, as you know, are the Supreme Leader of the Allied Command, General Eisenhower, and the Prime Minister of Great Britain, Winston Churchill, along with every man and woman who resists. We have 250,000 loyal German soldiers ready to march on London from those same camps and prisons to which you sent your parcels. They will be joined in their triumph by some of the Führer's most loyal friends.'

He paused for effect, smirking at the cheer that went up, accompanied by a clinking of glasses.

'I am talking about all of you of course.'

More cheers. She felt Max nudge her.

'To us, my darling,' he said, looping his arm through hers so that they drank from one another's glass.

'To the Fatherland,' Christine responded, untangling herself as soon as she decently could.

'Yes, yes. Of course.'

McMahon banged the gavel for attention before continuing.

'All of those people, all of us, will march upon the capital. We will take it and therefore take this country as well. Without a leader, the British people will quickly surrender. Then the Führer can reign supreme over Europe and, eventually, the rest of the world. Heil Hitler.'

As one, the assembly leaped to their feet, shouting out another chorus of Heil Hitlers. Christine caught McMahon glancing her way. Damn the silver dress. It was gorgeous but it caught the light, as did her hair.

She ducked her head, pretending to have dropped something, sinking back into her seat along with everyone else. When she raised it again, McMahon was once again addressing the entire room. If he'd recognised her, he showed no reaction.

'Now I believe there is a musical interlude before we eat. Thank you all for your loyalty and support.'

More Heil Hitlers as the band shuffled onto the stage in place of McMahon and struck up what sounded like a Strauss waltz to Christine's ears. She saw McMahon making his way through the tables, heading towards the doors, and quickly rose from her seat.

'Would you excuse me,' she murmured and made for the doors too, her eyes fixed on the back of McMahon's head, her fingers curled around the pistol in her evening purse just in case.

Across the salon that served as an anteroom to the ballroom, she caught sight of McMahon deep in conversation with a couple of men, both in white tie with a cornflower attached to their lapels. These must be the committee members of the Cornflower Club. She watched as Edward came through from a room beyond and joined them, shaking McMahon's hand with an enthusiasm she was sure he didn't feel.

'Can I help you, madam?'

One of the hovering footmen appeared at her elbow.

'I was looking for the ladies,' said Christine.

'Over there, madam.'

He pointed towards a door beyond the huddle of men that included McMahon. Damn. Now she would have to walk past them. There was nothing for it but to hold her head high and act natural.

In the event, the men ignored her, their business obviously far more important than some mere woman in search of the toilet. She gave it a good ten minutes in there before she emerged, hoping they might have dispersed, breathing a sigh of relief when she saw that they had.

'Well, fancy meeting you here.'

She whirled. So not all of them had disappeared. McMahon peeled himself from the wall where he'd been leaning, clearly waiting for her.

'I could say the same.'

'Yes but you won't. You won't say anything at all, in fact, about seeing me here or what went on at this meeting.'

'Or?'

She stared him down, steel clashing against steel as their eyes met and held.

'Or I'm afraid I would have to have you silenced. Permanently. Which would be a great pity.'

'It would be an even greater pity if you were to be silenced first.'

He bared his immaculate American teeth. 'I'd like to see you try.'

'You won't see me. That's the point.'

'Right. Well, good luck with that, Countess.'

She hated the mocking emphasis he put on her fake title. Hated everything about him, in fact.

'Good luck yourself, Agent McMahon. Or do you have some kind of German title now?'

'Agent will do.'

'What the hell is going on?'

They both whirled round to see Max, face pink with indignation and an excess of alcohol.

'I was wondering where you'd got to,' he added. 'Now I see you had some sort of assignation.'

Christine wanted to cry aloud with relief. He hadn't heard the part about McMahon being an agent. At least, she hoped he hadn't. He seemed far more incensed about the fact she'd left him alone at the table to talk to another man.

'My darling,' she cooed, weaving her arm through his and gazing up at him in adoration. 'I am so sorry. I know I've been an age but we haven't seen one another since the Right Club last met. Jim was just telling me that his wife couldn't be here tonight. Such a shame. We are the greatest of friends.'

'Oh. I see. Well, no harm done. The Right Club you say?'

'Yes, darling. You must have been a member too. Why on earth did I never see you at meetings?'

Out of the corner of her eye, she saw McMahon was leaving. She steered Max back towards the ballroom, stroking his arm all the while to keep his attention firmly on her.

'Don't know about you but I'm famished,' she said.

He looked at her, his eyes already glassy with drink.

'Isn't that where we started this evening?' He sniggered, his hand reaching once more for her breasts.

She suppressed an urge to kick him in the balls, playfully swiping away his hand instead.

'Now, now. Plenty of time for that later.'

Time too to slip that sleeping potion in his drink. Once he was asleep, she could think it all through. What on earth McMahon was up to and what that meant for their mission. The plans that had been revealed tonight and the details to come. She needed to speak to Suzanne, and the only safe way to do that was in person. Damn all this cloak-and-dagger stuff when it came to knowing what other agents were doing. It was all very well keeping things tight for security reasons, but not if it meant flying in the dark.

She glanced at Max as they took their seats once more, a plan forming. Up the dose. Steal his car for the night. Of course there was always the risk she might overdose him, but that would be a small price to pay when so many lives were at stake.

TWENTY-FIVE

12 DECEMBER 1944, PARIS

'You're nuts.'

Dan pushed himself up on one elbow, his olive skin gleaming with the sweat that soaked the sheets beneath us, rumpled testament to the ecstasy of the past couple of hours. We hadn't meant to tumble once more between those sheets before dinner. At least, I hadn't. But Dan had knocked on my door at the Scribe, where I was now ensconced, to escort me to the dining room and one thing led to another. Security at the hotel had been trebled, with troops permanently stationed in and outside to guard it. I was a lot safer here than in the apartment.

'Thank you. I will take that as a compliment.'

'I mean it, Juliette. Your husband sounds like a psycho. You were supposed to flush him out, not push him into finishing you off.'

'He won't. Not until he has found out where the children are at least.'

Dan pushed a lock of hair from his forehead. 'My God. You're playing with fire here.'

'I know what I'm doing.'

The anger was rising now, dissipating the glorious heaviness in my limbs, the languor of lovemaking. He must have detected that because he bent and kissed me softly.

'I know you do,' he murmured. 'That was all too obvious.'

I could feel my response stirring again as his hand moved across my body, caressing my breasts before travelling on down. I reached down and wrapped my fingers around his wrist, stopping him in his tracks.

'I mean it,' I said.

A fractional pause and then he pulled back. 'I know.'

'My husband is a psycho, as you call him, and that's something I can use to our advantage. Right now he is in control. Or he thinks he is. He can hide behind his rich friends and in places like the Jockey Club. I want him out in the open where we can watch him and follow him. The only way he'll break cover is if he loses that control and starts coming after me.'

Dan curled a strand of my hair around one finger then tugged it gently. 'That's a crazy idea. You might think you're tough but he'll break you just like this.'

He held up the solitary hair he'd plucked from my head and broke it in half. A memory rose unbidden, Philippe dragging me across the floor by that same hair. I shuddered.

'No he won't,' I whispered. 'I'm stronger now. He can't hurt me.'

'We both know that's a lie. Juliette, let me handle him.'

'No!'

I cried out louder than I intended, startling both of us.

'He's mine,' I muttered, the tears flowing freely now. 'I want him to know what it's like to suffer the way he made me suffer, to be terrified that you are about to die and that you will never see your children again.'

'Sweetheart, I'm so sorry he did all that to you, but it only makes you the more vulnerable.'

I felt something tighten in me then. Resolve. Mixed with hate.

'On the contrary, it makes me invincible. I'm not afraid of him anymore. In fact, I pity him. He's a weak man who takes out his pain on others, especially someone like me who was foolish enough to love him.'

'It's never foolish to love someone.'

I looked at him, at that sensuous mouth inches from mine, his eyes glowing with a fire I wanted to curl up next to and never leave.

'It depends who you choose to love.' His mouth on mine now, moving as he murmured. 'I choose to love you.'

I felt it then, that knell of something deep within me, a prescience that threw a shadow over my heart and only made me want to cling to him all the tighter.

I love you. My lips formed the words, but they remained there, unspoken. I knew if I unleashed them I would be at sea, adrift without an anchor. And as much as I wanted to be swept away with this man, to allow the wave to take me, I was also afraid that he and I might drown, that we would be submerged beneath something that was bigger than both of us. It was why the tears kept falling as much as I tried to stop them, snaking down my cheeks and dripping from my chin even as he tried to kiss them away.

'Why are you crying?'

'I don't know,' I lied.

Of course I knew. I had always known. Philippe had ruined me for any other man, just as he said he would. I couldn't risk giving my heart away again, especially as it wasn't just mine to give. A part of it belonged irrevocably to my children. To France. To so many things beyond this place, this time. This man. And yet he made me feel in a way I'd never felt before, a deep sense of coming home, a peace I'd known only as a child, safe and adored.

I reached for him, clinging to his flesh, his bones, crying out as we rode those waves together once more, shouting aloud the joy and the pain, the agony of loving him, the knowing that it couldn't last. I could hear myself sobbing. Heard him calling my name. But I was already plunging, falling into a pit where he could no longer reach me, the walls closing in until all I heard now was silence. Apart from the one word I whispered. His name.

TWENTY-SIX

13 DECEMBER 1944, WILTSHIRE, ENGLAND

They came for him in the shower block, as Jack knew they would. One moment icy water was streaming over his face, the next he was sprawling on it, a heavy foot in the middle of his back pinning him down while hands ripped off the shorts he'd prudently worn.

'Turn him over.'

'You. Move. Now.'

They were shouting at him and at one another in German, their accents thick. Bavarian maybe. He had two choices – resist and get kicked to a pulp. Possibly more. Or give in and talk his way out of it. Show them he wasn't afraid. It was the way of prisons and camps, even in this unholy war. There was a hierarchy, although this one was more lethal than most.

'What the hell do you want? Happy now?'

He jumped to his feet and snatched his underwear out of the hands of the short, powerfully built man to his left who stood, muscles flexed, his blood-group tattoo just visible under his left arm. Waffen-SS no doubt.

'You see – I'm no filthy Jew.'

Jack stepped into his underpants, keeping his back to the wall as they stood in a semi-circle in front of him, their eyes feral with suspicion, sizing him up.

'You're British?' snapped the short fellow in English, the veins all too visible on his shaved skull.

'Yes.'

'So why are you in here?'

'They suspect I'm a German agent.'

They eyed one another.

'They picked me up on my way back from Bavaria. I was helping out with a training camp there.'

'What sort of camp?'

Jack tapped the side of his nose. 'Special place where they're planning a surprise for the Allies.'

Shorty's eyes narrowed. 'What kind of surprise?'

'Can't say, old man. Not until I know you a bit better. Wouldn't want this sort of thing to get out and spoil things, if you get my drift. After all, we're on the same side you and I. We both want the same result.'

Jack stared back at him confidently, hoping he wasn't overplaying it.

The German frowned. 'Erich, have you heard of a British agent being sent to this camp before?'

The gangly sidekick who had until now remained silent shook his head. 'No.'

Shorty sucked his teeth. His feral friends didn't look convinced.

'Where are you really from?' he demanded. 'You don't speak German, so how can you be an agent for us? You have no blood-group tattoo, and I've never heard of a special training camp in Bavaria.'

'That's because it's top secret.'

Jack took a step, closing the gap between them, thrusting his face into the other man's to make the difference in their height all the more obvious.

'It's not the kind of place an ordinary soldier like you would know about. Although you might have been useful, seeing as you speak English. As for tattoos, some of us are working undercover, infiltrating the American lines. You think they'd send in someone with a blood-group tattoo to do that kind of work?'

A couple of the men shifted from foot to foot, a new respect dawning in their eyes.

'You're one of Skorzeny's men?'

The unit commanded by Otto Skorzeny acting on the orders of Adolf Hitler, whose brainchild it was to cause confusion by infiltrating the US troops. The fact that this man knew about it told Jack he was party to classified information.

'I am. Was on my way to procure some more uniforms for our boys when I was caught. Too bad I'm going to miss the main event.'

'Not necessarily,' said the gangly one. 'We have our own plans here. You're welcome to join in the fun.'

'Oh yes?' Jack eyed him keenly. The tall fellow appeared far better educated than his shorter counterpart and he knew about Skorzeny. An officer perhaps.

'We're having a meeting tonight, eight o'clock in Block B. Come along.'

It was an order rather than a suggestion.

'I will.'

They snapped to attention as one, thrusting out their arms in the Nazi salute.

'Heil Hitler.'

'Heil Hitler.'

Jack's salute was perfect, jaw jutting at just the right angle, eyes fixed on some mythical fascist future, but still Shorty shot him a final glare.

'I'll see you there,' he muttered.

Jack smiled. 'I look forward to it.'

It was only after they left that he noticed the discarded sheet they'd brought along now flung in the corner, a noose still neatly tied at one end.

TWENTY-SEVEN

13 DECEMBER 1944, PARIS

The roadblock was set up on the outskirts of Paris, on the road to Versailles where Eisenhower had his headquarters. I was officially there as a member of the press accompanied by Dan, notebook poised as the American soldiers standing sentry stopped and questioned any military vehicle that attempted to pass in either direction.

They weren't the standard questions you would expect at a roadblock. Instead, they demanded to know the shape of an Original Slider at the White Castle burger restaurants, the names of state capitals, the price of a packet of cornflakes back home or the details of American football tactics. Almost all got the square shape of the burger right, although some struggled with the cornflakes.

As a jeep with four stars attached to the gold pennant it was flying drew up, I could see the sentries approach with some trepidation. The passenger wearing those same four stars that designated him a general answered with professional patience.

'What is the capital of Illinois, sir?'

'Springfield.'

'It's Chicago. Sir.'

'I think you'll find it's Springfield.'

The general was growing increasingly impatient, but the sentry carried on undaunted.

'And the name of Betty Grable's current boyfriend, sir?'

General Omar Bradley looked askance. 'How the hell would I know?'

'Yes, sir. Absolutely, sir. Could you tell me the location of the guard between the centre and tackle on a line of scrimmage?'

'Oh well now, that's easy.'

As the general went into a lengthy explanation of American football, my mind drifted to the night before and to the man standing beside me, close enough that I could feel the heat from his body seeping into mine as we stood in the freezing December fog, although that might have been my imagination.

I was certainly not imagining the way he made me feel. I had to stop myself from reaching out to touch him even now. Dangerous. So dangerous.

I tore my mind from the possibilities, focusing instead on the task in hand. After this, we were driving directly to Versailles, to the heart of Eisenhower's command here in France, the Supreme Headquarters Allied Expeditionary Force. There we were meeting with Dan's contact along with Dick Ward, the MI5 chief in Versailles. Apparently they had information gleaned from the double agents they were running. What had started as a clandestine mission was rapidly becoming a joint op, although it looked as if our presence at the roadblock would prove fruitless.

I was beginning to wonder if this rumoured infiltration of

the US troops by Germans was just that, a rumour, when a jeep drew to a halt and the driver passed over his papers, teeth as white as any American's, accent placing him from somewhere in the Mid-West.

'Shape of an Original Slider, sir?'

The open, guileless smile the driver had been sporting contracted at its corners. Beside me, Dan stiffened.

'I'm sorry, what did you say?'

'Shape of an Original Slider. Sir.'

'Well, burger shape of course.'

'And what would you pay for a packet of Kellogg's corn-flakes back home?'

'I don't know. Maybe twenty cents? My wife does all the shopping.'

Twelve cents out. Not a total giveaway although his body language certainly was. He was sitting bolt upright, the easy posture he'd been affecting vanishing under questioning. Behind him, two other soldiers looked similarly discomfited.

'Your wife's name?'

'Barbara.'

'What size dress does she wear?'

'Forty. I think.'

Forty. Didn't matter about the number. He'd used European sizing rather than American.

'Get out of the car, sir,' said one of the US soldiers.

'Why? Listen, I'm in a hurry. I have to deliver an urgent message to General Eisenhower's staff. If it doesn't get to him in time, I shall make sure he knows that you are responsible.'

It might have been my imagination but I thought I detected a slight Germanic inflection now that he was talking under pressure.

'Get out of the car. I'm not going to ask you again.'

The soldier had his Tommy gun pointed at the driver now while his colleague covered the passengers. I felt rather than saw Dan reach for his weapon, and I did the same. All pretence of being a mere reporter could go to the wall if we were facing German infiltrators here.

All at once, he slammed his foot down and the jeep surged forward, the soldiers scattering to avoid being hit. I saw the two passengers raise their weapons and point them at us. At that moment, Dan opened fire, swiftly followed by the soldiers while my finger was already on my trigger, my pistol aimed squarely at the driver's head.

It all seemed to happen in slow motion, as it so often did. One minute he was wrenching at the wheel, turning it this way and that to try to zigzag his way through, the next his head was exploding, falling forward as the jeep slammed into the concrete barriers and came to a halt. The other soldiers spilled out, arms raised in surrender, to be cuffed by the Americans.

I looked at Dan. 'I guess the intelligence was correct then.'

His expression was grim. 'Unfortunately so. And they were on their way to Versailles. We need to raise the alert level there and at all American bases to critical. From now on, we consider this an imminent threat.'

I stared at him. 'Do you think they'll make their move before that gathering in London on the sixteenth?'

'They may do.'

We'd moved out of earshot of the soldiers. I could see more jeeps arriving, reinforcements this time.

'Let's get out of here,' I said. 'We need to call Suzanne. Find out what's going on at their end. Can you set up an encrypted line from Versailles?'

'I can do better. We have a SIGSALY phone terminal there that we can use to connect to the one in London. It's much more secure than any other system, although it's only used for the highest-level communications.'

'I think this counts,' I said.

'So do I.'

His voice was sombre, his eyes more so. We had witnessed the chaos and confusion the Germans were stirring up here, aided and abetted by people like Harry King. If they succeeded in the rest of their plans, the entire course of the war could be altered. And then all the sacrifices we and thousands of others had made, all the lives ruined or lost, would be for nothing. Hitler would win, along with people like my husband. I could not, would not allow that to happen, whatever it took. Even if it meant sacrificing myself.

TWENTY-EIGHT

13 DECEMBER 1944, VERSAILLES

The Trianon Palace Hotel which housed General Eisenhower's headquarters was set among trees and lawns, its architecture a reflection of Louis XIV's Grand Trianon palace in the same great park at Versailles. As with the Hotel Scribe, the Allies had taken it over from the Luftwaffe. If nothing else, Goering had good taste, I reflected as we swept up the driveway, past the sentries at the gates and stopped outside the fairy-tale facade I remembered from childhood.

'You've been here before?' asked Dan.

'My parents used to bring us here when I was a child.'

'Us? You have a sibling?'

'Yes. I had a sister.'

'Had?'

'She died of smallpox when she was nine. I was three years younger than her.'

'That must have been awful.'

I shrugged. 'More so for my parents.'

I didn't want to talk about the shadow it cast over me, the need always not just to fill her shoes but to excel in everything so my parents would be proud of me. I was doing it for both of us, I reasoned, although perhaps I was really doing it just for me. I so wanted them to see me there, still, even though she was gone. They tried. They really did. They were the best of parents, but I knew that, in their hearts, I could never make up for the daughter they'd lost or fill the aching void she'd left.

'Hard on you too.'

That was one of the many things I loved about him. He got it. He got me. He was the most exciting man I'd ever known and yet he also made me feel safe. I didn't know if I could bear to lose that.

'Yes, well, we move on.'

'Why didn't you tell me before?'

'Perhaps for the same reason you didn't tell me about Elizabeth.'

In truth, I had never told him because I didn't want to cast that shadow over what we had. And what we had was always in the here and now, as it was in wartime. Anything could happen and it often did. Snatched moments of pleasure had to be guarded carefully. So did hearts.

I felt him glance at me as we walked up the steps and into the grand entrance hall lined with pillars, the floor set in a black-and-white diamond pattern that instantly transported me back through the years. I could see the armchairs and tables where we were served coffee and gateau, although we children preferred a tall glass of cold milk with our cake. Somewhere in the background, beyond the sound of our feet marching across the floor, I fancied I could hear a piano playing and soft chatter above the clink of silver on crockery. Out of the corner of my eye, I thought I caught a glimpse of my sister, forever young, sitting elegantly in her chair as my mother had taught us.

'A penny for them.'

His voice was a gentle murmur in my ear. I was beginning to like the way he always said that, as if it was part of a language we shared.

'I was back there with them. My sister. My parents, all of us here, together. I almost thought I could see them. Silly, I know.'

'Not at all. They're here still, at least in your heart.'

He didn't touch me. Didn't need to. I felt his strength and, yes, his love seeping into me, assuaging the ache of loss. I straightened my back, feeling lighter, as we approached the reception desk.

A uniformed officer stepped forward to greet us, checking our names off before leading us deeper into the bowels of the building, past public rooms and the restaurant that had once hummed with genteel life but now housed desks behind which military personnel sat, heads bent over paperwork, while others bustled from room to room with an air of purpose.

Several corridors later, he opened the door to a room where two men sat at one end of a long table, papers spread before them, glasses of water set ready for us. The one in civilian clothes stood and shook each of our hands in turn. He was tall with an easy charm, bright blue eyes and a very British manner. He reminded me of David Niven.

'Good of you to come. Dick Ward.'

So this was our MI5 man in Versailles.

His companion merely nodded and gestured to the chairs set opposite them.

'Lieutenant Colonel Gordon Steed. Take a seat.'

He sounded like a New Yorker. Looked like one too. They all had that big-city air of business coupled with a sharp wit and eyes that matched.

'I understand you met my colleague, Agent McMahon.'

At that, we both sat a little straighter.

'Affirmative,' said Dan.

'He transmitted intelligence from POWs he's been interrogating in England. It confirms the information we already extracted from German prisoners here. They each tell the same story of an order that all English-speaking personnel report to a secret training camp run by SS commander Otto Skorzeny.'

I looked at the American. Not as irritating as McMahon but every bit as disturbing. After all, he was a counter-intelligence agent too.

'We were already aware of German infiltrators posing as American soldiers. We observed a roadblock on the way here that was acting on that information.'

Steed studied me for a moment. 'What you may not know is that this is the latest in a series of reports concerning Skorzeny. Back in October the Nazis tried to run something they called Operation Werewolf, another infiltration plot. It failed. Then in November I received a report from Sixth Army Group Headquarters. A group of engineers repairing a road were surprised by a German attack force dressed in American uniforms yelling "GIs".'

'What do you think Skorzeny is up to?' asked Dan.

'Straight up? All we have right now are rumours, the most disturbing one being that he's planning to take Allied Headquarters here and assassinate General Eisenhower.'

I caught Ward's eye and then his almost imperceptible nod. It was time to lay our cards on the table.

'We heard the same,' I said. 'In fact, we believe it's part of a wider plot for Nazi prisoners and factions to march on London and assassinate Churchill, probably on the same day.'

'Jesus. Why the hell didn't you people tell us this before?'

Steed's face turned in a few seconds from ashen to a dark, angry red.

'Because we're still working on verifying this information and tracking down the ringleaders,' said Dan.

'We are running parallel operations here and in London,' I added. 'So far there seems to be an organised programme of terror by collaborators and pro-Nazi fascist groups to cause chaos and spread fear before they carry out their assassinations. They appear to be trying to place the blame on the French Forces of the Interior, the Fifis, and especially the communists.'

'The commies are behind this?' Steed spat.

'No. The Nazis are behind it. Apparently, this is Hitler's brainchild, but they are trying to place the blame for recent incidents here in Paris on the communists to deflect attention and cause yet more chaos.'

'I see.'

'There is a planned gathering of fascists in London on the sixteenth of December. That's the day we believe they are going to attack.'

'Does Churchill know about this?'

'He is aware, yes,' said Ward.

'So where do you fit in?' Steed looked at me.

'I worked with the Resistance and SOE.'

'But you're not working with them now?'

'No.'

'Then what the hell are you doing here?'

'Hey, steady,' said Dan. 'Juliette is here in an official capacity just as much as you are, buddy.'

That wasn't strictly true. The Network was unofficial. Deniable. Operating outside of all known agencies. I had the feeling Churchill would approve. And I very much approved of Dan addressing Steed as 'buddy'.

'And you?' Steed turned on Dan. 'Who do you work for? OSS?'

'I did. Now I liaise with them.'

'Oh for Chrissake.'

Steed rocked back in his chair, gazing up at the ceiling as if looking for answers there before looking from me to Dan. 'Who the hell are you people?'

'They're agents, just like you,' said Ward. 'Very good ones at that. So you would be wise to listen to what they have to say and work with them.'

Well, this was a turn of events. An MI5 chief speaking up for us. Perhaps this odd entente cordiale could actually work between the various secret services.

Steed took a breath. 'OK. I hear you. My problem is that no one else is listening to me. Or if they are, they're not taking it seriously. You saw the security here. It's not exactly tight.'

It was true. Apart from the sentries on the main gates, the Trianon wasn't well guarded. We'd got in by merely announcing our names. Any decent German agent could do the same under an assumed identity.

'So what do you suggest we do?' I asked.

'We need to substantiate these rumours. Provide proof that Eisenhower and the entire Allied command here really is in mortal danger.'

'That's what we're trying to do in Paris,' I said. 'We're

infiltrating the circles and groups we believe are helping facilitate Hitler's plans. We also have contacts within the communists helping. We have nothing concrete as yet, but believe me, we'll get it.'

Steed threw me a sceptical glance. 'The commies are helping you?'

'It suits them to do so when the Germans are trying to throw the blame for terrorist attacks on them. Don't forget, they still have ambitions to govern France.'

'And the rest of the damn world.'

'Just like the Germans then.'

I met Steed's glare with my own. It gave me inordinate satisfaction to see him look away first.

'In that case, I suggest we all carry on doing what we're doing.' Ward was smooth, I would give him that. 'We can set up a direct line of communication to the Hotel Scribe where I understand you're staying.'

'That would be great,' said Dan. 'Until you can do that, we'd like to use the SIGSALY terminal here if we may to call our colleagues in London.'

Ward glanced at his watch. 'No need.'

As if on cue, there was a discreet tap on the door.

'Come,' Ward called out.

The door swung open.

'Suzanne.'

Ever composed, she glided into the room and took a seat at the table, nodding briskly at each of us. As her eyes came to rest on me, I felt my stomach lurch.

'Juliette, I wanted to come and tell you myself. There's no gentle way of putting this. I'm also sorry we can't do this in private, but we believe this is part of the operations you're investigating.'

I felt the ice seep through my veins even as a rush of heat engulfed my head. 'Just say it.'

My voice resounding from a long way off.

'Your children and your mother have disappeared.'

As I sank to the floor in shock, I knew in my heart they were already dead.

TWENTY-NINE

'What do you mean they disappeared? Did anyone see them go?'

'They vanished from their safe house last night. We're doing everything we can to find them. There was no sign of forced entry or a struggle so we believe they went willingly.'

'My children are too young to resist anyone. They wouldn't know bad from good when it comes to adults. I taught them to stay with my mother at all times. They would never have left her side.'

I was speaking like an automaton, my brain pounding against my skull. *Where are they?* I wanted to scream. To tear my hair from its roots so I could hear it rip from my skull as my heart ripped in two. Instead, I looked at them all sat around the table gazing at me. Dan's expression was a mixture of sympathy and horror, but the other three had assumed their mantles of professional interest. Professional. That was a good idea. I must stay professional.

'Who found the place empty?' I asked, my voice still sounding hollow to my ears.

'Their security detail.'

'So they saw no one visit the house? Didn't see them leave, willingly or unwillingly?'

Suzanne shook her head. 'They were last seen at 9 p.m. the night before. The guard checked and your mother had just read them a bedtime story. She assured him she would lock up, and the lights in the house were extinguished by 10.30 p.m. No one saw or heard anything more until the following morning at 8 a.m. when they made their routine check.'

'There was a guard on the door?'

'A few yards away. We didn't want to alert anyone that this was anything other than an ordinary house so we had covert surveillance at all times.'

'Surveillance that must have been asleep on the job.'

I heard my voice rising. Didn't care.

'Juliette.'

Dan speaking softly to me. A kaleidoscope of memories whirling. My daughter laughing, her baby teeth pearly white, the big bow she was forever trying to rip from her silver-blonde hair. My son so much the older brother, patiently disentangling her from her latest scrape. Memories. I wanted more than memories.

'I want my children,' I wailed, dropping my face into my hands, dimly aware of the hush that had fallen, the hand laid on my shoulder and then a face close to mine, the scent of a cologne that had grown so familiar.

'We'll find them,' murmured Dan. 'Wherever they are, we'll get them back.'

'Oh God. My poor mother.'

I could see her sweet face too, always so gentle. Too trusting, that was her problem. Or that was what Papa always said. Except the day Philippe came looking for me after I'd fled. I heard her from the upstairs landing where I crouched, listening. Papa was at work, the children safely playing in the nursery. When the maid announced Philippe's presence, my mother insisted on going to the door and dealing with him on her own.

'Don't you ever come looking for my daughter again,' she said. 'If she has anything to say to you, it will be through our lawyer. In the meantime, I will make sure you never lay another hand on her. Now get off my doorstep before I call the police.'

And then my kind, gentle mother slammed the door in his face. She might be the soul of compassion, but woe betide you if you harmed one of her own. Then the tabby cat turned into a tiger and I loved her all the more for it. For standing up to a man who towered over her and who she knew was capable of such violence. After all, she had seen the bruises, tended to them with arnica and soft words.

My mother would do anything for anyone, but she was no fool. Someone must have tricked her into this. I uttered it aloud, raising my head so I could see the discomfort now on their faces.

'Someone must have tricked her. My mother. Someone she knew. She's not stupid. She wouldn't go with just anyone.'

'Or to just anyone.'

I looked at Dan. Could see his mind working.

'You think someone might have sent a message?'

'It's possible.'

'There was nothing at the house,' said Suzanne. 'No note and no telephone at the property. We checked all post before it was handed over, but there was very little in any case.'

'Post? My mother knows no one in England. The only people she would write to are here, in France. But I cautioned her against that again and again. Why on earth would she receive any post?'

Suzanne and Dan glanced at one another.

'Who would she write to?' Suzanne asked.

'Her sisters in Marseille. My aunt in Paris maybe.' Even as I said it, my heart began to sink.

'Of course she would write to my aunt. She never quite believed Papa was dead. She would ask my aunt now and then if she had heard anything, if he was maybe being held in a German prison somewhere. She even went to the Gestapo headquarters to demand someone tell her where he was, but they sent her away again.'

My voice cracked. I took a gulp from the water glass in front of me, concentrating fiercely on it so as to stem the tears that threatened to spill over once more.

'My aunt is a fascist sympathiser,' I added. 'I visited her just the other day, and she made it clear I was not welcome. She blames me for my father's death.'

'Why did you visit her?'

I didn't like Steed's tone of voice.

'For that very reason – her political views. Although I doubt they're so much political as social. Many of her friends share the same views, although most are busy back-pedalling now the Germans have surrendered Paris.'

'Surely you didn't go to discuss her politics?'

'Of course not. I went there specifically so she would inform her friend, my husband's mother, that I was back in Paris.'

'Juliette is acting on my orders,' said Suzanne. 'We believe her husband is one of the ringleaders of the fascist sympathisers aiding Hitler's plot. We want her to act as bait to draw him out.'

'Bait? How come? I take it you are no longer together.'

I was beginning to despise Steed.

'No, we are not, but Philippe, my husband, made it very clear he would never let me go. He is a controlling, violent man. Oh my God. Of course. It's Philippe. He's behind this. He has taken our children.'

That man in the cemetery, Lucien. He'd taunted me about my children. The man I'd shot. Philippe's crony, happy to betray him for a price. The memory of him sprawled on that grave. It had to be Philippe.

'Now, Juliette, you don't know that for certain.'

I turned to Dan. 'Of course I do. They are the biggest weapon he has to use against me. He knows I would die for them. He never really wanted them, but he doesn't want me to have them either.'

'But he's here, in Paris.'

'He has connections all over Europe, thanks to the Nazis. You know as well as I do that he could simply get one of his cronies in England to arrange a kidnapping. Right now we don't even know if they're still in England. It's not so hard to smuggle them over the Channel. We all know that.'

'You don't think he would hurt them?' Suzanne's voice was as rock steady as ever, but her eyes were full of concern.

'He might. If he thought that would be a way to get to me. He could use them to lure me in turn. Frankly, he is capable of anything.'

'Then we'll use all our resources to find your children whether or not they're with your husband,' said Ward. 'You have my word on that and the word of the British government.'

'Screw that,' said Dan. 'It was the British government who were supposed to be guarding them. We'll find them, Juliette. Us. Your friends. The Network.'

'I don't care who finds them,' I cried. 'I just want them back.'

THIRTY

13 DECEMBER 1944, PARIS

By the time he knocked on my door, I knew what to say. All through the drive back from Versailles, I'd been composing this in my head, watching the raindrops snake down the car window in place of the tears I'd dried from my face. I would cry later, in private, when there was no one to witness my agony. Which was exactly what I did when we finally got back to the hotel and I retreated to my room, where I curled up in the same way my babies once had and wept until my guts ached, my hands wrapped around my belly as if to keep them there, in my womb, where they'd been safe.

I cried for all the mistakes I'd made, for choosing Philippe in the first place. Except then there would be no babies – or at least not my precious two. I wept for my mother, for all she'd sacrificed for me. Finally I cried for me, for the searing pain in my heart, the desperate need to see them, to hold them one more time. Selfish. I was so selfish. I'd left them to fight this damn war for an ideal, for my country, when I should have been with them, taking care of them. Kissing away scrapes and bruises. Rocking them to sleep.

I was rocking now, on the bed in this anonymous hotel
room, backward and forward as if to somehow rock away the
pain. Or maybe it was for comfort, except that nothing and
no one could do that. Not even Dan. Especially not Dan.
Another betrayal, loving him. Well, I wouldn't do that
anymore. From now on, all my love was reserved for my
mother and my children. Perhaps then the gods wouldn't
punish me by taking them forever. I pleaded then, bargaining
with the heavens.

'I'll be a good mother,' I whispered. 'A good daughter. I
will focus only on them. Just please, please bring them back
to me.'

Silence echoed back from the empty walls. The gods
weren't listening. But when had they ever?

I punched my pillows, shrieking aloud to rouse them.
And still nothing. At last I slumped on the bed once more,
spent. I must have slept then. Or at least fallen unconscious.
It was only when I heard a knocking that grew progressively
louder that I sat up, confused as you are when abruptly
woken. Then I remembered. I was still smearing a treacherous tear from my cheek with the back of my hand as I stumbled to the door.

'I was about to kick it down.'

Worry, fear, anger and love all chased one another across
Dan's face.

'There's no need. I'm all right.'

'You don't look it. Can I come in?'

Without waiting for an answer, he put an arm around my
shoulder and steered me back into the room. I pushed him
away as his other arm came round to join it. He took a step
back.

'Dan, I can't do this.'

'I understand. You need some time. It's been a hell of a shock.'

'No, you don't understand. I mean I can't do this at all.'

I wished I could reach out and wipe the hurt from his eyes as easily as I could a tear. But I had to do this. There was no other option.

'By that you mean us?'

'I do.'

'But why, Juliette? Oh wait, let me guess. You think this is your fault. You're blaming yourself for what's happened and you think somehow you caused it by being happy with me.'

For a man, he was astonishingly astute. It was one of the many things I loved about him, that ability to feel, to know just how I was feeling too.

'Maybe you're right, but this isn't right anyway. We're here on a mission, Dan. I told you before that we shouldn't become distracted. Now you see I was right.'

'Why? Because your kids and your mother have disappeared from their safe house in another country? That wasn't your fault, Juliette. You weren't the one guarding them.'

'Yes but I should have been. Don't you see? I let them down. I am here while they are there. Or they were. I will never forgive myself.'

'So you want to punish yourself by destroying something that brings you happiness?'

'Perhaps.'

He took a step closer, so close I could feel his breath on my cheek, his fingers stroking my hair from my face. 'Don't do this, Juliette. I love you. You love me. That's not a sin. It's a beautiful thing.'

'Is it?' I looked at him, feeling such a weight of sadness as

I did so. 'I destroy beautiful things. Did no one ever tell you that?'

THIRTY-ONE

'That's what Philippe told me anyway. That I destroyed our marriage. That it was all my fault.'

'Philippe's an asshole.'

We were inches apart, the gulf between us narrowing. Dangerous. So dangerous.

'He told me that the night I left him. The night he... forced me.'

I could hear his heart beating in the silence. Or was that mine?

'That was my fault too apparently. I had shut him out of my bedroom ever since my daughter was born. So he went elsewhere, except he'd always done that. Always told me how much better than me his other women were.'

'Juliette...'

I held up my hand, stoppering up whatever he was about to say. I had to get this out, had to tell him now. Something was forcing the words out of me. I needed him to hear my truth. The real truth. Not the pleasant parts we'd shared. Then, no doubt, he would be so disgusted he would be the

one to end this once and for all, sparing me the agony as well
as the guilt.

'I was packing. I had already decided to leave him, that
enough was enough. My father was coming for me in the
morning once Philippe had gone to work. That way, we
could keep it nice and calm for the children, tell them we
were simply going to stay with Grandmère and Grandpapa
for a while.'

I heard it again now, the slam as the door was flung open,
Philippe striding in, his expression as he saw what I was
doing.

'Bitch!' he yelled. 'You stupid bitch. You think you can
leave me? Who do you think will have you, you whore? Or is
there already some other man mad enough to take you?'

I gaped at him, wordless, my mind darting all over the
place. He was supposed to be out this evening, gambling
away our money. I had the house to myself, or so I thought.
The children were in bed. *The children.* He mustn't wake
them.

'Shhh. The children will hear you.'

Slap. I could smell the alcohol on his breath.

'The children? What do you care about our children?
You're a lousy mother as well as a whore.'

Slap, slap. Then a punch to my stomach, a blow that had
me doubling over, gasping.

Somehow, out of nowhere, I felt the rage rise in me.

'You're the whore, Philippe, with your fancy women.
Who was it tonight, eh? The dyed blonde or your best
friend's wife?'

A roar of rage and then he was on me, pinning me down
to the bed, his hands tearing at my clothes as he shoved his
knee between my legs.

'Get off me, you pig. Get off me.'

I couldn't scream. Couldn't shout for fear of rousing the children. If they came running in and saw what was happening, I would never forgive myself.

A grunt as he shoved himself inside me, his fingers wrapped now around my throat. I willed myself to float away, somewhere else, somewhere beyond this room and this man.

The room was spinning around me, stars exploding across my vision, a cloak settling, immovable, across my face as he choked the life out of me, all the while thrusting and grunting until, at last, he cried out and fell still.

Finally his fingers slackened. I felt the air rush back down my throat as I gulped it in. Then he stirred.

'Whore,' he slurred again, pushing himself off me, doing his trousers back up before he stumbled from the room, no doubt to sleep it off.

I waited, counting to 100 and then 200, but he didn't return. I felt the stickiness between my legs and wiped it away with the sheet, staggering to the bathroom and scrubbing hard with a cloth until nothing remained.

I stared at my face in the mirror above the basin, my eyes wide with shock, the shadows beneath them pits into which they'd sunk. My skin was so pale that I scrubbed at that too, trying to bring the blood back to it, the life.

Finally, with cheeks raw from my efforts, I limped back into the bedroom and swept everything into my suitcase, what had been neat piles laid out on my bed now as scattered as my thoughts. I snapped the suitcase shut and crept down to the front door where I placed it by my coat. Then I tiptoed back up to the children's bedroom, swaddling Natalie in her blankets and carrying her, head lolling against my shoulder, while I led Nicolas down by the hand, too groggy to protest.

Every creak of the stairs sent paroxysms of fear flooding through me, my legs almost giving way as I froze, listening hard, only moving again when I was sure Philippe wouldn't appear.

Finally, we made it to the bottom and I grabbed my suitcase, telling Nicolas to stay close as we crept out the door, pulling it shut as soundlessly as I could behind us and then marching briskly to the street corner where I hailed a cab.

'It was only then that I began to feel safe,' I whispered. 'When that cab drove off. Then when we got to my parents' house. I pretended to the children it was all a game. That we were going to surprise Grandmère and Grandpapa for fun.'

'Jesus, Juliette.'

I dragged my eyes to Dan's, anticipating his disgust. His rejection. Bracing myself for it.

It never came.

Instead, he pulled me against his chest, murmuring my name into my hair, his arms cradling me as if they would never let me go.

'You're safe now,' he said. 'You're safe with me.'

If only he knew.

If only.

THIRTY-TWO

14 DECEMBER 1944, PARIS

Tante Lucie looked at me as if I'd lost my mind. 'You think Philippe has snatched his own children? Don't be ridiculous.'

'You know as well as I do that is exactly the kind of thing he would do.'

Beside me, Guillaume snorted in agreement.

'That fascist bastard would do anything,' he sneered. 'So would you, Maman.'

At that, she paled. 'You forget who you're speaking to, Guillaume.'

'On the contrary, I could never forget,' he retorted. 'The same way I will never forget the way you ignored me all my life. It's a family trait, no? To think that children are just some kind of plaything to be taken out on a whim.'

I'd never heard Guillaume sound so bitter and yet so dignified. My heart twisted at his words. It was true that Philippe treated our children like adornments to be taken out as and when it suited him, but I had no idea Guillaume had suffered a similar upbringing. Then again, I only ever saw him with his nursemaid or at our home playing happily with his cousins. The lonely little boy who was my aunt's sole son and heir had grown up into this disaffected young man who wanted nothing to do with her or her money. It was no doubt what was behind his sudden conversion to communism. He knew it would annoy her more than anything if her son were a known communist while she entertained her fascist-loving friends.

'Well,' sniffed my aunt, 'if Philippe has the children then I'm glad. At least now they'll be in good hands. They've been allowed to run wild all these years. They could do with a little discipline.'

No concern for their welfare, or my mother's. More tellingly, no attempt to suggest any other scenarios. She knew what had happened to them. She might even know where they were, but there was no way she would tell me. I'd have cheerfully taken her by the neck and throttled her there and then, except she was one of the few people Philippe trusted on this earth. Chances were, he would be in contact with her at some point and then we would be waiting.

So would the bugs I'd installed while we were waiting for her to make her entrance, timing our arrival to catch her straight after her *petit déjeuner* when she prepared for her day, her maid aiding her with her toilette. Guillaume kept a watch out for the maid while I inserted one in the table lamp and another under her armchair. If Philippe came calling, we would know about it from the listening station within minutes. True to his word, Ward had put a couple of his covert communications team at our disposal while Suzanne was even now on her way back to London to coordinate the search from there.

It was my job to hold things together. I could either dissolve in a weeping mess or I could focus on finding my children. And the best way to do that was to dangle myself even more in front of Philippe. I knew in my bones that he was behind this, and my aunt had all but confirmed it. The one thing I feared was just how far he was prepared to go to hurt me. I could only hope that even Philippe would balk at killing his own children, but I also knew the terrifying lengths he would go to if it meant watching me break.

As we left the apartment, Guillaume slammed the door hard.

'That bitch never changes,' he growled.

'Right now, that's a good thing,' I said. 'Consistency makes her easier to watch and to follow.'

He brightened. 'You're right. I know her routine backward. I can write it all down for you. Where she goes. The people she sees on each particular day.'

'That would be most helpful. Then if she deviates from her routine, we'll know something is up.'

We were almost at the front door by now, my hand reaching for it when I heard a discreet cough from behind us. We both turned to see the concierge standing just inside the front door of her lodge. She beckoned to us to come closer.

'Inside. Quick,' she murmured, eyes darting right and left in case anyone should appear.

I pulled Guillaume by the arm and followed her into the tiny apartment, only stopping when she closed the kitchen door behind us and nodded to indicate we were safe.

'I saw him,' she said. 'Monsieur de Brignac. Your husband. He was here only yesterday.'

'I see.' I eyed her carefully, wondering where this was leading and how she knew.

'He was arguing with some man outside,' she went on. 'I heard him mention your name several times. He sounded very angry. It was as if he was insisting this man do something although I couldn't hear what. In any case, I thought you should know.'

'Thank you. What did he look like, this other man?'

'Tall. Skinny. With reddish hair. He was wearing peculiar trousers. Looked like a foreigner to me.'

Harry King. It had to be.

'Interesting. Have you ever seen this other man before with Philippe?'

She shook her head. 'Never. But then, your husband does not come here so often anymore. I heard that he is living with a lady friend, a duchess or something like that. You could always find him at his meetings.'

'Meetings?'

'They call them soirées but they are really meetings. My friend who works the other side of Avenue Foch told me. They often come to her employer's mansion there. Lucky thing, she only has one house to look after. Me, I have this entire block and at my time of life.'

I pressed a ten-franc note into her hand. 'I hope this may help a little.'

'No, no, really I couldn't,' she said as she pocketed it.

'Consider it a small gift for all your kindness over the years. If you see Philippe again, or if you hear any more about his whereabouts or his meetings, do you think you could let me know?'

I scribbled down the address of the Hotel Scribe along with the direct telephone number Ward had given us.

'Of course.'

She tucked her hands in her pockets, waiting.

'There'll be a little something in it for you to supplement your pension,' I added. 'I know that times are hard.'

'I am very grateful.'

Outside in the street, Guillaume snorted in disgust. 'That old bat was shaking you down.'

'Hush, Guillaume. What happened to equal shares for everyone? She's a widow scraping by on a meagre salary while the wealthy people in her apartment block treat her like dirt. If we can make life a little more comfortable for her and she helps us in return, then that is true socialism if you ask me.'

He grinned, reminding me in that instant of the cheeky little boy he'd been before life and his mother had sapped the light from his eyes. Now it was back, those eyes sparkling with new purpose.

'You're right. That is true equality, redistributing wealth so that everyone has enough. That's what we're going to do to people like my mother's friends once we're in power. We'll make them give up their damn mansions and turn them over to the people. Let's see how those aristocrats feel when they're forced to live like ordinary folk.'

'Careful, Guillaume. Don't let the Americans hear you talk like that.'

'Why not? This is our country, not theirs. About time they learned how a true republic works.'

Ahead of us, at the end of the street, I could see another checkpoint. In the two days since we'd returned from Versailles, the roadblocks had multiplied, but it was still not enough. Paris was a big city and the streets hid many secrets. It was entirely possible that the children and my mother weren't even here, although I felt in my gut that they were. There had been no reports of planes taking off unaccounted for from English airfields, and the coastguards hadn't sighted any suspicious boats other than the usual German vessels in the Channel.

That was another thing. Would my mother even be with them? On the one hand, she could keep the children calm and happy. On the other, she was a grown woman capable of raising the alarm. I suppressed a shudder. I wouldn't even consider the possibilities. We were dealing with facts here and evidence, targeting our chief suspects. I knew that over the Channel, my friends and colleagues were doing the same.

Despite what Lucie's behaviour had suggested, there was still a chance my mother had for some reason decided to disappear with the children of her own volition. If she had, she would be in touch at some point, I knew that. She would never let me suffer not knowing what had happened to them. But she hadn't been in touch. Which led me to the final and most terrible conclusion, the one I couldn't even contemplate. My mother and my children may already be dead.

I didn't even realise I was clenching my fists until we drew level with the roadblock and the sentry who challenged us flicked them a suspicious glance. I slowly unfurled them to show that there was nothing there save my empty hands.

'You're stopping pedestrians now?'

'Those are our orders, ma'am.'

'I see. Any special reason?'

'I'm not at liberty to say, ma'am.'

He threw Guillaume a look. 'Show me your hands.'

'Why?'

'Guillaume, this is not the time,' I muttered.

'It is absolutely the time. An Imperialist invader is questioning me in my own city. *Vive la France! Vive le Parti Communiste Français!*'

The sentry's eyes narrowed. 'You a commie?'

'He's an idiot,' I said, taking Guillaume by the arm. 'And I am taking him home.'

'Now just a moment, ma'am. We need to talk to your friend some more. The communists are responsible for acts of terror around this city.'

'Bullshit,' spat Guillaume. 'It's the fucking fascists you want to talk to. They're behind those attacks. Those bastards even took her children.'

Cold hands clutched at my throat, squeezing it. I wanted to scream once more, but I knew it would only make things worse.

The sentry raised his Tommy gun and pointed it at Guillaume. 'I won't ask you again. Step aside. You, ma'am, can carry on.'

'Oh for God's sake,' I snapped. 'I'm not going anywhere without him. Now put down your gun or I'll—'

'You'll what?'

The sentry's eyes hardened. Then I heard a voice from behind us.

'Drop your weapon, soldier. I can vouch for this lady and her cousin. Besides, you really don't want to take her on. I've seen what she can do.'

I wanted to fling myself into Dan's arms and weep. Then I remembered who and what I was.

'Captain Diaz. It's good to see you.'

If only he knew how good.

He steered me away from the sentry, Guillaume following in our wake. 'I have some news for you.'

My heart leaped and then juddered to a halt. He wasn't smiling. This could only be bad news.

'Are you following me again?'

Anything to delay what he was about to say.

'Yes and for a very good reason. We've put permanent surveillance on that apartment building you were just visiting.'

'So have I, in a way. I bribed the concierge.'

This time he did break into a smile. 'Of course you did.'

I glanced over my shoulder. Guillaume was slouching along a few metres behind us.

'So what is this news?'

'We've had a report of a vessel leaving Southampton bound for Étretat near Le Havre. A fishing boat that belongs to a member of the Right Club. According to the coastguard, it dropped anchor off the beach early this morning and a dinghy was seen bringing four people ashore. Two of those people were children. It might be something and nothing, but I think we need to get out there and take a look.'

My scarf suddenly felt uncomfortably tight. I tore it from my throat, taking in gulps of air as I did so. My God. It could be them. It had to be them.

'Please, please let it be them,' I whispered under my breath although I had no idea with whom I was pleading. The heavens maybe. Or fate. I took another shuddering gulp of air.

'Steady there. You OK?'

I shook off his hand. 'Yes. I'm fine.'

Étretat was less than 200 kilometres from Paris. We could get there in a few hours.

'Do we know where they went after they landed?'

'No but we're going to find out. I have a car waiting back at the hotel. You can grab some things and then we'll go.'

'What about the operation here?'

'We have people on top of that. Ward or Steed will

contact us if there's anything urgent, but right now, I can't think of anything more urgent than this.'

I wanted to kiss him. And then I remembered.

'What are we waiting for? Let's get back to the hotel.'

I was already striding in that direction, picking up speed. I wanted to run, but that would have attracted attention and, just as we had eyes on them, I had no doubt they had eyes on us. Let them. We would outrun them, outwit them and do whatever else it took to find my family.

THIRTY-THREE

I gabbled instructions to Guillaume as we neared the hotel. 'Your job now is to keep a watch on your mother and Philippe's mother as well as Philippe himself. But say nothing about the children to anyone.'

'No problem. I'll get my friends to help.'

'Guillaume, you can't tell anyone what this is about.'

He bridled without breaking stride. 'What do you take me for? Besides, my friends understand. This is for the cause. They don't need to know the details.'

People like Philippe and Harry King had a sixth sense for professionals tailing them. They wouldn't be so alert to a bunch of scruffy student types who hung around the Left Bank as well as the 16th.

We were nearly there now, Dan forging ahead to talk to the driver of a car that sat, its engine running, outside the main entrance. It looked like an ordinary Citroën, although I suspected it was armoured. I tore a piece of paper from the notebook in my bag and scrawled the dedicated phone number on it.

'I'll see you when we get back. If you need to contact us urgently, call this number.'

'Don't worry. You can rely on me.'

The sulky brat who'd hurled accusations at me was long gone, replaced by a young man with purpose.

'I know I can.'

I dropped a kiss on each of his cheeks and then I was racing into the hotel, up the stairs to my room, where I changed into a pair of slacks, threw some items into a bag and was back out the front door within minutes. The driver of the car was nowhere to be seen. In his place, Dan sat behind the steering wheel wearing a leather jacket over a sweater and jeans instead of his uniform.

'You're going incognito?'

'You bet,' he said as he gunned the engine. 'Don't want to give those bastards any idea that we're on to them.'

As we roared across the square and towards the outskirts of the city, I glanced at him, one hand on the wheel, the other on my knee, foot down hard on the accelerator.

'Well,' I said, 'at least you drive like a Frenchman.'

He looked at me and grinned. 'Do I make love like one too?'

I felt my cheeks grow hot even as my heart shrivelled into a tight, cold ball. I turned my head away and stared out the window, gazing sightlessly at the streets flashing past. I could feel the silence between us stretching.

'Was it something I said?' he quipped at last, removing his hand from my knee so that it immediately felt a little colder.

'Dan...' I stopped, choking on what I was about to say, biting back words that, once said, could never be retracted.

'It is something I said, isn't it?'

'No. You've not said or done anything wrong. It's me. All I can think about right now is finding my mother and the children. Finding out if they were on that boat.'

Not the entire truth, but it was good enough.

'Of course. I'm sorry. You must think I'm a heartless bastard. I was just trying to keep your spirits up.'

'I know. And you do. It's just very hard, you know?'

His free hand reached across again and squeezed mine. 'I know. Well I don't. I can't even imagine. But we'll find them, Juliette. I can promise you that.'

'Don't make promises you can't keep.'

'I don't. Ever. I can also promise that I will love you until the end of time.'

My eyes welled treacherously. 'Can you?'

'Yes I can. Can you?'

Another silence, one that hummed with heartbreak. I could literally feel mine cracking apart.

'I'll take that as a no,' he said, and I could hear the hurt in his voice.

'Dan, please. This is such a strange time for me. I can't promise anything other than that I will do everything and anything I can to find my mother and my children.'

Another squeeze of my hand. 'I know you will. Ignore me, Juliette. I'm being a selfish bastard. This isn't about me. It's about you and the people you love most. I'll do everything in my power to help.'

'You already are.'

Why did he have to be so damn decent? It made it so much harder. *You're one of the people I love most*, I wanted to shout, even though it was a new love compared to the others. A love born from war and the knowledge that it could all end in a heartbeat, or the blast of a grenade, which only made it the more intense. Instead, I withdrew my hand from his and folded it in my lap. Maybe I was punishing myself, as he'd suggested. Penance for the guilt of leaving my mother and the children alone while I went off to play secret agent. Except this wasn't a game and the consequences were all too real.

THIRTY-FOUR

The sign for Le Havre loomed out of the mist. We must be getting close. Étretat was nineteen kilometres or so further on, along the coast, according to the map.

'I wonder why they dropped anchor in Étretat,' I said.

'Le Havre was bombed to bits back in September. The harbour was destroyed as well. I believe there are around thirty-five sunken vessels down there still. It's not safe for any boat to try to dock there right now so I guess the nearest alternative is Étretat.'

I could scent the tang of sea air above the car fumes. I rolled down the window and breathed it in, oblivious to the dank December chill. It smelled of earth and salt and childhood memories.

'We spent holidays on this coast sometimes,' I said. 'Summer weekends and August. Papa's people came from Normandy so we stayed with my grandmother while she was alive. I remember playing on the beaches with my sister. The same beaches where they landed on D-Day.'

The seemingly never-ending ribbon of sand that ran

along the coast that ended up being the graveyard for so many, gunned down by German artillery safe in their pillboxes above. Thousands died, most of them in the first wave of landings, but still they kept coming until they'd taken all the beaches. D-Day seemed so far away now, as did Operation Dragoon, the southern landings we'd risked everything to support.

As we got closer to the coast, though, the signs were everywhere, abandoned vehicles and ruined buildings littering the landscape. Even now, all these months later, France was a living monument to her invaders and the forces that had fought to repel them. It was one of those bitter twists of war and fate that Le Havre had been destroyed by the Allies rather than the Germans. Thousands of innocent civilians also died during those two days in September, but no doubt they were considered collateral damage.

Just like my mother and children, I thought. Innocents caught up in a battle not of their making. Except that this one extended beyond the boundaries of military warfare and into a much darker fight, the type no one could ever win. Had peace reigned in Europe, Philippe would still have found a way to attack me. The fact that his fascist beliefs were fired up by his brethren in bloodshed only made him all the more ruthless.

But my little family were still alive. So far. Which meant he intended them to be. How long since they'd landed? It was now four in the afternoon which meant a good eight hours had elapsed since dawn. The light was once more fading into the pearly haze that passes for dusk in winter. Soon it would be completely dark.

Dan's profile was silhouetted against the dimming light

as he concentrated fiercely on the road, his foot still flat to the floor.

'Are we going to the beach or the town first?'

He flicked on the car lights. 'The town. No point going to the beach. There'll be nothing to see there.'

'Who sent the message?'

'Our boys stationed at Le Havre. They picked up the coastguard's report, but they have no idea what happened to the boat's passengers, only that it's there.'

'It may be worth seeing if the fishermen are still bringing in their nets. They would have been out at dawn, and they might have seen something that would give us more of a clue.'

'Good thinking,' he said. 'The beach it is.'

He turned the wheel just in time to send us hurtling along the coast road and down to the far end of the bay from where we could see one or two lights start to glow from the town as we parked up.

Down on the beach, fishing boats sat silent, their hulls looming against the inky sky. Pebbles crunched under our feet, waves slapping the shore, the wind whipping them along, white tips visible as they curled and broke.

I was about to suggest we give up and head for the town instead when I heard someone whistling. The next moment, a figure appeared from behind one of the boats carrying a couple of buckets.

'Monsieur! Monsieur, please, over here.'

As we drew closer, I could make out the eyes that peered at me from under a knitted cap. He was younger than he looked all trussed up in his oilskins and woollen layers. Good. Younger meant sharper.

'Monsieur, were you out with your boat this morning?'

'I was.'

Taciturn, like so many of his kind.

'And did you see anything unusual around dawn? Any boat you haven't seen before? Some people perhaps.'

He dumped the buckets down and folded his arms across his chest. 'Who wants to know?'

'I do.'

'I do too,' said Dan, his tone friendly enough but with an edge to it I knew all too well.

'American, eh? What are you doing with him?' The fisherman looked at me pointedly.

'I work with him,' I said.

'Really?'

He bent to his buckets again, evidently unimpressed.

'Yes, really. I worked with him in the south when we liberated it. I fought alongside him against those Nazi bastards. I'm still doing that now. And I need your help.'

He was once more standing erect, arms no longer folded. 'My apologies, madame. It's been a difficult time. How can I help?'

That was when I noticed his posture, one shoulder sloping significantly lower than the other, the arm on that side dangling loose.

'You were wounded?' I asked.

'At the Battle of Toulon, yes.'

'So you were part of Operation Dragoon.'

'I served with the 1st Free French Division. Now please tell me how I can help you.'

He had a true soldier's quiet pride along with the immense dignity with which he carried himself. It couldn't have been easy to return here, disabled, and try to scrape a living.

'My name is Juliette. This is Dan. We're here because we heard that a dinghy brought two adults and two children ashore early this morning from a foreign fishing boat moored off this beach. I need to find them.'

He frowned. 'I didn't see or hear anything, but I go out a little later than the others. It takes me more time. That's why I come back later too.'

He gestured to his buckets, where I could make out the glint of fish scales. The one nearest his injured side was noticeably emptier than the other.

'I understand. Can you think of anyone who might know?'

'I know exactly who to talk to. Come with me.'

Dan bent to pick up one of the buckets, but the fisherman stopped him with a gesture. We followed him up the beach as he lugged both, back as straight as he could manage. He stopped by a battered van, wedging both buckets in the back alongside the coils of rope and various bits of equipment there.

'You have a car?'

I waved towards ours, parked a little further along the beach road. 'We do.'

'Then follow me.'

THIRTY-FIVE

He led us to a cottage on the beach side of town, driving with the verve he must have shown as a soldier. We pulled up alongside him as he began to knock on the cottage door, the only sign of life in the place a solitary light in an upstairs window. More lights blazed as whoever lived there descended and flung the door open.

'What the hell are you doing here at this time, my friend?'

The old man who appeared looked dishevelled, a dressing gown wrapped around him as if he'd emerged from the bathtub.

'My apologies, but these people here are looking for two adults and two children who apparently came ashore early this morning in a dinghy. You're always out early. Did you see them? Or a foreign fishing boat at anchor?'

The old man peered at us and pulled the dressing gown tighter around him. The legs that poked out from underneath were spindly, the slippers he wore tattered, his toes visible in places. 'You'd better come in.'

Inside the cottage, an elderly woman, presumably his wife, sat sewing by the fire. She jumped up as we entered, her cheeks scarlet with embarrassment.

'*Mon Dieu.* You never said we were having guests. Monsieur, madame, please excuse the mess. I was not expecting anyone.'

'It is I who should apologise, madame, for dropping in on you like this unannounced,' I said. She reminded me a little of my grandmother; she had the same kindly countenance.

She continued to flutter, her fingers plucking nervously at her pinafore.

The young fisherman took a step forward. 'Don't upset yourself, Éliane. My friends here worked with the Resistance in the south. They fought there, just as I did.'

At that, the two older people visibly relaxed.

'Why didn't you say?' said the old man. 'Come, sit down. Have a brandy. It's cold out there. You need to warm up.'

'You're very kind,' I said. 'But we need to find the people from the dinghy as quickly as possible, before anyone can harm them.'

The old man looked at me more closely. 'These people mean a lot to you?'

'A great deal.'

'It was not I who saw them but a couple of the other fishermen who were out that side of the bay. They watched the dinghy leave the fishing boat and then row to shore. They thought it odd because we don't normally have foreign boats out there these days.'

'Do you know where they went after they came ashore?'

'I do,' piped up the old woman. 'I was talking this morning to my friend who runs the bakery near the beach. They're always there baking from 5 a.m. and it wasn't too long after that she saw them go past – a woman, two children and the man who was with them. She thought it strange because the man had his arm tight around the woman, as if he was almost dragging her along, but assumed it was because she was not well or something.'

I tried to swallow but there was nothing there, just the constrictor that was once more wrapping itself around my throat.

'Did she describe them to you?'

'She said there was a boy and a little girl. The woman was older, too old to be their mother. She noticed that too. Said she was very elegant.'

That was my mother, always elegant no matter what.

'How old did she think the children were?'

'She didn't say exactly, although she mentioned the little girl was blonde. Said she had lovely, curly hair.'

My Natalie. It had to be. We were so close.

'Did she see where they went after that?'

'She thought that was odd too. They went to the garage across the road from her, but they didn't come out again. They simply vanished. That place has been empty for ages. No idea why they would go there.'

'Did she mention seeing a vehicle? One she didn't recognise?'

'Now that you ask, she did mention a US Army jeep she saw a bit later this morning. She noticed it because the American soldiers left a while back, but she assumed they were a patrol or something. She was joking that perhaps they'd left a girl behind and came looking for her.'

I looked at Dan. 'It's them. It has to be. Can you tell us where this garage is?'

'Better. I can take you there.'

Ten minutes later, we were standing outside the garage in question while our new friend hammered on the door and then rattled the handle, twisting and turning it.

'*Putain*. The Germans were the last here. They left it locked,' he said.

'Is that so?'

I pulled out my pistol and shot the lock to smithereens.

'Bravo,' said the fisherman as Dan kicked the door open and I went in first.

'Stay back,' I ordered as we entered, sweeping my pistol in an arc to cover us, squinting through the gloom to make out any threat while at the same time hoping against all hope that they were still there.

'Anyone here?' I called out. 'Maman? Nicolas? Natalie?'

No response. Just the sigh of floorboards settling and the creak of metal upon metal. The fisherman cocked his head at that sound.

'Over here,' he said, making for the far end of the garage, where double doors swung slightly open. He prised them apart to reveal a yard beyond and gates which stood wide.

'This is how they got out of here.' He bent to wipe a smear from the ground and then sniffed it. 'Petrol. They had a car waiting. Like I said, this place was empty for years until the Germans requisitioned it. The old guy died, and his son was killed in the war.'

They'd been here only hours ago. I wanted to howl. We were too damn late.

'They used it as a depot?'

'For a time. But the place wasn't really big enough to be of any use to them. They established a garrison and kept their vehicles there.'

'It still means they knew about it,' I said. 'This coastline is vital strategically and for signals. I'm sure the Gestapo were well aware of this town. And whoever brought my mother and the children here this morning had a key.'

I was speaking my thoughts out loud. The fisherman looked at me, and the sympathy in his eyes nearly undid me once more.

'Of course. The Gestapo came here several times. Took away quite a few of the townsfolk on one pretext or another. Brave people who hid downed airmen and at least one Jewish family. That old couple you just met harboured several of them.'

'Is there a faster way to Paris from here than going along the coast road and cutting in?' I asked.

'There are some back roads I can show you that are more direct.'

'How busy are those roads?'

'Not at all. You mostly see military vehicles if any, American and British, along with farm trucks. People don't have petrol so they can't use their cars so much.'

'You manage with your van,' said Dan.

The fisherman kept his gaze steady. 'I do.'

'So where do you get the petrol for that?'

'I stole it from those German bastards. A few of us broke into their depot before they left and took the lot. You should have seen them when they discovered what we had done. We hid it so well they never found it. Now we use it for the townsfolk who are most in need. I need my van to earn a living and to keep bringing in food for people to eat.'

'Think you could spare us some of that petrol? We have to get back to Paris fast.'

They had to have headed for Paris. There was no point driving along the coast road where so many troops were still stationed and they could be picked up by a patrol. Besides, Philippe was in Paris. So was I. And whatever he was planning, I knew it would include me.

'Of course,' he said. 'I'll take you there now.'

'Thank you. You don't know how much this means.'

'I think I do, madame. I hope you find them.'

I looked at his face, noble under his woollen cap, his eyes steady as a soldier's going into battle. I'd seen that look before, many times. It helped to steady me.

'We'll find them, monsieur. Or I will die in the attempt.'

'That would be a great loss. For your family and for France.'

I'd given so much already for my country. I couldn't bear to give my mother and children too.

THIRTY-SIX

We followed his van to the clifftop this time, bumping along a rutted track until we came to a ruined chapel where we parked.

'The Germans bombed it back in '42,' said the fisherman, indicating the chapel. 'Local sailors and fishermen carried the stone up the cliff path to build it. You may have seen the picture Claude Monet painted of it.'

I looked at the neo-Gothic ruins, one arch still visible above the pile of rubble. 'I've not only seen the painting, I saw it before it was bombed. My parents brought me here when I was a girl. My grandmother lived not too far from here, near Fécamp.'

'Then you are one of us, a local,' said the fisherman. 'This is your church too, and we will rebuild it.'

'I'm certain you will,' I said.

He was already leading us away from the chapel, towards the cliff edge, the torch in his hand lighting the way.

'Careful,' he said. 'The path is steep here.'

We scrambled after him, keeping close as he led us down

towards the beach, stopping halfway. There he stepped off
the path, appearing to vanish behind a rock.

'In here,' he called, brandishing his torch to illuminate a
cave entrance behind the boulder.

Once inside the cave mouth, he led us back through a
tunnel to another cave opening. We passed through that and
into a much larger cavern stacked high with oil drums. The
stink of fuel was overwhelming.

'*Et voila*, our supplies,' he said proudly, picking up a
petrol can and filling it from one of the drums while
motioning to us to do the same.

Lugging a couple of cans each back up the cliff path was
no easy task, but we did it, pouring the contents of one with
care into our fuel tank while stashing the others in the boot of
the car, wedged in tight so they couldn't spill on the long
journey back to Paris. Once we were done, I turned to the
fisherman.

'*Au revoir*, my friend,' I said. 'I don't even know your
name.'

'It's Vincent.'

My papa's name. I smiled.

'Vincent, we will meet again. I look forward to seeing the
chapel rebuilt.'

'God go with you,' he said. 'And with your family.'

He and Dan shook hands and then we were off,
following Vincent back to the road in his van and then taking
the directions he'd given us, picking up speed as we hit the
road to Paris.

Fifty or so kilometres from Étretat we came upon a roadblock manned by US troops. Dan rolled down the car
window and leaned out, calling a greeting. He was greeted in
return with a row of carbines levelled at him.

'Get out of the car sir,' ordered the nearest soldier.

Dan obliged, raising his hands slowly as he did so, while I stayed put.

'Captain Daniel Diaz attached to SHAEF,' he announced. 'We're here on official business. You can check with Lieutenant Colonel Steed in Versailles.'

'Oh yeah? So how come you're not in uniform, sir?'

'This is an undercover mission. An urgent one. Two French children have been kidnapped along with their grandmother by fascist sympathisers. They may be in a US Army jeep travelling towards Paris. I need you to pass a message along to the next checkpoint.'

'I have to ask you some questions first, sir.'

'For Chrissake, did you hear what I just said? There's no time for your dumb questions about baseball teams and what-not. We're talking about two children and their grandmother here.'

'My children,' I added, stepping out of the car with my hands raised in turn. 'And my mother.'

'Is that so, ma'am?'

'It is.'

'What seems to be the problem?'

An officer appeared, the silver eagle insignia on his uniform marking him out as a colonel. 'Daniel Diaz. Well I never.'

Dan's grin matched that of the colonel's. 'Andy. What the hell are you doing here?'

'It's Colonel Gillman to you,' said the colonel, clapping him on the shoulder before addressing his soldiers.

'At ease, men. Lieutenant Diaz and I served in an opera-tional group together.'

'That's Captain Diaz to you.'

'Creeping up those ranks, buddy.'

The colonel's smile remained in place as he turned to me.

'May I present my colleague, Juliette,' said Dan.

'Just Juliette?'

'That will do.'

'So what can we do for you, Juliette? I overheard something about children.'

'My children and my mother were taken from a safe house in England and brought to Étretat early this morning, we believe by a pro-Nazi cell still operating in Paris.'

I didn't mention my husband. Better the colonel didn't assume this was merely some kind of domestic affair.

'I see.' His brows drew together. 'I can radio ahead. Alert the other checkpoints between here and Paris, but you say this happened early this morning?'

'They came ashore around 5 a.m. and a US Army jeep was later seen driving away from the place they'd been taken. According to the locals, there have been no US troops in the vicinity for weeks.'

The colonel drew us aside, out of earshot of his men. 'That's correct. We have divisions in Le Havre helping clear the harbour and others further along the coast, but none that I know of at Étretat. You think this was part of the enemy Trojan horse operation?'

'I do,' said Dan.

'How long has this roadblock been here?' I asked.

'Since 1400 hours this afternoon, following new intelligence. We were given orders to extend the checkpoints beyond the immediate Paris area.'

'Why?'

'There have been more reports of infiltrators in and

around the city as well as others approaching from further afield. We have unconfirmed reports that they've already infiltrated the front lines.'

I looked at Dan.

'Exactly what we expected. Colonel, it's hours since that jeep will have passed here, long before you set up your road-block. Could you possibly radio the other checkpoints as you suggested and ask if any of them saw it? That would confirm at least that they were heading for Paris.'

'Consider it done. Why don't you wait in my tent while I find that out?'

He ushered us into a field tent equipped with a camp bed and a couple of chairs. An orderly appeared with hot coffee in tin mugs, and I sipped at it gratefully. The fog had closed in, the kind that penetrated to the bone, but I felt as if I was on fire, my nerves jangling, head whirling with heady exhaustion. My mother and the children were here, in France. They had almost certainly travelled this very road only hours before. So near and yet so very far.

'Hang on, my babies. I'm coming,' I whispered.

'What did you say?'

Dan's eyes were full of concern.

'Nothing. Everything.'

I choked on my words. Took another gulp of coffee.

'I have some news. I'm not sure if it's good or bad.'

The colonel was back.

'Two checkpoints closer to Paris reported seeing them this morning, one at Vernon and another at Saint-Germain-en-Laye. After that, they probably took the backstreets to avoid detection. Same description from each checkpoint, a little boy and girl with an older woman and a US soldier driving, a civilian male alongside him. Soldier produced paperwork each time that bore out his story.'

'Which was?'

'The little girl was very sick. The male in the vehicle was a local doctor. There were no ambulances available so the army had been asked to help out and bring the family to a hospital in Paris where she could undergo an emergency operation. Something to do with her heart.'

I felt the blood drain from my face. 'Did they say what exactly was wrong with the girl? Did she look sick?'

'She was all wrapped up in blankets, apparently asleep. My guess is that it was a story invented to help them bypass the checks. And it worked. When they heard how urgent it was, they waved them through fast.'

Natalie. Ma petite. *Impossible.*

I stuffed my fist in my mouth to stop myself from crying out. He was right. It was probably just subterfuge. But probably wasn't good enough. What if it was true?

'Juliette, they just said that to get through the checkpoints.'

'I know.'

Intellectually I did. In my heart, I wasn't so sure. She was only a baby. Barely even six years old. She'd already been through so much in her short life and I hadn't seen her for months. I would never forgive myself if it were true. When this was all over, I was never leaving her side – their sides – again.

'We'd better carry on,' I said. 'Concentrate on the hunt in Paris. Find out what's been happening there.'

Hopefully Guillaume and his friends would have some information for me. If not, I would get it out of my aunt and her vile Nazi-loving friends if it was the last thing I did.

'We've raised an all points alert on them,' said the colonel. 'If there's anything else I can do, please just ask.'

'Thank you.'

I was already striding out of the tent, heading for our car.

'Juliette.'

Dan calling after me. I didn't falter.

If I thought before that our relationship was doomed, now I knew it for certain. It was superstitious nonsense to believe the gods were punishing me for loving him, but I couldn't help but think it was true. I was here, with him, when I should have been there with my mother and my babies, looking after them, loving them. Making sure they were safe.

Even as it tore at my heart to turn away from him, it was the only thing to do. They needed me more. Even though so much of me needed him too.

THIRTY-SEVEN

'Juliette's mother, Claudine, and children have been abducted. They were taken from their safe house to a fishing boat moored on the south coast and from there over the Channel to Étretat in Normandy. We believe they are now in Paris.'

Christine stared at Suzanne across the table she'd chosen precisely because there was no one else seated nearby. Fortnum's was usually quiet at this time, which was one reason they met here. Another was its proximity to Whitehall so Edward could easily stroll up and join them.

'Dear God. Poor Juliette. Do we know who's taken them? And why?'

'We suspect it may be her husband, Philippe de Brignac, who's behind it. He's a known Nazi sympathiser who visited Berlin very recently. We also believe that he's instrumental in Hitler's plot to assassinate Eisenhower.'

'Sounds like a charmer.'

'He's a thoroughly nasty piece of work but very well connected. The group he leads are responsible for a number of shootings and bombings they're attempting to pin on the communist members of the FFI.'

'Why on earth would they do that?'

'The communists would love to take over from de Gaulle. Philippe de Brignac is a member of the French aristocracy. They, like the Americans, can't think of anything worse. The Russians are making great advances on the Eastern front which means they're a real threat not just to Germany but to Europe. A fascist like de Brignac would far rather the Germans ruled than a bunch of Bolsheviks.'

'But why take his own children? Surely he would want them to be safe in England, come what may?'

Suzanne looked up and smiled as a lean figure approached their table. 'Edward. Good to see you.'

He didn't need to drop a kiss on her cheek. His eyes did it for him. Christine watched his lashes drop just a fraction, as if he was caressing her. They were extraordinarily discreet, these two. More so even than Marianne and Jack.

'Good to see you both too.'

He pulled out a chair and beckoned to the waiter with his injured hand, refusing as ever to hide it away. He kept his back to the room while Suzanne had full view of it. It was unlikely any of the Cornflower Club members would happen upon them here, but even if they did, they would simply appear to be taking tea with friends.

'I was just updating Christine on the news from Paris,' said Suzanne.

'Our man in Versailles is on it,' said Edward. 'Name of Dick Ward.'

'I understand help may also be arriving shortly from Lyon,' added Suzanne.

'Oh yes?' Christine pulled out a cigarette, lit up and took a long drag. 'Care to fill me in?'

'First, why don't you fill us in on what's happening with Sir Max Mytton?'

'As little as I can manage,' drawled Christine. 'No sign of the Red Book, although I'll keep hunting for it. He trusts me enough to have had me dine at his house a couple of times now.'

'Any more babbling in German?'

'Not since the last time. But he's been making and receiving some interesting telephone calls, often in French. He thinks I can't understand or maybe he doesn't care. Keeps mentioning the sixteenth of December along with Skorzeny's name.'

Suzanne's gaze sharpened. 'Skorzeny?'

'Yes.'

'Could Max Mytton be involved in the kidnapping of Juliette's family?' asked Edward.

'Possibly, although as yet we have no idea of a motive.'

'Do you think Juliette has been compromised?' Christine crumbled a scone between her fingers as she spoke, letting the crumbs fall to her plate. No sense in spoiling the figure that was her greatest weapon for the sake of a few bites.

'I think,' said Suzanne, 'that it's more likely her husband is working for Skorzeny, and therefore Hitler, along with your aristocratic friend. As for the children and Claudine, I suspect he's using them to get at Juliette on a personal rather than professional level, although of course those now cross over.'

'I take it their marriage ended badly?'

As far as Christine was concerned, most marriages ended

badly, one way or another. Especially if the people in it actually stayed married.

'He's a violent man,' replied Suzanne. 'Controlling and obsessive. He was infuriated when Juliette left Paris to help lead the Resistance in the south and sent their children to Switzerland with her mother. So angry, in fact, that he denounced her father to his friends in the Gestapo.'

'What happened to her father?'

Edward spoke quietly, his voice overshadowed by his own memories of torture. 'He was brutally interrogated, but he wouldn't tell them where Juliette was so they killed him. Her mother was told that he'd died of a heart attack.'

'Dear God.'

'Juliette's husband had many friends at the Gestapo headquarters on Avenue Foch. Rumour has it he personally assisted in torturing his own father-in-law.'

'Send me after him,' said Christine. 'I'd be delighted to put a bullet in his brain.'

Violent men were her speciality. She'd dealt with enough of them, starting with her bastard of a stepfather. The day she'd finally brought that iron pan down on his head had marked the beginning of a whole new life. The life that had led her here. The one she was born to live.

Suzanne shook her head. 'You don't go after someone like Philippe de Brignac. He's far too well protected. Instead, you reel him in.'

'So let me be the bait.'

Fishing was another of Christine's special skills, especially when it involved someone like this. Someone who had hurt her friend and sister in arms. Christine wasn't the sisterly kind. She was far too much of a lone wolf. But she made an exception for Juliette and Marianne. She would happily kill for either of them.

'We already have the hook baited. With Juliette.'

Christine gaped at her. 'You're using Juliette? The woman he abused? He killed her father, for God's sake. How could you do this to her?'

Memories ringing in her head, the sound of her own mother screaming as her stepfather rained down his blows. The thought of someone doing that to Juliette made Christine feel physically sick.

'She volunteered to do it.'

'Volunteered? Or was persuaded?' Christine spat.

'She chose to undertake this mission,' said Suzanne. 'Just as you did. You always have a choice, and if you now choose to leave then I will accept that.'

'We can't leave though, can we? Not with what's at stake. You know that and we know that. And she had no bloody choice for those exact same reasons, God damn you.'

Tears sparked in Christine's cobalt eyes, diamond bright with rage and pain. They were each trapped by their sense of duty. By patriotism. By their need to do the right thing even if it meant doing a lot of wrong things along the way.

'Christine, she knows what she's doing. She has Diaz there with her making sure she comes to no harm.'

Diaz. Another bloody man. They were all the same. They kept their brains below their belts and their eyes on the main chance. She wondered if they'd ended up in bed together yet. Probably. The heightened tension in the field, the constant sense that you could be dead tomorrow. It was inevitable that so many operatives ended up between the sheets. It was the same tension she used to entrap her own targets.

'Even so,' said Edward, 'I'll make a discreet call to Dick Ward. Ensure that we have eyes on her at all times.'

'She'll spot any surveillance,' said Christine. 'I've seen her operate. She's that good. You have someone following her around and she'll be furious.'

'Better furious than dead. Besides, I already have an extra pair of eyes on her.'

They both looked at Suzanne.

'Jean Levesque. We turned him some time ago. All it took was a hefty promise of payment and he was ours. I banked on the fact he has no scruples.'

'The right-wing newspaper proprietor?'

'The same. Juliette used to work for him in Paris. Her cover story is that she's writing features for *The Times* along with Levesque. She has no idea that he's operating as a double agent.'

'Why not? Why wouldn't you tell her?'

'Because if she knew, she would act differently towards him. Far better that she believes he's simply her old mentor, at least for now. That way we can truly test Levesque. See which way his loyalties lie when the chips are down.'

'I don't believe you. She's going in there blind with no idea of who or what she can trust. Obviously not you. I'm going over there now, to Paris. I won't see Juliette used like this.'

Suzanne regarded her, unperturbed. 'You'll stay right here or you'll put her in even greater danger. She's working undercover, remember? As of now, you are supposedly a right-wing sympathiser having a liaison with someone who is almost certainly working with Juliette's husband and, by extension, for Hitler. You steam in there now and everyone's cover is blown.'

'She's right,' said Edward. 'You're far more use to her here, exposing Max Mytton and the rest of that filthy bunch of fifth columnists. We're keeping a close watch on McMahon too. I'm not convinced he's working undercover at those meetings, although his people, of course, will neither confirm nor deny.'

Christine lit up a cigarette, tilting her head back to blow out a perfect smoke ring through scarlet lips, the only sign that she was fighting for control a slight tremor in her hand. She looked at them both through narrowed eyes, thinking hard and fast. She had no option but to follow orders. How she interpreted those orders was open to question.

'Fine. I'll work harder on Max. Find that bloody book and get more out of him.'

'You do that. We have very little time to crack this, Christine. Do whatever it takes.'

Christine looked at the woman who had taught her everything, including how to lure a man to his deathbed.

'It will be my pleasure,' she said.

THIRTY-EIGHT

14 DECEMBER 1944, PARIS

I spotted Guillaume as we drove up to the apartment in Saint-Germain, casually leaning in the doorway opposite having a smoke, the car lights picking them out. A pretty girl was cuddling up to him, all smiles. They looked every bit the young couple in love. I felt a pang as I looked at them. It was so easy to be in love at that age when you had no responsibilities and no memories to trip you up.

Dan parked a little further along the street, and we waited while they ambled along from their doorway, arm in arm, chatting. These two were really good. We should offer Guillaume a job when all this was done.

Once they'd passed the car, we got out and followed them to the Café de Flore, taking a corner table upstairs and waiting until Guillaume apparently noticed we were there. He left his companion where she was and slid into the seat opposite us.

'How did you get on in Normandy?' he asked.

I fumbled for words. It felt as if aeons had passed since we left Paris this morning and yet it was only eleven hours.

'I suppose you could say it was productive. We talked to witnesses who saw them come ashore. We're now certain they're in Paris. Two checkpoints on the road in remembered them passing through. They had Natalie all bundled up in a blanket, pretending she was ill and needed urgent hospital treatment. At least, I hope they were pretending.'

I stirred the martini Dan had ordered for me, struggling to compose myself. It had been a long day. A hard day. And there would be more of them ahead until we found them. I had lived through hard days before, so many of them. But none like this – a day that had left my heart in shreds and my reserves of hope so low.

'She's only a baby,' I muttered. 'They both are.'

'I know.'

Guillaume's hand, rough and calloused on top of mine. *He used to have such soft hands*, I thought absently. That was before he learned that there was life beyond the 16th and that some fights were worth more than worrying about calloused palms.

'Did King appear at all today?' asked Dan.

'No sign of him. No sign of Philippe either. We've been swapping shifts between the apartment buildings all day. I have more friends keeping watch in the Deux Magots. King goes there sometimes. He's a slippery one, that fellow, but we're getting an idea of his movements.'

I mustered up a smile. 'Thank you. You're helping more than you know.'

'Juliette, I'll do anything to help. You're family. Your mother was always far kinder to me than my own. I just wish I knew where they were right now. I tell you, when we find that bastard Philippe, I'm going to teach him a lesson he'll never forget.'

'Join the queue,' said Dan.

I looked at them both.

'He's mine,' I said quietly. 'If anyone teaches him a lesson, it will be me.'

I could see in Dan's eyes everything: acknowledgement, regret. Understanding. Above all, love. It nearly undid me.

I felt rather than saw someone approach our table.

'Guillaume.'

We looked up at the bearded young man who'd appeared, evidently out of breath.

'Guillaume, that man you mentioned has just left the Deux Magots. A couple of the others are following him. You need to come.'

We were on our feet within seconds, Dan throwing some money on the table to cover the bill. Outside in the street, another young man pointed across the Rue Saint-Benoît, beyond the Café de Deux Magots.

'He went that way,' he said. 'Paul and Chloe are following him.'

We walked up the Boulevard Saint-Germain in the direction he indicated, careful to appear as if we were simply a group of friends out for an evening stroll. I could see a couple ahead, sauntering in a similar fashion, and then, ahead of them, the unmistakable figure of Harry King. He was once more dressed in his plus fours, a cap on his head and the slight limp more pronounced than before.

Just past the church of Saint-Germain-des-Prés he stopped, looked around and crossed the wide avenue, doubling back on himself on the other side of the road. Had he seen us? More likely he was simply being careful. He didn't glance in our direction or that of the other couple following him – they'd also stopped, pretending to admire the church, then carried on as if they didn't have a care in the world. The girl glanced back at Guillaume, who gave her a tiny nod.

'Let's go,' he said, also crossing the Boulevard Saint-Germain and then turning back so that we were once more following King, taking up the baton from the others.

We kept him in our sights as he marched at a good pace ahead, apparently unimpeded by his limp, turning left when he reached another side street that led off the boulevard.

'We should split up so we don't look too obvious. I'll take this side,' said Guillaume, crossing the road once more, hands in pockets as he sauntered along.

Dan took my hand. 'Come on,' he said. 'Act like you love me.'

He was joking and yet he wasn't.

Out of the corner of my eye, I saw King stop again and look over his shoulder. I half-turned and pressed myself against Dan.

'Can you see King? Is he on the move again?' I murmured, lifting my face to his.

'Not yet. He's pretending to tie his shoelace. This guy definitely thinks he might have a tail. No, wait. He's on the move again. Damn. He's disappeared around the bend.'

I could feel Dan's reluctance as he released his embrace. I felt it too. But King was the priority right now. I broke into a half run as we too rounded the bend in the road, picking up our pace.

'I see him,' I said. 'He's heading for the Boulevard Raspail.'

I glanced over the road. Guillaume was maybe thirty metres ahead of us, moving like a cat in the shadows. I felt a surge of pride. I'd been wrong about him all these years. He wasn't spoiled or petulant, just lost and in search of something that mattered to him. Weren't we all, in one way or another.

King was well ahead now, speeding up, apparently intent on getting to wherever he was going. We paused when we saw him reach the crossroads and turn left again, along the Boulevard Raspail.

I beckoned to Guillaume, who crossed back to join us, and together we took that same left turn.

King was nowhere in sight.

'*Merde*,' Guillaume spat.

'I think I know where he's going.'

I headed in the direction I was sure King had taken, stopping outside the Hotel Lutetia.

'This is where he used to meet his Abwehr and then SS contacts,' I said, gazing up at the vast art nouveau facade of the hotel that sprawled across an entire corner of the block, its glamour a little faded but still unmistakably there.

'Well, they're long gone,' said Guillaume.

'Yes, but maybe some of the same staff remain? Who occupies it now?'

'US and some French troops took it over at first,' said Dan, 'but de Gaulle handed it over to be a reception centre for returning prisoners of war and displaced citizens. Apparently he honeymooned here and has a soft spot for the place. Thinks it's not as intimidating as some other luxury hotels.'

'I always loved it too,' I said. 'The Lutetia is the grande dame of the Left Bank. So many writers and artists came here before the war, as well as Jewish families from Germany who were fleeing the outbreak.'

'A lot of secrets hidden within those walls then,' said Dan. 'Maybe King is hiding a few more.'

'Let's find out, shall we?'

I pushed my way through the revolving door, not waiting for their response. Inside, the place looked much as it had always done, the furnishings a little tattier perhaps but still lovely in their own way, just like an ageing movie star who refuses to concede to the passage of years. On second glance, the clientele looked out of place, the bohemians and intellectuals of yesteryear replaced by weary faces that looked far older than they should.

They were everywhere, wandering through the foyer like ghosts, slumped in armchairs or simply standing, staring sightlessly at more spectres, most likely from their recent past. Repatriated French prisoners of war, swapped like for like with German prisoners held in France.

'What the hell?' muttered Guillaume.

'That's exactly what they've been through,' I said. 'Hell. The Nazis are notorious for mistreating their prisoners. Some of them were probably forced labour as well.'

I looked around. No sign of King.

'Let's split up,' I said. 'Search the public rooms on the ground floor and any other areas we can access. We can meet back in the bar in an hour. That way it will look as if we're simply getting together for a drink if anyone is watching.'

'Good idea,' said Guillaume. 'I'll go this way.'

He disappeared into the labyrinth of corridors towards the rear of the hotel.

'I'll take this side,' I said, which left Dan to cover the area where we'd entered that bordered onto the Boulevard Raspail.

The place was vast, more like a village than a hotel, shops lining the ground floor, designed so that its clientele need never leave its environs. The decor straddled the periods between art deco and art nouveau, the effect not as grand as the Ritz, and the atmosphere less charged than the Scribe. Here, the inhabitants I passed appeared unaware that I did so apart from the odd curious glance thrown my way, and now and then a mumbled greeting.

They seemed reluctant to be in their rooms, preferring to wander the corridors and public areas. I came across one in the library adjacent to the Borghese salon, running his finger along the bookshelves as if feeling their spines would enable him to absorb all their knowledge.

'Pardon, monsieur, but did you see a man pass through here? Tall with red hair and trousers that look like pantaloons.'

He peered at me for a second and then his face broke into the loveliest smile. 'I am afraid not, madame, but it is so good to hear you speak. It has been far too long since I heard a woman speak as you do. Forgive me for any impertinence.'

'There is nothing to forgive,' I said, noticing his pallor and the way his eyes had sunk into his skull. The man had obviously been half starved, and but his voice and manner were educated.

'Have you just arrived here?' I asked, itching to carry on with my hunt but reluctant to appear dismissive to this fragile soul.

'A few days ago,' he said. 'I think. I escaped from a camp near the border along with some of my men. We came across a detachment of American soldiers who brought us here. It is just as I remember it.'

'You are from Paris?'

'Originally, yes. I moved with my wife and children to Toulouse before the war. I was captured during the Battle of France.'

I stared at him. 'You spent four years in a German camp?'

'I did, but now I'm home, and I hope very much to be reunited with my family soon. That is why I prefer to be down here rather than upstairs, alone in my room. I am not used to being alone, you see. I had to share everything with my fellow prisoners for so long.'

His quiet nobility was impressive, the suffering he'd endured all too evident.

I held out my hand to shake his. 'It is an honour to meet you. My name is Juliette.'

'Juliette. I hope you find the man you're looking for.'

'So do I. *Bonne chance.*'

It would take more than luck to find Harry King in this maze. Possibly a miracle.

I left him there with his books and carried on searching through the salons, coming back round on myself to where we'd started. There was no sign of Dan or Guillaume so I made for the bar where I'd spent many an evening arguing philosophy, art and the meaning of life. The bar was still magnificent, its art nouveau frescoes adorning the sculpted walls, a grand piano set at one end of the long room. Dan and Guillaume were already seated, and I could tell from their faces that their searches had been as fruitless as mine.

Inside the bar, life appeared to be going on a little more normally than in the rest of the hotel. There was a mixture of locals and the dispossessed, although the students and intellectuals who'd once used this as their watering hole after lectures were nowhere to be seen. Hemingway, too, was long gone, preferring the Ritz these days.

Dan signalled to one of the waiters. 'A martini and a Scotch on the rocks, please. What will you have, Guillaume?'

There was no response. Guillaume was no longer listening. Instead, he kept throwing looks at another waiter, surreptitiously taking mental notes as he passed.

'What are you doing?' I murmured.

'I've seen that guy before,' muttered Guillaume. 'With Harry King, leaving his apartment.'

'Oh really?'

The waiter came towards us and I got a good look. He was young, nondescript. A weak chin that had barely sprouted hair. The perfect patsy for the Germans. The kind of contact they could leave behind to service men like Harry King and my husband. While there were people like Meier at the Ritz who did their bit for the Resistance, there were others who succumbed to the threats and bribes of the occupiers. I couldn't blame the boy. His family were probably starving, along with so many other Parisians.

'It's nearly ten o'clock,' I said. 'What time do you think he'll finish his shift?'

'I don't know,' said Guillaume, 'but I can hang around and follow him when he does.'

'Good idea. Just make sure he doesn't spot you. If he's working with King, he's likely to have some very nasty friends.'

'What do you take me for? Haven't I done well so far?'

I patted his hand. 'You've done extremely well. Forgive me. I'm tired and I don't know what I'm saying.'

Tired was an understatement. I was weary in a way I'd never felt before, my spirits every bit as depleted as my body.

Fighting in the field was one thing, fighting for your family quite another. Especially when that family had vanished into the greater labyrinth that was Paris. The Lutetia might be a maze, but it was nothing compared to the streets beyond that stretched for mile after mile in a city that was long practised at harbouring secrets, never mind the whereabouts of a woman and two small children.

'We should also check with the listening station,' I said. 'Find out if there are any reports from my aunt's apartment.'

I was clutching at straws, I knew. But it was better than doing nothing. The chances of those bugs I'd installed picking up anything useful were remote. My husband might be a pig but, like all pigs, he was clever. It was how he'd managed to stay alive this far while doing deals with the devil.

'I've asked them to alert me immediately if there are,' said Dan. 'Why don't we go back to the Scribe and see if there are any messages? We also need to liaise with the surveillance teams. Find out if they've turned up anything.'

'I feel so helpless. All we are doing is watching and waiting.'

I glanced around the bar once more as if King might miraculously have appeared.

'That's all we can do. King is long gone from here. If he's not, we can't properly search the place without raising suspicion. My guess is, he came to touch base with his buddy over there and then scuttled out into some back alleyway like the rat that he is. We'll pick him up again. We have eyes all over the place.'

'Yes but every hour that passes means they have another hour to do what they like to my mother and my babies.'

I clamped my mind down again, trying not to torture

myself, but images rose unbidden no matter how hard I tried. My little girl smiling up at me, so tiny and so innocent. My boy kicking a ball in that determined way of his, shouting to me to watch. Damn this war. Damn that bastard husband of mine. Damn everything. I could feel what little energy I had left draining away as I let my head fall into my hands.

'Come on,' said Dan. 'You look exhausted. Let's get you back to the Scribe. Get some food inside you. You haven't eaten all day.'

'Nor have you.'

Rather than argue, he took me by the arm and helped me to my feet.

'Guillaume...'

He waved a hand. 'Don't worry about me. I know what to do.'

'Are you sure you'll be all right?'

'Go before I prove to you how tough I can be.'

I managed a weary smile in his direction. Then we were pushing through those revolving doors, Dan propelling me as much as they did, hailing a taxi which had miraculously appeared, not caring about the extortionate price quoted.

Ten minutes later, we were back at the Hotel Scribe and twenty minutes after that ordering what passed for room service.

'Makes sense,' said Dan. 'The restaurant is shut. They said they would do their best to rustle something up. Besides, we can speak more freely here.'

I looked around his room. It was tidier than mine, his clothes neatly folded in military fashion, his toiletries laid out in precise ranks on the dressing table. I had no idea how I ended up in his room instead of mine. Maybe it was easier. Or maybe I wanted it. Wanted him. I had no idea what to think or say anymore. My head was reeling from the day, my mind fuzzy with exhaustion and raw emotion.

I'd been in far more dangerous situations many times but none that terrified me like this, fear pulsating beneath every thought, marring every moment. The worst part was knowing that there was little or nothing I could do until we tracked them down through one or other of our suspects. I knew there were people on them day and night and yet I wanted to be there too, making sure that no one looked away at the wrong moment or blinked, following each and every lead, never letting up until I knew they were safe.

'Juliette, eat.'

Dan's voice, gentle with concern.

I looked down at the plate the waiter had brought. Pushed the food around some more with my fork. Then set it to one side and drew in a long, shuddering breath. 'I can't. Not until we find them.'

'You have to. You need your strength. For them, Juliette, if not for you.'

He always knew the right thing to say. I picked up my fork again and forced in a few mouthfuls, each morsel as hard to swallow as a lump of gristle. I washed the lot down with a glass of the wine Dan had also procured. It permeated the edges, softening them.

'Stay here tonight. With me.'

I looked at him as he topped up my wine, pushing a plate of patisserie towards me. The chef had done his best with what ingredients he could obtain and these were no doubt left over from this morning. I thought of the people waiting patiently in the rain outside the city's bakeries, queueing up with their ration books for bread, never mind cakes. I picked up a tiny tarte and bit into it. Not bad, considering. Then I brushed the crumbs from my mouth.

'I can't do that,' I said.

'Just to hold you. Nothing more. You look as if you could do with being held.'

Such a tempting idea. Too tempting.

'I need to sleep,' I said. 'I have to be fresh for the morning so we can start looking for them again as soon as it's light.'

'Then let me take you back to your room at least. Make sure you're OK.'

'I'm OK, Dan. Really. I can look after myself.'

'I know you can. But I want to look after you too.'

Such simple words, but they were words I'd been waiting to hear half my life, if only I'd known that. I'd never thought a man could or would take care of me. Never wanted one to. It was only when I heard him say it that I realised how much I longed for it. At least, from him.

'I have to go now,' I muttered thickly, not daring to say much more. If I did, the floodgates would open and then everything would be lost, including my soul. My heart was already his. The part that loved in that way, at least, the other part reserved for my family.

He rose and took my hand across the table as I stood too. 'Don't.'

'I must.'

'You don't want to.'

'I do.'

A lie. And he knew it.

'Very well then – I'll walk you to your door.'

His tone brooked no argument.

It took a couple of minutes to cover the twenty metres or

so to my room, far longer to tear my eyes from his face as he stood there, silent, his eyes saying everything.

'Goodnight then,' I said at last.

'Goodnight, Juliette. Sleep well.'

He dropped a featherlight kiss on my forehead.

I was already closing the door when I heard him murmur, 'I love you.'

'I love you too,' I whispered as it clicked shut and the tears finally began to fall.

THIRTY-NINE

14 DECEMBER 1944, WILTSHIRE, ENGLAND

Marianne looked up from her borrowed desk at the prison barracks to see a guard hovering.

'You ready for the next one, ma'am?'

She nodded and glanced down at her list as the guard brought him in. Erich Koenig.

The tall, gangly fellow who now stood to attention in front of her looked more like a scholar than a member of an elite fighting force.

'Please, sit down,' she said. 'Would you like a glass of water?'

Koenig shook his head.

'Do you speak English?'

He gazed at her mutely.

'Very well. Let's begin. I represent the Red Cross and I'm here to ensure that you're being treated in accordance with the Geneva Convention. Do you understand?'

Still no response. This one was going to be hard work, just like the others. They all wore black armbands, marking them out as Category C prisoners, the highest category.

Mostly Waffen-SS with a few from the Luftwaffe para-
trooper division. Fanatical, diehard Nazis. They had to be, to
survive not just this prison but their own rules. She bent her
head, about to make the same note that she'd made about all
the rest being unwilling or unable to engage in conversation
when a commotion from the hallway outside the office
brought it snapping back up.

Koenig was already rising from his seat.

'Sit down,' she ordered.

He ignored her completely, lunging across the desk to
grab her and pin her arms to it while from behind him she
heard the door smashing open.

More shouts and cries. The sounds of a struggle. Marianne's mind went into overdrive, working out what to do
next. This was some kind of mutiny or insurrection. They
would use her as a bargaining tool. That meant they wouldn't
kill her straight away. *Think, Marianne, think.*

A hand grabbing the hair at the front of her head and
yanking it up. Another voice shouting in German. Another
prisoner, shorter and stockier than Koenig.

'Look at me, bitch.'

She pretended not to understand.

He tried again, in English this time.

She spat in his face.

His answering slap sent her ears ringing.

Next thing she knew, he was pressing a pistol to her
temple. Where the hell had he managed to get that? Off a
guard, probably. Where were the guards? The soldiers?

Another voice shouting, this time in English. One she
recognised.

'Leave the bitch alone. She's not worth worrying about.
We need to get to the governor.'

A laugh and then she was being dragged round the desk, hauled to her feet, her arms pinned behind her. She could see him now, the man who'd yanked her by the hair, a chunk of it still in his grip.

He laughed again and threw it in her face. 'There you go. Stick that back on.'

He was short, powerfully built, his eyes sizing her up even as his mouth twisted in a sneer. Behind him, Jack was also staring at her. *Don't do anything stupid*, his eyes seemed to say. Well, too bad. There was no way in hell she was going to let this German scum treat her the way he had.

She threw her head back and up, hearing the satisfying crack as it met cartilage and bone. The man holding her let out a yelp. Not so tough then.

She twisted in his grip, raising her knee so she got him hard in the balls, just as her instructor at Arisaig had taught her.

'Just kick him in the balls and chop him in the side of the neck.' Good old Sykes. She could hear him now, in her head, even as her hand sliced into the side of the German's neck.

He gurgled and staggered.

She kept the momentum going forward, twisting and turning so the short one couldn't get a clean shot. He tried anyway, the sound of it ricocheting around the room.

'Hold your fire!' someone yelled.

Jack maybe.

More shouts. The sound of running feet, boots thudding on wooden floors. More bodies bursting into the room, the shouts and curses English this time. Hands reaching for her and pulling her free, out of the slackened grip of the German.

'You all right, miss?'

A more cultivated voice ringing out.

'What the bloody hell has been going on here?'

She caught sight of an officer's insignia, British this time.

'Dear God, what have they done to you?'

The officer was staring at her hair, then at her wrists, where livid bruises were already appearing.

'I'm fine – really,' she protested. 'It all happened so fast.'

Over his shoulder, she could see Jack, his arms raised in surrender. She watched as one of the guards cuffed him and led him away with the others.

A sudden thought struck her.

'One of them had a pistol,' she blurted out. 'There could be others.'

Her words died on a yell of pain, one that came from deeper inside the prison, the sound of a pistol shot still ringing under it like a death knell.

FORTY

I was still sleep-blurred when the phone rang in my room.

'Someone to see you, madame,' said the receptionist. 'A gentleman by the name of Antoine. He says he is a friend of yours from Lyon.'

'I'll be right down.'

I threw on my clothes and splashed water on my face. What the hell was Antoine doing here? Last time I saw him was in Lyon. As far as I knew, he'd taken over there after we left, tracking down collaborators and those spies who remained.

'Antoine.'

He was standing just to the left of the reception desk, evidently ill at ease, his cadaverous face thinner than ever.

'Juliette. It's good to see you.'

As his face brushed mine, I felt his tension. He pulled back, holding me at arm's length.

'I am so sorry about your mother and your children,' he said.

That was when I realised why he'd come. Antoine of all

people would understand. His own family had been taken, transported to the camps. The tension I felt was him holding back his own grief in empathy with mine.

'We'll find them,' I said.

I sounded more confident than I felt.

'We will and that is why I've come. To help you do that.'

'Who sent you?'

'Suzanne. She thought I might be the right person to assist. We're also working with displaced people in the south, you see. Helping them trace their children and other family members now that they're returning home, although many don't have a home to go to anymore.'

I thought of the soldier I'd met the night before in the Lutetia, his voice full of yearning as he spoke of his family.

'My God, Antoine, that must be so hard.'

It had always been easy to read Antoine's soul simply by looking in his eyes. Now I saw a new depth of compassion in them. The suffering he must have seen.

'It is, but your situation is even more difficult. I'm here for you, Juliette, as a friend as well as a colleague. I understand that Captain Diaz is here too. Perhaps we could sit down over a coffee and make a plan.'

'Sounds good to me.'

I looked up to see Dan, freshly shaven, a file tucked under his arm, handsome in his uniform. He smiled at Antoine and held out his hand.

'Great to see you, Antoine. Thank you for coming.'

'You knew he was coming?'

'Suzanne sent a message.'

Another detail he'd kept from me. Last night, Dan hadn't avoided my gaze like this. Did they seriously think I couldn't handle it? That I was going to fall apart over my mother and the children? Well, they would have to think again. If anything, it only made me stronger and more determined to find them.

I suppressed my irritation. 'I see. Well, let's order that coffee and bring you up to date with what's been happening, Antoine.'

By the time we'd finished filling him in on the details, Antoine's face was alive with indignation.

'And you say you believe it is your husband who has taken them? Your own husband?'

'Yes, but I also believe he's not acting alone in this. Philippe might hate me and want revenge for my leaving him, but he has always loved power more than he ever loved me. He wants to reinstate his Nazi friends in France so he can regain that power and rule alongside them.'

'But that's insane.'

'He is. Which means he could do anything.'

My breath juddered and died, my words tailing off. Another image rose, unbidden, in my mind – my mother's face, her gentle smile. She was no match for Philippe, although I knew with absolute certainty she would give her life to protect her grandchildren. I could only hope she wouldn't have to.

'The problem is that our mission here is unofficial, at least in the eyes of de Gaulle's government. Apart from a couple of agents based at Versailles, we have very few resources.'

'Agents?'

'One American and one British, CIC and MI5. Or so I believe.'

I didn't want to glance at Dan for confirmation. I was

already annoyed at being sidelined. I felt rather than saw him give a slight nod to Antoine.

'My cousin Guillaume has been helping with surveillance, along with some of his friends,' I continued. 'I bugged his mother's apartment, and the agents at Versailles have someone listening in. His mother is my aunt and a good friend of my mother-in-law, who shares her son's fascist beliefs.'

I didn't mention Guillaume's communist connections. Antoine liked them about as much as he liked fascists, which was not at all.

Dan gave Antoine a frank look. 'We could really do with your assistance.'

'Consider it done,' said Antoine. 'Where do I start?'

'Philippe has never seen or met you,' I said. 'I think you're the perfect person to track him down and follow him. You have all the skills that Guillaume and his friends lack. As for the British security services, they were the ones who were supposed to be looking after my family when they were kidnapped.'

I tried not to sound as betrayed as I felt.

'You really think your husband will lead me to them?'

'I know he will. He has my mother and children somewhere in Paris – I know that too. I lived with the man for years, remember. At the right moment, he's going to use them to get what he wants out of me.'

'And what is that?'

'Ten times as much pain as I inflicted on him by leaving him and taking them with me.'

'You think he will harm his own children to achieve that.'

It was a statement, not a question.

'He will do whatever it takes.'

'Then we must do whatever it takes to stop him.'

I looked at Antoine, hearing the passion in his voice, seeing the fervour on his face. He, of all people, knew how it felt to have your own family torn from you. His wife and children had been taken to a German camp somewhere, transported there because they were Jewish. Too many tales had filtered through from those camps for Antoine not to be aware of what might have happened to them. At least I knew that my mother and children were still alive. For now.

I took his hand between mine. 'Thank you,' I said. 'For coming.'

'You would do the same for me.'

His eyes were bleak. We both knew that I might never get the chance.

FORTY-ONE

Antoine pulled a notebook and pen from his pocket. 'Tell me everything you can about your husband. Description, habits, last known addresses and contacts. I will need to speak to this aunt of yours as well and your cousin.'

'That should prove interesting.'

'Don't worry. I'll think up a watertight cover story for your aunt. I will try to get to speak to your mother-in-law too.'

'Good luck with that.'

Antoine's smile briefly lit up his face. 'I can be charming when I want to be.'

'I'm sure you can. There is also the concierge at my aunt's building. A bit of a busybody, as they all are, but helpful. I slipped her ten francs and told her there would be more if she passed on any useful information.'

Antoine made a note. 'Excellent. I'll start with her. Do you have a photograph of your husband?'

Dan produced the file Suzanne had given us at our briefing, the one that contained pictures of all the likely and known suspects.

'That's him,' I said, extracting the relevant photograph.

Antoine studied it for a second, taking in Philippe's handsome, dissolute face, the set of his mouth and the supercilious sneer in his eyes.

'Thank you,' he said, handing it back. 'I've memorised it. Do you also have photographs of your mother and children?'

I reached for my bag and pulled out the pictures I carried in my purse.

'Only these,' I said. 'This is my mother, Claudine.'

Her sweet face was set in an uncharacteristically stern pose as she gazed into the camera. She hated having her picture taken and it showed.

'Normally, she's smiling.'

'I can see that,' said Antoine. 'She has little laughter lines around her eyes. A beautiful woman.'

I then passed him the one of the children. The picture was far less formal than the one of my mother, the children laughing up at me as I snapped away with a borrowed camera. I had to stop myself from stroking their little faces as I handed it to Antoine. He studied it carefully too.

'Nicolas and Natalie. This was taken when we were reunited in November after four years apart. At first, they were so shy, afraid of this stranger who claimed to be their *maman*.'

'How old are they?'

'Nicolas is eight and Natalie six. Still babies. They were only four and two when I last saw them before that, and I wondered if they would even recognise me. But within a few minutes we were all cuddling as if nothing had happened. Children are so resilient, you know.'

'I hope so.'

I wanted to bite my own tongue.

'How long did you have with them?'

'Only that one afternoon, playing in the park. I flew back that night, to London, and they followed a few days later. They were taken to the safe house the British promised in return for my continuing to work for them. Only it wasn't so safe after all.'

'She looks like you,' he said, handing the photographs back to me. 'Your daughter.'

'You think?'

I looked at her face framed by blonde hair, lighter than mine. Her eyes as large as pansies and just as velvety, rosebud mouth open as she giggled. Beside her, Nicolas was acting every bit the big brother, one arm around her shoulders. For once, he too was smiling. I worried more about him than her. He was so serious for his age. Old beyond his years. But then, he'd been forced to grow up fast, fleeing across the border to Switzerland with my mother, his sister too young to know what was happening. Nicolas looked like Philippe, but there the resemblance ended. He was kind through and through, always trying to look after his sister and his *grand-mère*, even though he was only eight.

'What makes you think they were kidnapped rather than went of their own free will?'

A good question. But then, Antoine always got straight to the heart of the matter.

'My mother would never have brought the children back to France voluntarily. She was so relieved to get to England, away from the chaos and misery here. As you know, people have been going a little crazy after liberation with their reprisals. All that hair-shaving and marching collaborators down the street to mock them. Or worse. Then there's Philippe. Maman was always afraid of what he might do.'

My voice tailed off. It wasn't just what he might do now. It was what he had done and what he was going to do next. Philippe always had a plan, even if it was a warped one. Until he made another move, we had no idea what that plan might entail.

'Madame, a package for you.'

I looked up to see a bellboy hovering.

'Thank you.'

I took it from him, knowing immediately who had sent it from the feel of the envelope, never mind my name written across it in Philippe's unmistakable hand. The envelope was thick, of good quality, a rarity when there was a paper shortage. But this envelope had been made before the war and stockpiled in a bureau along with others of various sizes and matching cream notepaper, all embossed with the family crest. Philippe's family crest.

I ran my thumb over it before I slit the envelope open. Inside, there was a book.

The Werewolf of Paris.

The cover was lurid, depicting a devilish man looming over a blonde woman slumped on the ground, a pool of blood beneath her head and her clothes half torn from her body. I remembered it well. It sat on our bookshelves for years, alongside his other books on strange sects and even stranger beliefs. At least this one was supposed to be fiction. Supposed to be. It always troubled me that the woman on the cover bore more than a passing resemblance to me.

I flipped it open, looking for a note. Some kind of clue. There was nothing.

'It's from my husband,' I said. 'How does he know I'm staying here?'

'Maybe King told him?'

I looked at Dan. 'Maybe.'

I could feel ants crawling under my skin and across my scalp. *He knows where I am. He's watching me. Of course he is. He told me over and over that he would never let go.*

Dan held out his hand. 'May I?'

The pages fluttered as I passed the book to him. I couldn't stop trembling, my whole body shaking as if I had a fever, although I felt icy cold to my very core.

Dan examined the cover and then flicked through the pages. 'You know this book?'

'Yes.'

The word emerged from my lips as a rasp.

'Looks like some cheap horror story.'

'It's more than that. It's his favourite book. Philippe is sending a message. He's always been fascinated by the occult. It's another thing he has in common with the Nazis. Somewhere in this book I am sure there's a hint as to where he's holding my mother and the children. It's the kind of thing he would do, forcing me to solve a puzzle in order to find them. It makes him feel even more in control.'

'Do you have any idea what that puzzle might be?'

'None at all. The book is the story of a man called Bertrand Caillet who is the descendant of a cursed family. He has strange dreams and desires he cannot control. It turns out he's a werewolf. It's mostly set during the Franco–Prussian war and then in Paris during the Commune when the people tried to overthrow the government, a little like now.'

'I know this story,' said Antoine. 'It's very graphic.'

He took the book from Dan in turn, glancing at it with disdain, his eyes flicking from the blonde on the cover to me.

'*Bâtard,*' he muttered. 'May I look at the envelope?'

He scrutinised the writing on the front and then the crest on the back.

'This is his family? They are some kind of nobility?'

'Yes. Minor aristocrats. But important enough to get him membership of the Jockey Club and to make him believe he is entitled to rule France along with his German friends.'

I spoke bitterly, my words tinged by every blow he'd landed in the name of bringing me up to his standards, of beating the bourgeois out of me as he called it. I was proud to be bourgeois if it meant my family had worked for what we had instead of being handed it on a silver plate. One day, he would scream into my face as he throttled me, his son would inherit his title and all that went with it. And I, his mother, would have to make sure I didn't embarrass him the way I'd embarrassed his father.

'He's toying with you,' said Dan. 'Playing mind games. Don't fall for it, Juliette.'

'I know his mind games all too well,' I retorted. 'They're almost worse than the ones he likes to play with his fists.'

Antoine's shock was written across his face. 'He hit you?'

'It was a long time ago, Antoine, before I learned how to stand up for myself.'

'Or maybe before you found yourself again.'

I looked up into Dan's eyes. Those beautiful eyes. Eyes in which I would happily have lost myself forever.

'Maybe.'

The truth was that I was already lost, or at least lost to him, if only he knew it. Although it was far better he didn't – preferable he believed my lies and half-truths. My head had to rule my heart, now and always. Even if it meant that same heart shattering into a million pieces at the very thought of being without him. But be without him I must.

A voice sliced through my thoughts, one that was familiar and so very English. 'I thought I might find you here.'

Dan stood, holding out his hand. 'Good to see you, sir. To what do we owe the pleasure?'

Dick Ward smiled genially, immaculate as before. 'I had to bring some papers over from Versailles. Didn't want to trust a courier, if you know what I mean.'

'Please, join us,' I said, indicating an empty chair. 'This is our colleague Antoine from Lyon. Antoine, this is Dick Ward who works at Versailles.'

Ward's eyes swept over him in one cool, professional glance. 'Thank you but I must be getting back. I just wanted to say hello and to let you know that if there's anything you need, anything at all, then all you have to do is say the word.'

I looked at him. So he knew too.

'Thank you,' I murmured, my voice thick with unshed tears. 'That is very kind of you.'

'Not at all.'

A nod to us all and he was gone, gliding towards the door in the way of men like him everywhere – imperturbable, sure of his place in the scheme of things.

'Let me guess – the British agent,' said Antoine.

Dan sat back down in his chair, reaching for the photograph of Philippe and tucking it back in the file. 'Got it in one.'

Antoine quirked an eyebrow. 'In that case, we had better move as fast as we can.'

'Why?

'Because if that stuffed shirt is our backup, we've got no chance.'

FORTY-TWO

15 DECEMBER 1944, WILTSHIRE, ENGLAND

The two men stood back to back in front of the open window, stark naked, handcuffed. Their jaws were rigid with the effort of maintaining self-control. Even so, one involuntarily cried out as their interrogator picked up the pail of icy water and threw it over them. Another and another followed until their skin was puckering and turning blue. The temperature outside was below zero, but in there it must have felt even colder.

On the other side of the door, Marianne bit the inside of her cheek to stop herself crying out too. The interrogators had arrived early this morning from London, and it was clear they meant business. She'd overheard one of the officers saying they were from a clandestine unit. From the glimpses she caught through the barred window, they evidently knew what they were doing.

In one corner of the cell, McMahon looked on, his expression impenetrable. He knew as well as she did that Jack had to withstand this torture if he was to maintain his cover story, but she trusted McMahon about as much as she would a rattlesnake.

'Where did you get the gun?'

The interrogator was shouting into Shorty's face. The German grimaced but said nothing.

Smack.

A punch to his kidneys.

Smack, smack.

Two more blows, one to each side.

Shorty doubled over, gasping, pulling Jack with him. It would almost have been comical except that this was deadly serious. A guard was fighting for his life with a bullet wound to the head. Two more had suffered injuries that would put them out of commission for weeks. Shorty had managed to achieve all of that in the thirty seconds it had taken him to pull the other pistol from his belt where he'd concealed it and start shooting at the guards attempting to get them back to their cells.

Why the hell they hadn't searched him properly before they started to march them back from that debacle in her office was anyone's guess. She'd shouted a warning but too late. Now Jack was implicated too simply because he'd been the one closest to Shorty. And there was nothing she could do but hope he could maintain his cover long enough to survive until Shorty finally broke. The trouble was, he showed no sign of doing so. Damn Nazi code of honour or whatever it was called.

She turned her head away as the interrogators started in on Jack and felt a tap on her shoulder. She turned to see an adjutant standing there.

'The camp commander wants to see you, ma'am.'

'What, now?'

'Yes, ma'am. If you'll follow me.'

She had no alternative.

Leaving Jack to his fate, she followed the adjutant along what felt like miles of corridors to the commander's office. Evidently he didn't like to be disturbed by the screams and cries that emitted from certain cells.

The commander looked up as she entered. 'Please, take a seat.'

He nodded at her and then motioned to his adjutant to leave. 'Shut the door behind you, there's a good fellow.'

The moment they were alone, the mask dropped. The commander steepled his fingers and regarded her over them.

'I've just had a telephone call from London. They've asked me to treat this conversation with you as top secret. Apparently we have a problem with our American friends. Do you have any idea what that might be?'

'I think the clue is in the top secret. Sir.'

For a second she thought she might have gone too far and then the commander let out a bellow of laughter. 'Didn't think you were the Red Cross type,' he said. 'You have that look about you. Someone who's seen combat.'

'I've seen way more than that, sir.'

'I bet you have. So how can I assist? It seems we need to be a little more open with one another.'

'Did London say which American friends specifically?'

'Yes. The one currently supervising the interrogation of two of my prisoners.'

'That would be McMahon. American counter-intelligence. I had some dealings with him in France.'

'Did you indeed? Well, London have asked me to keep this strictly between ourselves. McMahon, it appears, has been here under false pretences. His presence is unauthorised, and it looks very much as if MI5 would like a word with him.'

'I see.'

Marianne wondered who exactly had sniffed out what McMahon was up to this time. Her money was on Edward.

'So what do you intend to do about him, sir? McMahon?'

'The same car that brought those men from London will be taking him back with them.'

'What about the operation here, sir? My colleague is currently being rather roughly interrogated by those men. If you have something I can use to put a halt to that, please do share it.'

The commander cleared his throat. 'Ah, yes. I do have some information for you. Again, top secret.'

'Which is?'

'They've transcribed and translated some of the conversations they picked up with the hidden microphones in the cells. It appears that the man currently being interrogated is not the ringleader. That honour falls to his compatriot, a man called Erich Koenig.'

'I know him. He's the one who first grabbed me across the desk.'

'Indeed. It appears from the transcriptions that Koenig helped to mastermind a plan to break out of this prison, seize weapons and tanks and use them to liberate other German prisoners in camps on their way to London, where they intended to assassinate Churchill and facilitate the landing of German troops.'

'I see. That is absolutely insane.'

And not exactly news to her ears, although she couldn't let on that she already knew.

'I know but they had every intention of carrying out their

plan. They've been stockpiling weapons. That's how Koenig's friend managed to have not one but two pistols on him.'

'Not very bright then, giving the game away.'

'Apparently not, but it appears they thought they could overpower you easily and break out using you as a hostage. Their mistake. It does mean that we can now round up the perpetrators, warn the other prison camps and stop them carrying out this ghastly plan. I trust you now have what you need to stop the interrogation of your colleague?'

Marianne rose from her chair and saluted. 'I do indeed, sir. Thank you.'

She was out of the room and running down the corridors before the commander could return her salute. Under her breath, she chanted one name: Jack. She was coming to save him all over again. And, together, they had once more helped save the day – or at least Churchill's skin.

FORTY-THREE

15 DECEMBER 1944, LONDON

Christine stared at the picture above the mantelpiece. It was of a house, at first sight a charming neo-Gothic villa, until she noticed the gargoyles above the door, the whole painting lit up by the fire that burned in the grate beneath, lending it a sulphuric glow. Come to think of it, there was something about the place that repelled her, although she wasn't quite sure what.

'Where is this?' she asked.

Max came up behind her, his arms snaking round her in a way that made her want to deal him a sharp backward blow with her elbow. She had to content herself with a moan that he would assume was lust.

'Paris. It belongs to a friend of mine.'

'Unusual building.'

He chuckled, more at the way she writhed under his touch than her words. The man really did think he was irresistible. 'Some people say it's haunted.'

'Gosh. How exciting.'

He was licking her ear now, poking his tongue in it and

rotating it like a large slug. 'Not as exciting as you,' he breathed.

'Won't your guests be here any minute?'

He'd invited a group of his chums to his townhouse in Mayfair for what he called 'an evening of cards and games'. The timing was interesting, the night before another significant social gathering, the one they suspected was in fact a rallying cry for fascist insurrection.

'They will,' he sighed, pulling away as a discreet tap on the door signalled that the first of them had arrived.

Christine arranged herself to best advantage by the window, sipping at the cocktail a footman had served while another admitted the guests. A French 75. One of her favourites. She felt the champagne bubbles pop in her mouth, tasting the gin and lemon notes.

Just the one, Christine. These things were lethal and she needed her wits about her tonight.

'My dear, may I present Lord Rattray? You know Lady Rattray of course.'

Christine felt her smile tauten at the edges even as she held out her hand. The notorious Nazi-loving MP himself. The evening was already more interesting. Accompanying him, his unlovely wife, whom she'd last seen at the Cornflower Club meeting, her lipstick perhaps more vermillion than before, a slash of blood across her face.

As the other guests filed in, Christine recognised faces from the Rattrays' house as well as the Cornflower Club. Here was the couple they had sat alongside, the husband who'd leered at her and the wife who'd exuded disapproval the moment her eyes lighted on Christine.

Christine beamed at her. 'How lovely to see you again.'

The woman sniffed and pretended to inspect the curtains.

Evidently embarrassed, her husband thrust out his hand and pumped hers vigorously. 'Good to see you too.'

Over his shoulder, Christine caught a glimpse of Max deep in conversation with a newcomer, a rather dull-looking man who appeared to be foreign. Dull or not, there was something about the way they were talking, heads close together, that intrigued her.

'Excuse me.'

She slunk through the other guests, bestowing an even more alluring smile upon the two men as she sidled up to them.

Max's manners were impeccable, if not his politics. He immediately broke off his conversation to introduce her to his companion.

'My dear, may I present the Duc d'Aquitaine?'

'*Enchanté.*'

The Duc did not sound at all enchanted, but Christine wasn't fazed. 'You're French?'

'You are astute, madame.'

She emitted a tinkly laugh, the one she reserved for men like him. 'I do so love France. Especially Paris.'

'Everyone loves Paris, although I fear it is not what it was. These awful queues of people in the streets outside the shops. The lack of law and order. It is chaos, I tell you. Anarchic.'

'That does sound worrying.'

No doubt he, too, was hoping his German friends would march back at any moment to instil a fascist sense of discipline once more on the city, although, in her experience, they were more than capable of debauchery as well.

'There is no need for you to worry. We will have the situation under control soon enough.'

He might as well have patted her on the cheek.

'I'm sure you will,' murmured Christine. 'My dear, are the games about to start?'

Out of the corner of her eye she'd detected a number of the guests moving towards the oval table set near the fireplace, taking their seats. A footman placed two packs of cards on the table, fanning them out to demonstrate that the cards were pristine and brand new. Max took up his place in the centre and motioned to Christine to sit beside him.

'I propose we start with a few rounds of gin rummy before we get a little more serious.'

There was a murmur of agreement around the table, and the footman took up the cards, shuffling them well before dealing them out. It gave Christine a chance to scan the faces before her, all of them male apart from Lady Rattray and the sniffing wife. Eleven in total, including her. An odd number. She wondered if someone was missing or arriving late.

'Another cocktail, madam?'

She put her hand over her glass. 'No thank you.'

Max glanced at the footmen. 'That will be all for now, thank you.'

The moment they'd left the room, he threw a card down on the pile in the centre of the table. The four of clubs. The Devil's Bedpost. A card that many players considered cursed. It didn't seem to dismay him.

'Change of plan. We're all meeting at 11 a.m. tomorrow by Admiralty Arch,' he announced as if he was discussing the weather. 'You will, of course, conceal your weapons until the appropriate moment, although I hope it will not be necessary to use them. Apart from the, ah, necessary eliminations, we intend this to be a bloodless coup.'

'Fine sentiments,' said Lord Rattray, 'but do you really think the hoi polloi won't put up a fight? Remember Cable Street.'

'That was a long time ago, before people got sick of the war. They want this over as much as we do.'

'What about these German troops?' piped up the man with the sniffing wife.

His lordship glanced at the clock. 'The first contingent should already have started breaking out of their prison camps. They will liberate the others. The authorities, of course, will try to keep a lid on it and clamp down on all communications, but I'm confident they'll succeed. There are over 250,000 of them after all. Provided they manage to procure enough vehicles, they should reach London at around 11 a.m. too.'

'Where are they supposed to find these vehicles?'

'We have people on the inside in the barracks. They have orders to make sure jeeps, armoured vehicles and some tanks are readily available.'

Tanks? This was a new one on Christine.

She, too, glanced at the clock – 8.35 p.m. She wondered how Marianne and Jack were getting on at that prison camp and whether the prisoners there had actually succeeded in their breakout. She was itching to get to a telephone and call Suzanne, find out what was what, but she knew that Max's was most definitely bugged, not just by their people but MI5 and possibly his own people too. It was simply too risky to contemplate, and there was no other way of getting in touch. Suzanne had designed it that way. They each had their tasks. Carry them out successfully and the entire plan would succeed. Slip up or fail and that put everyone at risk, not least the people of London and Churchill himself.

As for the Paris end of things, she could only imagine what Juliette was going through. Knowing her, she would carry on with their mission at the same time as trying to track down her mother and children. At least she had Diaz with her. He completely adored Juliette. It was as plain as day to see. Had done since the moment he set eyes on her, although Juliette appeared to be oblivious. He was a good man, Dan. An excellent man to have on your side when the chips were down.

From the chatter at the table, it seemed that these people thought the chips would be falling all over the place come the morning. They talked about the arrangements as if they were planning a picnic or a day at the races.

She listened hard without appearing to do so, making mental notes. Once they were done here, she would insist on sleeping in her own bed that night to be fresh for the morning. That would give her the chance she needed to get a message to Suzanne.

'Now that we have all the details in place,' said Max, 'why don't we play something a little more exciting?'

He pulled a wooden box from under his chair, opening it out to reveal a board with the words 'yes' and 'no' written on it along with the letters of the alphabet and the numbers from one to ten. Beneath them, one word: 'goodbye'.

She gazed at it in fascination. A Ouija board. She'd heard about them but had never actually seen one.

There was a murmur of excitement around the table and not a little glee. These people were as deranged as the Nazis they professed to admire so much.

He tucked the box back under his seat and, as he did so,

something in the bottom of it caught Christine's eye, the corner of what looked like a file or a ledger. A ledger. The Red Book. Not a bad place to hide it.

'My dear?' He was looking at her quizzically. She hastily rearranged her smile. 'Anything wrong?'

'Not at all,' she said. 'I've just never seen one of those before.'

'A bit of fun. That's all.' He picked up a glass and placed it in the centre of the Ouija board.

Of course, the first question Max asked was to do with their planned coup. Much as he tried to get a straight answer though, it seemed the Ouija board wasn't playing ball.

'Damn thing must be asleep or something,' he declared. 'My dear, why don't you try?'

To her horror, he pushed the glass in her direction. There was nothing for it but to place her fingertips gingerly on it.

'Nothing,' she said, quietly relieved.

'Give it a moment,' he said.

She could sense eyes upon her from around the table, like a circle of malevolent crows. All of a sudden, the glass almost shot from under her fingers and moved rapidly across the board, spelling out letters so fast she could barely keep up.

'R-O-N. It says his name is Ron,' exclaimed Lady Rattray.

Christine felt as if someone was pouring liquid nitrogen through her veins. It couldn't be. This was some kind of trick.

The glass was moving again, spelling out another message: 'Hello Chrissie.'

She screamed and wrenched her fingers off the glass. It felt as if they were stuck there with some kind of glue.

Chrissie. No one had called her that in years. It was almost the last word her stepfather Ron had ever uttered, turning in surprise and disbelief as she brought the heavy iron pan down on his head. She still had no idea if she'd meant to kill him. It was her brother who'd helped get him to the river, hauling him in the cart he used to buy and sell scrap. Their mum had stayed home tending to the latest wounds he'd inflicted on her. The last ones he ever would.

Except that he was back. Or at least, someone was pretending he was.

Now that she had a moment to recover from the shock, Christine's mind went into overdrive. Who knew about her abusive stepfather, let alone his name? No one. Certainly not her recruiters at SOE. Not even Suzanne. She'd been careful to wipe every trace of the East End from her accent and her bearing, soaking up all that Suzanne and the other girls had taught her so that she could pass as a lady, or at least a woman of substance. The girl Chrissie was long gone. She'd died aged seventeen along with her stepfather. Someone was playing games here and she had a shrewd idea who it might be.

She pulled out her handkerchief and dabbed at her eyes as if overcome, then reached out with her foot, pulling the wooden box towards her from under his chair. A fake drop of the hankie and she was bending down, extricating the ledger and slipping it under her skirt, tucking it into her waistband so it sat snug against her stomach.

Pushing back her chair, she stood, clutching her stomach as if she was in pain. 'Excuse me. I'm not feeling too well.'

Their eyes followed her as she left the room and kept on walking, retrieving her coat from the footman, breathing again only once she was safely out the door. There, she hailed a cab.

'Pimlico please. As fast as you can.'

She was going straight to Edward's flat. It was the plan they had already put in place in case of an emergency like this.

She pulled the ledger from her waistband. It was all there, names, some of which she instantly recognised, a number of them still sitting at His Lordship's table, as well as His Lordship himself. The Red Book at last or, at least, a copy of it.

Christine pressed her fingertips to her throbbing temples, squeezing her eyes shut as she tried to block out their eyes, the knowing smiles on their faces. Perhaps she was imagining it all. It was just a silly parlour trick, a game for bored house-wives. And yet he'd called her Chrissie. He'd said his name was Ron.

No, Christine. Ron is dead. Lying at the bottom of the Thames, weighed down by the chains they'd nicked from the dockside and wrapped tightly round him.

Ron would never hurt their mum again. He would never hurt Christine either.

Another image now, his face purple with rage and lust as he thrust into her, taking her virginity along with her belief in humanity. He had done her a favour then. There were very few humans alive she trusted, Edward and Suzanne among them. She would give them the Red Book, and by morning the lot of them would be rounded up. She felt a twinge of satisfaction at the thought of His Lordship in a cell along with the odious Rattrays. Fascist beliefs were one thing, something that was scarcely punished any more so long as you were of the right class and had the right connec-tions. Treason – that was something else altogether. They should all swing for it. Unlike her, they would not escape the hangman's noose.

She flipped through the pages again, smiling with satisfaction at some of the names of those who would hang, working all the way through to the back. That was when she noticed a Manila envelope tucked into a flap.

Extracting it, she unwound the string sealing it to find a collection of more envelopes, each one an airmail letter from the United States, addressed to Juliette at a PO box address here in London, all of them slit carefully open.

Alarmed and intrigued, she pulled one from its envelope and scanned the contents, her heart contracting as she realised who it was from. Diaz. He had written these letters, pouring out his thoughts and fears at being back home, so far from her, telling her how much he missed her and how he hoped to see her very soon. Love letters all of them, as she discovered from scanning a couple more.

Tucking the thin airmail paper back where it belonged, she resealed the Manila envelope and secreted it in her bag. These letters were personal and she felt bad for reading them. It would be far worse though if they came to light. She could only imagine what Max Mytton had intended to do with them or how on earth he got his hands on them. Blackmail probably. An attempt to compromise the Network.

'Foiled again,' she murmured as they drew up outside Suzanne's house in Pimlico. And she would make sure it stayed that way. First opportunity she had, she would get these to Juliette. It would remain their secret, hers and Diaz's. Although Christine couldn't help but feel a pang of envy at the depth of emotion he'd expressed. He obviously loved her a great deal, hardly a surprise given the way he used to look at her. The surprise was that Juliette had reciprocated, given her circumstances. Wonders would never cease. Perhaps love really did conquer all.

FORTY-FOUR

'Drink this.'

Edward handed Christine a tumbler of whisky. She took it gratefully and knocked it back. Suzanne was busy on the telephone, issuing instructions. She replaced the receiver with a smile of satisfaction.

'Your boys are there now,' she said to Edward, 'along with a fine detachment of His Majesty's constabulary. Good work, Christine. You got them. They can't wriggle out of it with the Red Book proving they were members of the Right Club along with all the other evidence.'

'Thank you.'

She swilled the last of the whisky around in the glass, watching the amber liquid whirl. It reminded her of the river with its whorls and eddies that night as they tipped Ron in by the bridge. A high tide, and a treacherous one, but those chains should have made sure he didn't shift much with it. Bodies often ended up downstream but, with any luck, Ron's would sink into the mud, never to be seen again.

'Are you all right?'

'What?' She looked up, seeing the concern on Suzanne's face. 'I'm fine. Really.'

Edward and Suzanne glanced at one another. They had evidently dressed in haste, not expecting her knock until much later, but they were still calm and in control. She wanted to slap herself around the head. How could she have been taken in by such a cheap trick? And it had to be a trick. There were no such things as ghosts or ghouls, and the only things that went bump in the night were the sort of men she used for target practice. She could kick herself for her reaction to that Ouija board, even though Max and his friends would have other things to worry about right now.

The phone rang again.

'Yes? I see.'

There was a new note to Suzanne's voice, one Christine didn't like.

'That was Marianne,' she said after she'd hung up. 'She's still at Le Marchant barracks along with Jack. Apparently they've rounded up the prisoners who were in on the plot to break out and march on London, but there was something their ringleader shouted out as they cuffed him that concerned her.'

'Which was?'

'That we wouldn't be able to stop them in Paris. That no one could stop Skorzeny.'

'Have you heard from Juliette or Diaz?'

Suzanne shook her head. 'Not since yesterday.'

'Do we know what's happening with her mother and children?'

'Not a word. We're in touch with Versailles, but nothing from there either. It's not like Juliette to disappear like this.

As for Diaz, you couldn't shut him up if you tried. Something's wrong. I can feel it in my bones.'

You and me both, thought Christine. The letters were safe in her bag, and there they would stay.

'What are we going to do?' she asked.

'The operation here is pretty much sewn up. We have the organisers and the perpetrators in custody, thanks to you, Marianne and Jack. By morning we'll have more. Churchill and his cabinet were warned and have already left London as an extra precaution. We can either watch and wait to make sure there are no loose ends or leave it to the authorities here and head for Paris.'

'I vote for Paris.'

'Me too,' said Suzanne.

'I'll stay here,' said Edward. 'Then I can coordinate things from this end and liaise with Marianne and Jack. Don't be surprised if they follow you.'

'I guess that settles it,' said Suzanne. 'We're going back to the city of lights.'

A city that contained some dark memories for them both. One where Christine had learned almost everything she knew and then some, a lot of it from Suzanne. Things the average person would never understand. But then, she wasn't average and nor were the people she considered family as well as friends. If one of them was in trouble, they all were.

'Let's go give Juliette a hand,' said Christine. 'Prove that German wrong and stop Skorzeny in his tracks.'

She only hoped they weren't already too late.

Something in her gut told her they might be.

FORTY-FIVE

15 DECEMBER 1944, PARIS

I carried on flicking through the book while Dan took Antoine to the equipment store to be kitted out, trying to remember anything Philippe had said about it. He was scornful of the writing style, calling it clumsy, but he was fascinated by the story all the same, not least because it mentioned the cemetery where some of his ancestors were buried after they were guillotined during the Revolution. Picpus. That was its name.

I flipped through the pages faster, searching for it. Here it was, along with an account of the Picpus affair.

By the time I'd read it through, my heart was racing.

'You look as if you've found something.' Dan slid back into his seat beside mine. 'Care to share?'

'I think I've found the clue. It's to do with the Picpus affair.'

'Tell me more.'

'The Picpus affair involved three women imprisoned in a fictitious convent that stood on the site of a cemetery that actually exists. They were found in barred cells in the attic, driven mad by years of solitary confinement.'

'How is that a clue?'

'Philippe's ancestors are buried in that cemetery along with over a thousand others who were guillotined during the Reign of Terror. He's visited it several times. Philippe is obsessed with his ancestry and the noble line. This is precisely the kind of puzzle he would set.'

'Or a trap.'

I shrugged. 'But of course. He's hoping to lure me in. It's exactly what I would expect him to do.'

'So where is this cemetery?'

'Not too far. It's in the 12th near the Place de la Nation where the guillotine was set up. Handy, you see, for all those headless corpses.'

'Very convenient. And a little too convenient for Philippe. You can't just walk in there, Juliette. You have no idea what he's got planned. He has that lunatic King on his payroll along with half the right-wing thugs in Paris from what we've already seen. He could have the entire place wired with explosives.'

I shook my head. 'That's not his style. He wants to see me suffer, remember. Blowing me to bits is too swift for his taste. He wants a death by a thousand cuts.'

Dan leaned forward, grabbing both my hands as he stared deep into my eyes. 'Listen to me, Juliette. Your husband is crazy, that much is obvious. But he's also cunning enough to have covered his tracks this far. The guy is the original Scarlet Pimpernel. We can't ever pin him down. He's always been one step ahead of us. I don't think a man like that is going to make it quite so easy for you.'

'You think I'm clutching at straws? That this isn't a clue at all? I have to at least try, Dan. These are my children. My mother.'

'I know that, sweetheart, but I also know he's leading you up a blind alley. Or worse. You think you can turn up and there'll be another clue there like some treasure hunt or maybe even, just like in the book, he's got them imprisoned nearby and you can get them out.'

I felt the tears prick. Blinked furiously to hold them back.

'Maybe,' I whispered. 'What else can I do? Time is running out, Dan, for us and for them. Tomorrow is the sixteenth, when all hell could break loose. Philippe is a key part of that too. If he can help assassinate someone like Eisenhower, he's capable of anything.'

'We'll find them. I promise you that.'

'How?'

I could see in his eyes something that shot an arrow of dread through me. Doubt. Dan never doubted himself. It was at that moment I felt the tiny residue of hope I had left evaporate, leaving me empty of anything save the gnawing sense that I had to do something, anything.

'I'm going to the cemetery,' I said. 'And you can't stop me.'

'In that case, I'm coming with you.'

'No. He won't come anywhere near me if he sees you there.'

'Isn't that the idea?'

I sighed. 'Dan, he wants to see my face as he tells me what he's done with them so he can watch me beg. It's the only way I have of getting any information out of him. There's been nothing useful picked up by the bugs. He

hasn't been near his mother's apartment. All of that tells me
he's weaving one big spider's web he wants me to walk into,
and that is exactly what I'm going to do.'

'No way. Not on your own.'

'You can't stop me.'

'I can make sure you're protected. If you won't let me
come with you, I can follow you. Put Guillaume and his
friends on it too.'

'Absolutely not. If he sees Guillaume, he'll know something is wrong. And how are you going to follow me without
him seeing you? I can't risk the lives of my children and my
mother. He thinks this is between him and me. If there are
other people involved, he might cut his losses to save his own
skin.'

'He wouldn't expect you to call in the authorities? The
police?'

'Why? There's no ransom note, no evidence they were
even in that safe house. That's what safe houses are there for,
remember. To help people vanish. I have no proof of
anything, and Philippe would simply tell the police that I'm
some crazy woman. Don't forget that I am still legally his
wife.'

Dan fell silent for a moment, thinking. 'Maybe we're
going about this the wrong way. At best, it's an educated
guess about the cemetery. He could have meant something
else entirely. I think we should focus on finding Philippe. He
has to surface somewhere. Even rats need air.'

'Dan, I have to do this. You would understand if you had
children of your own. The umbilical cord never quite breaks,
at least not when it comes to a mother's intuition. And mine
is telling me to do this.'

It was also honed by years of learning to listen to it and to trust it. It had saved my life many times, that sixth sense warning me not to go in a certain building or turn a particular corner where the Gestapo were waiting. It was screaming at me now. I knew it had something to do with that cemetery. I also knew I had to go there.

'You're wrong, Juliette. For one thing, I do have children. Well, a child. I may not be her mother, but I know what's best for her. Just as I know what's best in this situation. You go blundering into your husband's trap and you could get all of you killed.'

'You have a child?' I was staring at him, trying to digest this bombshell.

'Yes. A daughter. She's seven years old and her name is Grace.'

'But... how? You told me your fiancée died. You had a daughter with someone else?'

'I told you I had been in love before and that she died. Elizabeth was my wife. You simply assumed she was my fiancée. Gracie is our daughter. That's what I was doing back home, apart from work. Seeing her.'

'I see.'

Except I didn't. I thought we knew almost everything about one another by now, but never once in all our long chats deep into the night had he mentioned Grace.

'I – I have to go,' I said.

'Juliette...'

I was already out the door, my thoughts crashing into one another. A daughter. He had a daughter. What else hadn't he told me? Was he holding back other secrets? Where there was one, there were usually others. And once doubt started creeping in, it found all kinds of corners to invade. He might have lied about those letters after all. He was back home with his daughter when he said he wrote them. His focus would surely have been on her rather than me. I could understand that. Just as my focus was on finding my children, totally and completely. I was doing what it took. If Dan didn't like that, too bad.

FORTY-SIX

The cemetery was closed when I got there, the gates locked and bolted. I looked around in vain for a sign with the opening hours. Perhaps there were none. Like many places in Paris, it might have been closed up to try to prevent the Germans from looting any treasures.

'It opens at two o'clock.'

I turned to see an old man, his overalls proclaiming him to be some kind of manual worker in spite of his age.

'Are you the caretaker?' I asked.

He straightened his back, his moustache bristling. 'I am.'

'Monsieur, my family are buried here. I have to leave Paris today, before two o'clock. I wanted to see their grave one last time before I go. Our name died with them.'

I was pressing every button I could think of, appealing to his evident sense of pride in this place and to the history that lay behind it.

'I'm sorry...' he began.

I let my lip tremble and dabbed at one eye. 'Monsieur, please. I will only be a moment.'

He looked around the empty street as if someone might appear to castigate him. 'Very well,' he sighed. 'But just for a moment, mind.'

'You are very kind.'

I gave him my sweetest, most grateful smile, containing my impatience as he laboriously unlocked the gate and then pushed it open, standing aside to let me through before closing it after him and relocking it once more.

'I will wait here,' he said, 'to give you some privacy.'

'I cannot thank you enough.'

He waved a hand as if to say it was nothing. 'Take your time. I have nothing else to do. I can wait.'

It felt oddly reassuring to have him there as I made my way past an old well towards the chapel that stood at the far end of the courtyard. The cemetery lay beyond that, through an avenue of trees, their branches starkly bare in the grey December light, leading up to an ivy-clad wall that marked the boundary of the graveyard. The graves were arranged in rows, many with the names of noble families etched on them. It was the mass graves at the far end I had come to see, although they could only be glimpsed through another rusting blue gate at the far end of the cemetery. Here Philippe's ancestors were interred along with their fellow victims of the guillotine.

I passed the tomb of the Marquis de Lafayette, adorned with an American flag. He was buried there under American soil, a mark of respect for his part in fighting the Revolutionary War under George Washington. The flag had been placed there during the First World War and I paused a moment, sending a silent prayer to another French citizen who'd fought alongside Americans, although, as far as I knew, he hadn't lost his heart to one.

The blue gate was a few metres from his grave and I pressed my face to it, peering through at the mass graves beyond. There was nothing out of the ordinary to see. I don't know what I expected. A sign maybe.

Don't be a fool, Juliette. That's not Philippe's style. He likes to confound and talk in riddles.

I turned away from the gate, wandering back through the gravestones, glancing at each one as I passed, but there was nothing that stood out, no hint or message anywhere that I could see.

The avenue of trees stood like sentries on either side of me, guardians of those who lay under the earth behind.

At the chapel I paused. The caretaker was nowhere around. Might as well take a look.

I pushed open the door and glanced at the statue that gave the chapel its name, a carving of the virgin known as Notre-Dame de la Paix. Our Lady of Peace. I only wished she could bring me some. Carved into the walls of the chapel, the names of those in the mass graves, including twenty-three nuns. Only the descendants of these people could be buried in the cemetery.

I scanned the names, searching for Philippe's ancestors. There they were. The entire family – father, mother and two sons. The daughter had been spared as she had married and left Paris.

A sudden thought occurred to me. The daughter was Philippe's maternal great-great-great grandmother or something like that. I remembered him telling me the story over and over again. His bloodline was so important to him. It was one of the reasons he professed to hate me, the fact that I had polluted it, or rather that of our children. How or why he hadn't noticed there was a problem before we married was anyone's guess, but it certainly helped explain why he loved his Nazi friends so much, with their obsession with racial purity and hatred of those they found wanting.

Andlau. That was her surname. She married a man from Alsace, from an old and noble family there of course. She died in Paris. I knew that much because Philippe had told me how she and her husband returned to take over her old family home, a place some believed was cursed. Only a year after she and her husband moved in, he died of a mysterious illness. Then one of their children died too. I wondered aloud if the house wasn't so much cursed as an inheritance she didn't wish to share. My reward for that was a punch in the stomach that left me so winded I couldn't speak, which was, I'm sure, what Philippe intended.

I peered out of the chapel door. The caretaker was still nowhere to be seen. I could risk a dash back to those grave-stones. Yes, it was a hunch, but hunches had paid off for me before and I wasn't about to ignore this one.

I raced back through the trees, skidding to a halt by the wall and then taking a slower pace back through the rows of graves, concentrating on the ones that appeared to be the oldest. And there she was, her name still just about visible along with the others on the family tomb.

'Found you,' I breathed.

Andlau, Henriette Josephine Marie.

At the foot of the tomb, hidden on the far side so I couldn't see it until I moved around it, a fresh-looking posy. I picked it up and examined the card attached.

1 Avenue Frochot.

That was it. Nothing else.

I turned the posy around in my hand. Where had he managed to get flowers like this in the depths of winter? They were deep red roses, their petals perfectly formed, lavish curls that were plush and soft to the touch.

'Ouch.'

I gazed at my thumb, with which I'd carelessly caressed the bouquet. A drop of blood was welling from it, as red as those roses. I hadn't even noticed the thorns, so shocked was I by this discovery. An address. The message I'd been trying to find.

'Bravo, Philippe,' I muttered under my breath, tearing the card from the roses and stuffing it in my pocket before hurling the bouquet to the ground, a few petals clinging to my sweater. He hadn't placed it there with any thought other than to taunt me. His flowers deserved nothing but contempt.

Sucking at my thumb to stop the bleeding as I passed through the cemetery gate, I didn't notice anything different about the avenue of trees at first. Then I saw it. A figure apparently leaning against one. The old man. The caretaker.

'Monsieur,' I called out as I broke again into a run, slowing when I realised what I was seeing. 'Oh no, monsieur, no.'

He was smiling but not at me, his lips drawn back in a grimace that extended beyond the corners of his mouth right to his ears. It matched the slash on his neck. The blood was still pooling at his feet, soaking into the rope that tied him to the tree, his head lashed so that it remained upright. Whoever had done this had acted with surgical precision. Whoever. I knew exactly who had done this. I threw back my head and roared.

'Philippe.'

There was no answering cry, no sound save the wind whispering through those bare branches.

A memory of that other cemetery in London. The man lying on Karl Marx's grave. The man I'd shot dead. Was this retribution?

I thought I heard a footstep hitting the path behind me. Whirled round. No one there. I turned back to see the poor caretaker once more, only this time he wasn't alone.

'You took your time,' said Philippe.

FORTY-SEVEN

Too late. He knew it the minute he found the body of the old man tied to the tree, the earth at his feet soaked with his blood, which was damp to the touch, his corpse still limp, the wound across his throat no longer weeping. He must have just missed her. Missed them. Of course that husband of hers would have come for her here. She knew it and he knew it. Dan cursed the phone call that had held him up – the one he had to take. But the news from Versailles was useless if she died. She wasn't going to die. Not Juliette. His Juliette.

'I won't let you,' he murmured to the wind that sighed through those bare branches, singing through his bones, wrapping its frosty fingers around his heart. He would find her. He had to. That bastard wasn't going to win.

He looked about in vain for any indication of how he might have taken her, but there were no scuff marks, no foot-prints on the frozen ground. Nothing to indicate anyone else had been there save the poor old guy sagging against the tree and a couple of rose petals spinning in the air, probably from one of the graves in the cemetery.

There was one thing he could do.

He reached inside the man's overalls and pulled the keys from the capacious pocket on the front.

'I'll send someone for you,' he said, averting his eyes in respect.

As he pulled the main gate to behind him, he locked it carefully to ensure no one disturbed the old guy.

It took him thirty minutes to get back to the Hotel Scribe, and in that time a plan began to formulate in Dan's mind.

Once he'd made the necessary phone calls, Paris was all but closed down, every checkpoint in and out of the city on red alert. It was a start, but he was well aware that, in all likelihood, Philippe wasn't taking her anywhere. Twenty-four hours until showtime and he would want to have a grandstand seat.

Too bad for him Dan had also made sure that Versailles was well and truly locked down too, ringed by tanks and doubly protected by an entire new detachment diverted from the coast. Apparently General Eisenhower was none too pleased, but better he was furious and alive than dead from an assassin's bullet. If Skorzeny wanted to try anything, he would have a fight on his hands. And so would Philippe de Brignac. By the time Dan was finished, that precious name of his would be mud everywhere.

The office door flew open. 'Dan, I got your message.'

'Antoine. Thank God they found you. Juliette has gone missing. She set out a couple of hours ago for this cemetery she was talking about, somewhere she believed she might find a clue to where her husband is holding her family. I think he's now taken her as well.'

Antoine gaped at him, then collected himself. 'I see. Then we need to move fast.'

'I already called Versailles. There's an all points alert right through and around the city as well as on all roads in and out. They can't get past a checkpoint, but I suspect he won't even try. I think he's keeping them in Paris until his buddy Skorzeny comes marching in tomorrow or whatever it is he's planning to do.'

'I think you're right. Why did Juliette believe there was a clue at this cemetery?'

'That damn book he sent her. She said he had a connection to the cemetery because some of his family were guillotined and buried there.'

'The Cimetière de Picpus?'

'That's the one. But it gets worse. I went there. Found the caretaker with his throat slashed, tied to a tree. My guess is that's her husband's handiwork too.'

'*Putain*. He truly is insane. Did you inform the police?'

'Better than that. I sent Ward's men to clean up. Made sure they'll treat the old guy with respect. They'll find his family and give them a sanitised version of events. We don't want any scandal or the press getting a sniff of this. It could compromise everyone, especially Juliette.'

He lowered his voice as he spoke, aware that the Hotel Scribe was crawling with journalists.

'Agreed. So what do we do now?'

'We go back there. To the cemetery. Retrace her steps. Check the place out thoroughly. Whatever she found might still be there, if she found anything apart from her husband. Ward's boys should have done their work by now so we won't be treading on their toes.'

Antoine took the extra pistol Dan was holding out and tucked it in his belt along with the one he kept there permanently. 'Let's go.'

FORTY-EIGHT

My head was splitting, the throb in my temples reverberating through my skull. I pressed my fingers to my jaw, where he'd landed his first blow. The second had knocked me out. I was lying on my side on a bed, a coverlet over me.

I moved my hand from my jaw to feel the sheet beneath my aching body. Linen. I wriggled my fingers and then my toes experimentally. Everything seemed to be working. Except the leg that was stretched out under me – that felt wrong. I tried to move it and discovered why. There was something around my ankle tethering me to the bedpost.

I tried to turn my head to see what it was and a shard of white-hot pain sliced through it. I licked my lips and tried again.

'You really should try to sleep, Juliette.'

He was there, somewhere in the room. I pushed myself up from the pillows, fighting back the nausea, the world spinning as I squinted at the corner where he was sitting in a carved chair, perfectly at ease.

'Now that wasn't so clever, was it?'

His voice was always so damn reasonable, especially when he was pointing out something that was my fault. It was always my fault. Even this would be down to me.

Sure enough, his tone turned a little uglier as he said, 'You really should have listened to me.'

I licked my lips again. So dry.

I could see it now, the chain around my ankle, the other end wound around the bedpost. I tried to tug my foot away. It held tight. My eyes travelled up the bed, taking in the silk nightgown that was all I was wearing. Sky blue. His favourite colour.

'What the hell have you done, Philippe? Where are my clothes?'

He laughed, as much at my croaking voice as my words. 'You'll find out soon enough. You always were too nosy for your own good, Juliette.'

'*Salop*,' I spat. 'Son of a whore. Take off this chain.'

He stood, strode over to the bed and dealt me a slap across the face that set my ears ringing. 'Shut up. You are the whore.'

A trickle now of something by my mouth. I tasted it. Blood.

'You won't get away with this. I'm not alone any longer, Philippe. I have friends.'

'Oh really? So where are your friends now?'

I stayed silent, not wanting to goad him any further. Although silence was something he couldn't stand. I should have remembered that.

'Tell me, bitch,' he sneered, readying himself to hit me again. 'Where are your precious friends now?'

'Papa.'

A tiny voice from the door. Hastily, I brushed my arm across my mouth to wipe any blood away.

'Nicolas, my darling,' I breathed. My precious son. After all this time. How could he see me like this?

'Maman.'

He hovered, his little face filled with anxiety, his eyes darting from Philippe to me.

'Come here,' I said, opening my arms. 'Maman has just been having a rest.'

'Stay right where you are,' snapped Philippe.

Nicolas rushed right past him and into my arms. 'Maman. Papa said you were dead. I was so sad and so afraid.'

'Did he now?'

I stared at Philippe over our son's head, stroking his hair as I pressed it into my chest, snuggling as we always did to try to make him feel safe.

'Nicolas, go back to your room.'

'I don't want to. I want to stay here with you.'

He spoke into my heart, his cheek nestled next to it. I could feel his mouth moving, hear the beat of his own heart. My boy. My brave little boy.

'Leave him alone,' I snarled as Philippe made a grab for him.

Nicolas cried out as Philippe got hold of his arm and pulled him away from me. He was sobbing now, crying in those great gulps and gusts only a child can make, writhing as he tried to break free from his father's grasp.

'I told you to go to your room.'

My thoughts were slamming around my head, my heart threatening to burst from my rib cage. I took a breath, trying to slow them down, to think rather than react.

'Nicolas, do as Papa says. I'll be along in a minute. I just need to have a word with him.'

Nicolas shook his head, mute now, the tears still streaming from his eyes.

I tried again, sweetening my voice as much as I could. 'It's all right, darling. I'm all right. I'll be there in a minute. I promise.'

He dropped his eyes and allowed his father to push him through the door, shutting it firmly behind him.

'Happy now?' I spat. 'Our son thought I was dead. How do you think that's going to affect him?'

'He'll be fine,' growled Philippe. 'He needs to toughen up. You've mollycoddled him.'

'No, Philippe. I've loved him and nurtured him and taught him how that feels. That's something he could never learn from you. I expect you told my mother and Natalie I was dead too. How on earth do you live with yourself?'

He laughed. 'Easy. Much easier than living with you.'

'Then why the hell did you bring me here?'

'Well, it certainly wasn't to live with you, my dear.'

I stared at him in mounting horror, the glee on his face sending darts of alarm shooting through me. He was enjoying this far too much. It could only end one way.

'So what was it for?'

He smiled. 'I think you know.'

I looked away, unable to bear his expression a moment longer, focusing instead on the room, taking in the silk drapes above the bed, the decorative armoire, the vase of roses on the dressing table. Red roses, just like those in the cemetery. A dozen of them. I counted them one by one, as much to steady myself as anything. Twelve red roses. The kind of bouquet you send to declare love. Come to think of it, this room was decked out like a boudoir or a bridal chamber.

'Like it?'

He was watching me with amusement still glinting in his eyes. I hated his games. Hated him.

'Not especially.'

He laughed again. 'You'll get used to it. But now I must leave you, my dear. Things to do before tomorrow.'

With that, he was gone, the door slamming shut behind him, a key turning in the lock. He never cared how he moved through the world. As far as Philippe was concerned, the world did his bidding. And so did I. Alive or dead.

FORTY-NINE

In the gathering dusk, the cemetery seemed more sinister, its chapel looming over them as they locked the gates behind them and crossed the courtyard, skirting the well that stood in front of it and passing a house on the left which, like everything else in this place, sat in darkness. There were no lights at the windows and nothing to illuminate their way as they moved through the avenue of trees, pausing by the one where the caretaker had met his end.

'See, here,' said Dan, 'where the earth is darker. That's where he bled out.'

Aside from that, there was no sign that a man had been tied to a tree and his throat slit. Those clean-up boys did a good job. They carried on to the cemetery itself, peering through the twilight at the gravestones, looking, as Juliette must have done, for some kind of clue.

'I can't see anything unusual,' said Antoine. 'Aside from that American flag over there.'

They stooped to read the plaque in front of the grave of the Marquis de Lafayette.

*America has joined forces with the Allied Powers, and
what we have of blood and treasure are yours... And here
and now, in the presence of the illustrious dead, we pledge
our hearts and our honor in carrying this war to a
successful issue. Lafayette, we are here.*

Dan's voice was sombre as he read out part of the
inscription.

'*Plus ça change*,' murmured Antoine. 'Here we are, still
fighting a war together.'

Something stirred beyond the gates beside the tomb.

'That's where the mass graves are located,' said Dan.

'It's probably a fox, searching for food. They are as
hungry as many of the people.'

More rustling as the wind picked up and a few drops of
rain started to fall.

'There's nothing here. Let's head back,' said Antoine.

They were passing another tomb when something fluttered into Dan's face, blown there by another gust.

He brushed his cheek and then stared at his hand. 'Rose
petals.'

They looked like drops of blood against his skin, their
deep crimson colour appearing almost black until he looked
closer. 'They must have come from here.'

Antoine bent and picked up a bunch of roses from the
ground, some of them looking a little worse for wear. He
replaced it on the tomb.

'Andlau,' he read out. 'A good Alsatian name.'

'This place is so quiet it's giving me the creeps. There's
absolutely no sign Juliette was even here.'

'Except we know she was. She must have been. She told
you this was where she was going.'

'She did. But we argued. I was about to go after her when the phone rang. I would have been right behind her if it wasn't for that damn call from Versailles.'

'You weren't to know what was going to happen here.'

Antoine's face appeared as carved as any of the statues in the cemetery, its planes and hollows made more prominent by the half-light. His eyes gleamed from pits that seemed as deep as any dug as a mass grave. He'd seen so much during this war, including the loss of his own family.

'Thank you for saying that. But it's my responsibility. *She* is my responsibility.'

'You love her, don't you?'

'Yes, I do. Very much.'

'Then we will find her. Love always finds a way.'

'Spoken like a true Frenchman.'

'That's because it's true.'

From somewhere beyond the walls, a songbird filled the air with a few, heartbreaking notes before it once more fell silent. Dan hoped it was perched, free, in a tree somewhere instead of imprisoned in an elaborate cage. The Parisians did love their songbirds. Was Juliette also trapped in a gilded cage, locked behind the doors of some Belle Époque apartment or one of those mansions? Philippe had so many well-connected friends. It wouldn't be hard to conceal two women and two small children. If she was with them at all. He hoped for her sake that she was. That, somehow, like that songbird, she still had the strength to sing out in spite of the cold and dark.

'Juliette, we are here,' he murmured.

Maybe the wind would carry his words to her.

FIFTY

16 DECEMBER 1944, PARIS

'The Germans have attacked in the Ardennes. Thousands of troops along with tanks. They caught us on the hop.'

The young lieutenant was breathless, eyes wide behind round glasses. The office door was still swinging where he'd burst through it moments before.

'Slow down,' said Dan. 'Tell me exactly what happened.'

'They struck early this morning, sir, in the forest where four divisions of our troops were trying to rest up. Our guys didn't have much of a chance, but they're fighting back. That's all I know.'

'What about Versailles? Is everyone there safe?'

'I've had no reports of anything happening there, sir.'

At least that was something.

'OK. Can you set me up an encrypted call to Versailles? I need to speak with Dick Ward and Lieutenant Colonel Gordon Steed. Patch us all in on the same call.'

'Right away, sir.'

While Dan waited for the call to be set up, he summoned a bellboy to alert Antoine.

'Goddamn Germans caught us by surprise,' he said when Antoine appeared. 'Attacked four US divisions that were resting in the Ardennes forest. I've asked for a call to be set up with Versailles so we can find out the latest. Our friend Skorzeny might also be about to spring a surprise, along with his buddy Philippe de Brignac.'

'Do you think this poses a direct threat to Juliette?'

Dan ran a hand through his hair. 'I have no idea. Possibly. Probably.'

He didn't want to think too hard about those possibilities, not with what he already knew about Philippe de Brignac. He couldn't bear what that bastard had already done to her. Could be doing to her all over again.

No sense in thinking like that. He had to concentrate on finding her, along with her family. But the idea of Philippe laying a finger on her made him sick to his stomach. Five minutes alone with the guy and he would make sure he never hurt anyone, let alone Juliette, again.

A discreet cough disturbed his train of thought. The lieutenant was back.

'Come this way please, sir.'

He and Antoine huddled around the telephone equipment set up in another side room.

'You're connected now, sir.'

'Thank you. Ward, can you hear me? And Steed?'

'We're both here.' Ward's mellifluous voice sounded surprisingly clear. It was almost as if he was in the next room. 'I gather you already know about the attack this morning?'

'Affirmative.'

'We're also getting reports of infiltrators behind our lines causing chaos. Signs being turned around. Orders not passed on. I understand Skorzeny himself led the first detachment early this morning, but now he's disappeared. The general is at present in the bunker beneath the building. We insisted, but he's not too happy about it.'

'I'm sure he's not. I'm also sure he'd rather stay alive right now. Do we know when and where Skorzeny disappeared? The Ardennes forest is quite some way from Paris.'

'This is Otto Skorzeny we're talking about. The man landed a glider on top of a mountain to rescue Mussolini. He's capable of anything.'

Dan glanced at Antoine. 'I understand how dangerous he can be. I think Philippe de Brignac may try to facilitate Skorzeny's entry to Paris and then Versailles, possibly by using hostages.'

Silence hummed down the line.

'Are you still there?'

'Yes, we're here.' Steed's voice now. 'We cannot allow any negotiations. We have to view potential hostages as collateral damage.'

It was Dan's turn to fall silent while Antoine struggled to control himself.

'Roger that,' he said finally.

'You understand, Captain Diaz? We cannot risk the lives of General Eisenhower and thousands of his men, no matter who these hostages might be or your relationship to them. I will keep you apprised of the situation as it develops. You are to await further instructions.'

The moment the line was cut, Antoine exploded. 'How dare he? How dare they? He's talking about the life of a woman who has saved so many other lives. Who fought for France and the Allies. Her life and those of her family are every bit as important as Eisenhower's.'

Dan raised his weary head from his hands. 'The thing is,

Antoine, he's right. The Germans have attacked right where they know our lines are weakest. They're trying to push us back towards the Normandy coast, which means they'll retake Paris and, with that, control of France. We cannot allow that to happen, no matter the consequences.'

Antoine stared at him. 'You would let them die? I thought you said you loved her.'

'I do, Antoine, with all my heart, body and soul, but she would say the same thing. This is war, and in war you have to make tough decisions. I can't disobey orders and nor can you. There's too much at stake.'

'So what do we do? You're just going to sit there and wait for your orders while God knows what happens to Juliette?'

'Hell no. I'm going to get out there and do everything I can to find them before the Germans get within fifty miles of Paris. That way de Brignac has no leverage.'

'Perhaps we can help?'

They both looked up to see a small, slender figure standing in the doorway. Behind her, another figure, platinum-blonde hair framing her face like a halo.

'So,' Suzanne continued, 'where do we start?'

FIFTY-ONE

'Tell us everything you know about Philippe de Brignac.'

Guillaume looked at the woman across the table, her hands folded as she waited for his response. She reminded him a little of Juliette. The same quiet confidence. A poise that could only be gained by facing down danger again and again.

'He's always been a vicious bastard. I could never understand why Juliette married him. Yes, he's good-looking, but that's about as shallow as his beliefs. Philippe is only committed to the Nazis so long as it benefits him. He did very well during the occupation.'

'Do you have any idea where he might be holding them?'

'None at all or I would certainly tell you. He seems to have gone to ground. There has been no sign of him at his mother's apartment or at any of his usual haunts. Believe me, my friends and I have kept a close watch.'

Suzanne inclined her head. 'Thank you for all your help.'

'I did it for Juliette. She was always kind to me even

when my own mother was not. And for the cause of course. I hate those Nazi bastards.'

A knock at the door interrupted his impassioned outburst. Dan had to bite back his impatience. They were sitting here around this conference table when they could be out there, finding Juliette.

'Levesque.'

He couldn't conceal his surprise at this new visitor.

'I asked Jean to come,' said Suzanne. 'He may be able to help us.'

Levesque executed a little bow and took the last remaining seat, squeezing his bulk behind the table and settling himself with a grunt. His eyes darted round the assembled group, lingering on Christine before he turned his attention to Suzanne. 'How can I help?'

'Yes, how exactly can he help,' demanded Dan, 'when he's friendly with fascists like de Brignac?'

'For the record, I loathe Philippe de Brignac,' said Levesque.

Suzanne glanced at Levesque then at Dan. 'He also works for us.'

'Since when?'

'Since I recruited him.'

She gave that a moment to sink in and then carried on. 'Jean, you know de Brignac's friends and supporters. Juliette's mother and children were taken from their safe house in England and brought, we believe, to Paris. Now Juliette herself has gone missing and we're pretty sure de Brignac is behind it. Can you think of anywhere he might be holding them? Anyone who would be helping him?'

For once, Levesque looked taken aback. 'But that is horrible. I cannot think of anyone in particular, no. Philippe has many contacts but only a very few he would trust with something like that. His inner circle, if you like, and no one springs to mind.'

'Maybe this will help.'

Dan pushed a book across the table to Levesque. 'Someone sent this to Juliette yesterday. She was absolutely sure it was her husband and that he was sending her some kind of message or puzzle to solve.'

Levesque picked up the book. '*The Werewolf of Paris*. I have never read it. It's really not my kind of thing.'

Dan could barely conceal his impatience. 'Well, perhaps you should read it now. See if there's anything that leaps out at you.'

'This woman on the cover looks a bit like Juliette. As for that devil above her... that could be de Brignac. He's very interested in the occult, you know, like so many of his friends.'

Christine let out a gasp, and they all turned to look at her.

'That's what Max and his chums were up to before I left. Playing with a Ouija board. And he made frequent trips to Paris. We have no evidence of who he met and why except that he also visited Berlin. I wonder if he's in de Brignac's inner circle?'

'Bound to be,' said Levesque. 'They're all connected. What's this Max's full name?'

'Lord Maximilian Mytton.'

Levesque nodded, his face sly as if privy to some special knowledge.

'That is not quite his full name. He is, in fact, Maximilian Mytton von Hohenburg. His family moved to London before he was born, but he is Alsatian by descent on his father's side.'

'That explains why he would sometimes sleep-talk in German.'

'His father grew up in Alsace so yes, I am sure he would speak German to him. I saw him off and on during the occupation, attending soirées and the like. I got the impression he and de Brignac were close.'

A memory tickled at the recesses of Christine's mind. 'Does he have a house in Paris?'

Levesque shook his head. 'Not as far as I know. He always stayed at the Ritz when he was here.'

Dan could see her thinking hard. 'Why do you ask?'

'There was this painting at his house in London, of a villa that he said was in Paris. Spooky-looking place. Gave me the shivers.'

If it had given Christine the shivers, it must have been sinister. She didn't scare easily.

'Do you recall any of the details?'

'Only that it appeared quite charming at first, small but perfectly proportioned and with a courtyard in front. Then I noticed these gargoyles above the door. There were also turrets. It was all very gothic.'

Dan turned to Levesque. 'Can you think of anywhere like that?'

The Frenchman spread his hands and gave a Gallic shrug. 'There are hundreds of houses in Paris that could match that description.'

'Hundreds? Really? Think, man. Think harder. Juliette's life may depend upon it.'

He was yelling now, but he didn't care; nor did he care

that they were all staring at him. All except Antoine, who gazed down at his hands.

'Regretfully, I cannot think of anywhere in particular. There is no house I know of like that.'

'You'd better not be lying to us, Levesque.' Suzanne's voice was soft, but the threat rang out loud and clear.

'I swear on all that is sacred to me, I am not lying to you.'

'That gives me little comfort when I suspect that nothing is sacred to you except saving your own ass,' snapped Dan, pushing his chair back from the table and standing in one swift move. 'I don't know about you, but I'm done with sitting around and talking. We need to do something or Juliette and her family are as good as dead.'

'How do you know they're not dead already?'

Dan's fist met Levesque's cheek with a satisfying smack. 'I don't but I do know that you're a lying piece of shit. Now you tell me where that house is before I beat it out of you.'

Levesque laughed. 'Is that the best you've got? No wonder the Germans caught you sleeping in the Ardennes.'

'How do you know about that?'

'I'm a journalist. I have my sources.'

'There are dozens of journalists in this hotel. All of them seasoned war correspondents. None of them know about that attack yet. The only people who do are party to privileged information.'

'I suppose you'll have to consider me privileged then.'

'I consider you a traitor.'

Suzanne's cool voice cut through Dan's fury. 'I see now where your loyalties lie. You'd better start talking or we'll do what we do with all traitors in wartime. We'll take you out and shoot you.'

'Do it,' said Levesque. 'It would be a blessing.'

FIFTY-TWO

I could get as far as the middle of the room but no further. The chain on my ankle bit into my flesh as I strained against it, trying to reach the window. If I could only reach it, I could work out what floor I was on and if there was any chance of escape through it.

But no matter how much I tugged and twisted at that chain, I couldn't free myself from it. The links were small but thick and strong, made of what looked like steel, the chain padlocked at one end to the bedpost and at the other around my ankle so that it sat tight. There was nothing within reach to pick at the lock and no way of prising it apart through brute force.

'*Putain*,' I swore through gritted teeth.

There had to be a way. *Stay calm, Juliette. Think.*

A noise from outside the door. The unmistakable sound of a child screaming in fear. My child. My little girl.

'Natalie,' I called out.

She couldn't hear me above her cries.

'Natalie,' I shouted again, louder this time.

A heartbeat and then an answering cry. 'Maman!'

Another voice now, Philippe's, shouting above her, yelling at her to shut up. Finally, something that sent terror spiralling through me once more – the sound of absolute silence.

'Natalie,' I called. 'Natalie, are you there?'

I could picture her tiny face wet with tears, her cheeks pink with pain and anger and fear.

'Natalie.'

I sank onto my haunches, the sobs tearing through me. To hear her and not be able to comfort her. It was the worst agony. Philippe knew that. Of course he did. This was yet another of his mind games. Well, I wasn't going to let him win this one either. I would not give in. I would stay strong.

I dashed the tears from my face with the back of my arm and got to my feet, holding on to the bedpost for stability.

The bedpost. It gave a little under my grasp.

I wiggled it experimentally. The thing gave some more, twisting now as I turned it, finally pulling it out of its seat on the bedframe. It wasn't nailed in but simply slotted.

I froze as I thought I heard a creak from the corridor, waiting until I was sure it was nothing. Then, slowly and carefully, I pulled the chain from the bedpost.

I was free, although it remained locked tight around my ankle. I would deal with that later.

I padded over to the window and peered out cautiously. I was one storey up above the ground. An easy climb down via the tree branch that arched tantalisingly close to the window, although I had no idea what awaited me beneath. Then there was the fact my mother and the children were in this house somewhere and I had no doubt Philippe would make them pay if I escaped. There was only one thing for it and that was to free them too. I tried the door handle, turning it as gently as I could.

Still locked. Of course.

It would have to be the window then so I could get into the rest of the house and find them.

I looked out at the tree branch again. It was thick enough to take my weight, the tree trunk itself sturdy.

I tried to push the window open. Locked too. Or maybe it was nailed shut.

I felt around the frame with my fingertips. Nothing. He could have nailed it shut from the outside. In which case, I would have to break the glass. I looked around for something to use, ripping a pillowcase from the bed to wrap around my elbow, ready to punch my way out.

I was just examining the glass when I heard the unmistakable sound of the key in the lock and the door handle turning. I was just in time to ram the bedpost back into place and throw myself under the covers.

But the person who came through the door wasn't Philippe. It was a man I didn't recognise at first. And then I remembered. The man who'd hosted the party Levesque had taken me to, where I'd first seen Philippe again. Louis. He was no longer wearing his monocle, but the swagger was still there, along with the air of entitlement.

'Well if it isn't, Philippe's troublesome wife,' he said. 'We meet again.'

I stared at him, not saying a word.

'What's the matter? Cat got your tongue?'

I waited him out, wary as said cat.

He turned and locked the door behind him, pocketing the key.

'Wouldn't want the children running in now, would we?'

All at once I grew very still. A deep, primeval sense spoke to me from within, warning me of what lay ahead. I wasn't about to let it happen, not again.

As he lunged towards the bed and ripped the covers from me, I lunged too, towards the bedpost, tugging at it with all my might.

'What the...?'

He slammed his hand into my chest, pushing me back, sending fresh darts of pain through my healing wound. 'Lie still, you little bitch.'

That was when I brought the bedpost down on his head.

He opened his mouth as if to scream so I brought it down again. And again. His hands groped for my face, my hair, clawing at me, but I kept going. At last, he let out a long, shuddering gurgle and slumped on the bed, bubbles at the corners of his mouth, which now hung open, slack, blood seeping into the sheets from his broken skull along with what looked like lumps of matter.

'You were brainless anyway,' I snarled, wiping the bedpost on the sheets. It might come in handy for Philippe.

I extracted the key from his pocket and inserted it in the lock, wrenching the door open. If anyone was out there, I would catch them before they had a chance to react.

But the corridor was empty.

I crept along it in my bare feet, the bedpost in my hand, trying each door in turn. One opened into a bathroom, another into a linen store. With the last one on the left, I struck lucky. There was a key in the lock.

I glanced down the corridor to the landing, where I could see the top of a stairwell. There was no one to be heard or seen. I unlocked the door and eased it open.

'Maman,' I whispered.

The woman sitting in an armchair looked up, her expression changing from resignation to shock as she realised it was me. I held a finger up to my lips and locked the door behind me.

'Juliette. *Mon Dieu.* Can it really be you? He said you were dead. I cried so many tears for you.'

I was holding her shaking hands between my own, soothing her as best I could. 'As you can see, I am very much alive. Now, let's get you out of here.'

My mother clutched at the thin nightgown I was wearing, its scanty folds no protection against the cold. The house was like an ice box, my nipples standing proud against the silk. I didn't want to think about Philippe undressing me. He'd seen it all before anyway. At least, unlike his friend, he hadn't tried to rape me again. Not yet, at any rate.

'It's all right,' I murmured. 'There is nothing to fear.'

It was a lie and we both knew it.

'The children,' she said.

'Where are they?'

Just then I heard delighted shrieks from outside, unlike the ones I'd heard earlier. Maman's window looked out onto a back garden and the children were out there, dancing around in the snowflakes that were falling from the sky. From what I could see, there was no one with them, but that didn't mean Philippe wasn't watching from the house too.

'Is there anyone else here? Besides the children and Philippe?' I asked.

'I haven't seen anyone, although I heard a different voice today. A man speaking with Philippe on the landing. I couldn't hear what they said.'

I could imagine though, I thought grimly.

'I think I know who you mean. Does Philippe ever leave the house?'

'Not that I am aware. He seems to be hiding out here. At least, that was the impression I got. I didn't dare ask. You know how Philippe can be.'

'I do indeed,' I said. 'Come on. We need to get moving.'

She glanced at the bedpost as I picked it up but didn't say anything.

'Put on your warmest clothes,' I added. 'It's bitter out there.'

She pulled open a drawer and hastily threw on another sweater, a woollen hat and a pair of gloves, handing me her one remaining sweater.

'Take this, Juliette. You must be freezing. Here, take my hat too.'

I tugged the sweater over my nightgown. 'You keep it. You need it more than I do. Slowly now,' I murmured. 'Follow me.'

I opened the door once more with extreme care. Out on the landing, the only sound was that of a grandfather clock ticking in the hallway below.

We made our way down the stairs as quietly as we could, staying close to the wall rather than the banister so he would be less likely to spot us. The stairs were lined with portraits as was the fashion, each frame filled with a likeness that stared out, eyes as unseeing as those of the man I'd left lying in the bedroom at the other end of the house. I didn't feel the slightest twinge of guilt.

It was him or me, same as it was in the cemetery in London, in the fields and on the roads of Provence where I'd led my band of Maquis for so long, and now with Philippe. I was coming for him just as he'd come for me, with no mercy and no compunction. The man had tried to take everything and everyone I loved. Now he would pay for it.

At the bottom of the stairs, there was a salon to the left and another to the right with a corridor leading off the hall into the bowels of the house. From what I'd divined from the position of my mother's room, he would be somewhere at the back of the house, from where he could see the children playing in the garden.

Not that he cared about their welfare. That was all too obvious. But he couldn't risk them shouting too loud and attracting attention or attempting to get away over the garden wall. And try to get away they well might. I'd seen the look on Nicolas's face. He was terrified of his father. Then again, he wanted to protect me just as he tried to protect his sister and grandmother. That meant staying close even if he was scared. I loved my brave boy so much. He was everything Philippe wasn't – kind, loyal and loving.

I held up a hand to my mother to warn her to stay still while I listened, holding the bedpost firmly in my right hand. It was all I had to protect us against him. He had my pistol, my clothes and everything else he'd stripped from me. Luckily that didn't include my courage or my fight. When I was as sure as I could be that he wasn't lurking nearby, I beckoned again to Maman and we crept on down the stairs, pausing once more at the bottom before I signalled to her to wait where she was, by the front door. It was, of course, locked too and there was no sign of a key. Philippe probably carried it on him.

The corridor that led off the hall was short. I could see another couple of doors ahead of me, one of them half-open. I chose that one, betting that Philippe would keep it ajar in case his friend needed him. His dead friend upstairs. The thought gave me some grim satisfaction. No doubt they had plans for after he raped me. Too bad those plans would never be carried out.

I rounded the door fast, banking on the element of surprise. Philippe was standing with his back to me, gazing out through the French windows. It must have once been a glorious garden room, although most of the furniture was now covered in dust sheets apart from a small table and armchair next to Philippe.

He half-turned as I entered, did a double take and then the mask dropped once more as he recalibrated.

'Expecting someone else?' I asked, wielding the bedpost.

He indicated that I should look out the window. 'I wouldn't do that if I were you.'

I could see the children playing, their faces glowing with excitement and the cold, trying to catch the snowflakes that whirled all around them, sticking their tongues out to taste them as they landed. They were the picture of innocent fun. Then I looked again. At the far end of the garden was a summerhouse, decorated as the house was in a neo-Gothic style. But that wasn't the most sinister thing about it for just inside it there was a man, also watching my children. A man I recognised immediately. The Italian heavy who'd trained his gun on us at the Ritz. Harry King's friend.

'Anything happens to me and they die,' said Philippe. 'As do you and your mother.'

'How can you be so sure? Maybe I can offer him more than you can.'

Philippe laughed. It wasn't a pleasant sound. 'I very much doubt that, my dear. That man there is in the pay of the SS, along with several others. They all want one thing and that is to make sure we retake Paris.'

'We? When did you cease to be a Frenchman, Philippe?'

'I have never ceased to be a Frenchman. I simply learned how to be on the winning side.'

It was my turn to laugh. 'You think? The Germans will never retake Paris.'

'Ah, yes. I forgot. You were out cold when they attacked the American lines in the Ardennes this morning with Panzer divisions. The Americans were outnumbered and outclassed. They're fighting as we speak, but I can confidently predict that the German troops will push the Allies all the way back to the Normandy coast within days.'

I looked at him, trying to work out if he was lying. I wouldn't put it past him but, then again, his words held the ring of truth. And if that was so, it could mean that Skorzeny was also on his way towards the capital.

'So what do you say, Juliette? Shall we sit down and discuss this like adults? Oh and congratulations by the way on somehow eluding my friend. What have you done with him?'

'The same as I'm going to do with you.'

I saw it then, the flicker of something in his eyes. Not fear exactly but doubt along with disbelief that I would actually turn the tables on him.

He reached under the table at the same moment I brought the bedpost down on his head. It caught him a glancing blow on the side of it, and he roared in pain.

'What the hell do you think you're doing?'

I could see the pistol in his hand now. My pistol. The one he'd secreted under the table. Over his shoulder, the children were still playing, oblivious. Beyond them, the Italian thug, who was no doubt also armed.

Philippe levelled the pistol at me. 'You stupid bitch. You thought you could take me on?'

A cry from outside. 'Papa!'

His eyes darted to the French window where Nicolas was hammering on it, his eyes wide with fright.

'Papa, what are you doing? Stop!'

Philippe's eyes moved back to me.

'Go on,' I said. 'Shoot me in front of your son. He will never forget or forgive you, no matter what you tell him.'

The certainty had gone. He didn't know what to do.

I pressed home my advantage. 'Come on, Philippe, don't tell me you're scared to pull that trigger? A man like you. So brave. So fearless.'

The rage was back, suffusing his face, filling the veins on it so they bulged from his forehead. 'Scared of you? Don't make me laugh.'

His lips were drawn back in a smile that was more a snarl, his hand shaking very slightly. Good. Emotion had him in its grip. That's when I lunged forward, striking out with the bedpost again, knocking the pistol from his hand, diving for it as it skittered across the floor, then snatching it up as we both scrambled for it.

He struck out, knocking me off my feet and then kicking me to the ground. I rolled over onto my back, aiming the pistol up at him. He roared again, grabbing for it as I pulled the trigger again and again. Philippe slumped forward and fell, lifeless, on top of me.

I shoved at his dead weight, crawling out from under him. I could see Nicolas still at the window, his face creased, his mouth open in an endless scream. The Italian. He was still out there with them. I could see him staring at the house.

He must have heard the shots. I had to head him off before he did anything to the children.

Keeping low, I darted across the room, signalling to Nicolas to keep quiet, to get back from the window. Somehow he understood my frantic waves, running back to his sister to take her hand and lead her to the other side of the garden, to the furthest corner from the Italian.

Except that the Italian got there first, snatching Natalie up and holding her under one arm as she kicked and screamed.

I yanked at the French windows. Locked. They couldn't be. Tried another that flew open, slamming back as I dived through it, pistol aimed squarely at him.

'Go ahead, take a shot,' he jeered, holding Natalie in front of him like a shield as she cried out over and over for me, her face crumpled, the tears dripping off her chin.

'Maman.'

Her mouth was moving soundlessly now.

'Put her down,' I growled.

'Not a chance. Now you put your gun down.'

'No way.'

'Then she dies,' he said, pressing his gun to her ear.

'All right. All right. I'll put the gun down.'

'Very sensible. Throw it here.'

I looked at him, then at Natalie, still squirming in his arms.

At that moment, Nicolas ran up from behind him and grabbed at the arm that was holding the gun. I heard a shot and then Natalie screaming at the top of her lungs. I saw Nicolas lying on the ground, the Italian turning to fire at him, opening up the way for a clean shot. It was now or never.

I squeezed the trigger, saw the bullet hit its target, watched as the Italian staggered and spun in the opposite direction, dropping Natalie, fired again and caught him square in the chest, a dark red stain spreading across his jacket as he finally hit the ground and lay there, still. I kicked the gun away from him and bent to check if he was breathing.

No sign of life. I gazed for a moment at his pockmarked face, brutal even in death.

'Good riddance,' I murmured under my breath.

'Nicolas, Natalie.' I scooped them up as they ran to me, checking they were unscathed, carrying them inside and kicking the French window shut behind us, shooting the bolt just to make sure.

'Don't look,' I said as I gently deposited them on the floor.

'Don't look at what?'

'Close your eyes. Come on, Nicolas. Do it for Maman.'

I turned, thinking maybe I could cover him up, could divert their gaze so they wouldn't have to see their father lying dead in front of them. But Philippe was no longer there.

FIFTY-THREE

An unearthly howl told me where he'd gone.

'Stay here,' I commanded. 'Don't look out the window.'

Nicolas looked at me solemnly and then led his sister to the armchair, seating her so that she faced into the room, ignoring the spatters of blood on the floor. *They're in shock,* I told myself. Everything right now was surreal.

I looked back as I reached the door, holding a finger to my lips and nodding at Nicolas. He nodded back, his eyes dark with a wisdom that was beyond his years. I pulled the door to and moved as quickly as I could up the corridor, keeping my back to the wall, pistol held out in front of me.

They were by the front door, my mother with a carving knife still in her hand, staring at it in disbelief as if she couldn't comprehend what she'd done. At her feet, Philippe lay in a pool of his own blood.

'I stabbed him,' she said, her face paper white. 'I heard him shouting at you, came to try to help and found this knife in the kitchen. Then I heard the gunshots and thought I'd better stay out of the way until all that stopped. Did I do the right thing?'

'You did exactly the right thing.'

'He came for me, you see,' she went on, 'came stumbling towards me, tried to get the knife off me. I could see he was already wounded but I had to stop him. May God forgive me.'

She was trembling now, the shock of what she'd done sinking in. I took the knife from her and placed it by the grandfather clock, still ticking inexorably.

'Of course God will forgive you,' I said. 'You were protecting us, and I won't tell anyone. Besides, he was already dying. Look, one of my shots hit him in the head. He would have died from that anyway. You simply hastened things so, in a way, it was a merciful act.'

She looked at me in the same way the children did, searching for answers, for affirmation. 'Really?'

'Yes, really. Now I want you to go and find the children while I clean up here. They're down the hall in the room on the right. Don't look through the windows.'

I didn't want her to see me rifling through Philippe's pockets for the keys and whatever else might be in there. She'd suffered enough without having to look any longer at the body of the man she'd stabbed, albeit in self-defence. My mother was such a good soul. Once it all sunk in, she would never forgive herself, never mind expecting God to.

I found a bunch of keys in his trouser pocket along with his wallet and a folded piece of paper. I unfolded it to see a note, written in a hand I recognised immediately. Jean Levesque's hand.

1 *Avenue Frochot.*

It was the same address that had been written on the card in the cemetery. The card I'd stuffed into my pocket.

My clothes. They must be somewhere in this house. But first I had to work out why Levesque had scrawled that same address down. I could only imagine it was the address of this house, which meant he knew something of Philippe's plans. Probably even facilitated them. That double-crossing bastard. I would deal with him later. Right now, I had to find my clothes so I could get us all out of here and to safety without freezing to death. The sweater was helping, but it was well below zero out there. Not ideal conditions for my current attire.

I ran back up the stairs, heading for a room I hadn't so far searched, the one across the landing from the others, its door unlocked. Sure enough, Philippe's things were there, neatly arranged, a pile of books beside the bed. I caught a glimpse of the one on top of the pile, a novel by Karl May, a popular German writer who penned westerns. It conjured up a memory. An article I'd read before the war, written by a journalist who had toured the Berghof in Hitler's absence and discovered a pile of novels by Karl May beside his bed. It looked as if Philippe had done his best to emulate his hero. Too bad he hadn't lived to see him retake Paris. And I would make damn sure that never happened, especially now that Skorzeny had lost several of his key players in Philippe and his friends.

I glanced around the room. There were my clothes, in a heap in the corner. Evidently they didn't merit the same care as Philippe's things.

I threw them on, pulling my thicker sweater over my head, then stepping into the sensible trousers I'd worn to the cemetery. I looked about for my bag and eventually found it stuffed beneath the bed. It looked as if he'd gone through my notebooks, the pages scuffed and some torn. Much good it would do him now.

Another memory, one of Philippe reading my diary behind my back, ripping out pages from it and stuffing them in my mouth. Anything he hated, he destroyed. Well, he hadn't succeeded with me.

One final look around the room to make sure I hadn't missed anything and I was galloping down the stairs again, surefooted in sturdy shoes, desperate now to get us all out of there.

I was about to call out to my mother to bring the children when I heard someone banging on the front door. I stood stock-still, listening hard.

More banging and then someone calling my name. Not someone. Dan.

I scrabbled for the keys I'd retrieved from Philippe and flung the door open.

'Juliette. Oh thank God.'

Behind him, Jean Levesque, who stood between Marianne and Jack, both of whom had their guns trained on him. I looked beyond them, across a paved yard to where a couple more familiar figures stood. Antoine was just closing the gate behind them.

'Well,' I said. 'You had better all come in.'

FIFTY-FOUR

Levesque stared at the body of Philippe lying in the hall and grunted. 'No great loss.'

'There are two more,' I countered.

'Oh really?' He looked at me, almost amused, and then at his escorts. 'You heard what the lady said. Shouldn't you take a look? Wouldn't want to miss anything after all.'

His manner was strange, at odds with what was happening. *He's enjoying this*, I thought. The bastard. How could I have been so blind?

'You won't stop him,' he added. 'Skorzeny. You think this will change anything? He's way ahead of you.'

'What do you mean?'

Levesque smirked in response.

'I know this house,' said Christine. 'I saw a painting of it in London. At Max Mytton's place in Mayfair. I thought then it looked spooky.'

'That's why they chose it,' said Levesque. 'It's known locally as the haunted house. One owner was murdered and a servant killed. People say they hear footsteps from inside when the place is empty. That made it the perfect place for Philippe's purposes, especially as I believe some ancestor of his once owned it too. No one was going to come looking.'

'You're being too modest, Jean,' I said. 'I found the note you wrote for Philippe with this address on it. Was it your idea for them to use it? How much did he pay you for all your help?'

'And you were always too smart for your own good, Juliette. Too bad you outwitted them. You could have been part of this place's history.'

'Well, now there are a few more bodies to add to that history,' I said as Dan threw a dust sheet over Philippe.

'Who are the others?' he asked.

'There's one upstairs,' I said. 'In the bedroom at the far end of the corridor. Some Italian heavy is also dead. I left him in the garden out back.'

Levesque stared at me. 'You did what?'

'I killed him. And the bastard who tried to rape me. The one upstairs. That friend of yours and Philippe's, Louis. The arrogant little man who held the soirée you took me to. He had it coming.'

For once, Levesque was speechless.

Dan pushed past him and headed for the stairs. 'I'll take this one. You check out the other two.'

Suzanne and Christine came up behind Levesque.

'No funny business,' said Suzanne.

'Don't worry,' said Marianne. 'We won't let him try anything.'

'Juliette, darling, are you all right?'

I looked at Christine. 'I'm fine.'

I heard someone calling my name.

'Nicolas?' I called back.

'Are your mother and children here?' asked Antoine. 'Shall we go and find them?'

'I'll come too,' said Suzanne, 'and take a look at the one in the garden.'

Levesque snorted but, luckily for him, said nothing.

I smiled at Antoine. 'Yes they are. Come with me.'

Together with Antoine, we headed back to the garden room. Maman was sitting in the armchair, Natalie on her lap, telling them both a story. The story of Bluebeard. I could have wept. It was a story she'd told me a hundred times as a child. I wished I'd listened more closely.

'Maman!'

Natalie beamed the moment she saw me, hopping off her grandmother's lap to throw herself into my embrace. Nicolas stayed where he was, one arm resting on the chair, the other dangling by his side as if he wasn't quite sure what to do. My dear, sweet boy. Always so watchful.

I held out a hand to him. 'Nicolas, come here.'

He obeyed with one, shy glance at his grandmother, sidling up to me and nestling into my side so I could hug him close without letting go of Natalie.

'Hello,' said Antoine. 'My name is Antoine. Who are you?'

'I am Natalie,' my daughter announced. 'This is my brother, Nicolas.'

'Well, Nicolas, would you like to come with me so that Maman can help your grandmother?'

'We have a couple of cars waiting outside,' said Suzanne. 'Why don't you take your mother and children out and put them in one of them? Antoine can drive them back to the hotel.'

I glanced involuntarily at the French windows and the garden beyond. 'Good idea.'

Levesque was still in the hall as we passed through.

'Such lovely children,' he said. 'Your son is so like his father.'

Antoine ushered my mother and the children out the door.

I stopped and looked at Levesque. 'My son is nothing like his father. He's good and kind and decent. Three things you never really were and will never be. You sold your soul to the devil, Jean, and there is no god anywhere who will forgive you. I certainly won't. Nor will I forget.'

He looked at me, unrepentant. 'You may eat your words, Juliette,' he said. 'Do you really think this is over?'

'What do you mean?'

'You think this whole plan was about Philippe using you as hostages? That was only one option.'

I stared him out. He didn't blink, like the reptile he really was.

Suzanne's voice rang across the hall. 'You'd better start talking, Levesque, and fast.'

'Or what?'

'Or we'll do to you what we threatened to do earlier.'

Dan, descending the stairs, his contempt for Levesque unconcealed.

Jack nudged him in the ribs with his gun. 'You heard them,' he growled.

Levesque looked from Suzanne to me and back again.

'You leave me no choice,' he said. 'But I can tell you that you are too late. If that clock is accurate, Eisenhower could already be dead.'

FIFTY-FIVE

'They're safely on their way to the hotel with Antoine,' I said, taking in the scene that confronted me as I came back in from seeing them off, Levesque on his knees with two pistols levelled at his back, Dan standing over him, his gun aimed at his forehead.

'Do you want to do this or shall I?' Dan asked me.

I was suddenly weary of violence and pain. I'd experienced enough of it in the past few hours to last me for quite some time.

'He's all yours,' I said.

'It's all right. I'll talk. I'll tell you anything you want to know,' whimpered Levesque.

'You'd better talk fast,' snapped Suzanne.

He looked up at her. 'You've changed. You were always so shy. But that was a long time ago, wasn't it?'

'Shut up.'

Her words were cut off with a yelp from Levesque as Dan's boot slammed into his belly. He landed on all fours, curling over as he snivelled.

'He has someone in Versailles,' he stammered. 'A plant. High-powered. Someone you would never suspect.'

'Who has?'

'Skorzeny. It's all part of the master plan.'

Dan yanked his head up by the hair, reminding me horribly of Philippe.

'The name. Give us the goddamn name.'

'Dick Ward.'

'Say that again.'

'Dick. Ward.'

Dan looked at the rest of us. 'We have to get to Versailles.'

'Shouldn't we call? That would be quicker.'

'Call who? We have no idea now who we can trust. Steed could be in on it too.'

I looked at Levesque still on his knees, his face set now as if he was resigned to his fate.

'Are there others?' I asked.

He shrugged. 'I don't know. I swear. That's Skorzeny's genius. Only one known contact in each place.'

'Then you're right,' I said to Dan. 'But I have an idea. Those jeeps that brought you here, they're US military, right?'

'Correct.'

'So they have radios?'

'Also correct.'

'What are we waiting for? Let's call up help.'

FIFTY-SIX

'Andy's onto it,' said Dan, stashing away the radio set. 'You were right. They were moved in from the coast along with the other divisions to guard Versailles. He's got his best guys looking for Ward now. Don't worry. I used a secure channel.'

'That's great but we still need to get there,' I said. 'For one thing, you and I know what Ward, or whoever he really is, looks like.'

'That's true,' said Marianne. 'I bet you there's a connection to McMahon's lot. They picked him up, you know. MI5. It looks like he had something to do with the jailbreak plan at Le Marchant barracks.'

'I saw him in London,' said Christine, 'at one of the meetings where Edward spoke. I couldn't work out if he was undercover or not.'

'I suspect we may never find out the truth,' said Suzanne. 'We'll need all of us at Versailles. It's a big place. Unless you would rather stay with your family, Juliette?'

'They'll be fine,' I said. 'My mother will look after the children. She's stronger than she seems.'

Much stronger, although that would remain our secret.

'Juliette and Dan, we'll go together. The rest of you can follow us.'

On the way to Versailles, Suzanne filled me in on what had been happening.

'So the plot against Churchill failed?'

'Completely,' she said. 'The group Christine penetrated along with Edward were all arrested, as were the German ringleaders in the prison barracks and McMahon.'

'I can't believe it,' I said. 'I knew he wasn't to be trusted, but to this extent?'

'There's a lot at stake,' replied Suzanne. 'American interests in Europe. The Russians threatening the West with communism. In the middle of it all, France, along with Belgium and the Netherlands, desperately trying to rid themselves of the fascists once and for all.'

'Do we have any more news from the Ardennes?' I asked Dan.

'Andy said that, as far as he knew, the fighting is still fierce. The line is holding for now, but the next few hours and days are crucial. They're getting ready to mobilise as we speak, but he still has his men looking for Ward until they do.'

'What about Skorzeny?'

'It seems his operation is working behind the lines. There are fake US soldiers causing more chaos. We'll have to wait and see how well it's worked at Versailles.'

I checked my watch, its chunky masculine strap oddly reassuring. Papa's old watch, the one he'd given me before I left for the south, strapping it on my wrist with that sweet smile of his. It had seen me through the worst situations imaginable. I had no doubt it would see me through this one too.

'Forty minutes since we left. We should be there soon.'

Sure enough, another five minutes and we were driving through the great Parc de Versailles, passing through a ring of tanks that hadn't been there before, then more security checks before we were finally allowed through the gates, an officer striding out to greet us.

'No sign of him yet,' said Colonel Andy Gillman. 'But I have all-areas passes for you. You're going to need them to get anywhere in the building. The security is tighter than a bull's ass at fly time.'

'But not tight enough,' I said. 'To stop an imposter getting through.'

'That's true, ma'am, but at least we're on to him now.'

'Let's split up,' said Dan. 'Proceed in pairs.'

'Sounds like a plan to me. Dan, you go with Juliette.'

I looked at the colonel. 'If it's all the same to you, I'd like to go alone.'

'No chance,' said Dan. 'Look what happened last time you went alone. Besides, I'm in uniform. I can get you through doors a lot faster, and we don't have a moment to lose.'

'Where's General Eisenhower?' asked Suzanne.

'Safe in his bunker and hopping mad about it. He wants to be up here, directing operations in the Ardennes. Instead he has to hide away from some lunatic.'

A lunatic who'd proved so cunning he'd managed to pass himself off as the head of MI5 at SHAEF. I wondered who he really was and how he'd infiltrated the supreme Allied command. He must have friends in very high places. The same high places that spawned Philippe's friends, as well as their counterparts across the Channel, all hellbent on ensuring that their beloved Führer triumphed. Well, he'd failed spectacularly so far when it came to this particular master plan. Now all we had to do was make sure he failed completely.

In each room we passed through, people were working away, apparently oblivious to any threat. The place was a warren of offices, command centres and control rooms. I heard accents from all over the globe as we systematically checked for any sign of Ward, turning up nothing except quizzical looks. The staff had been told the building was in lockdown because of a general high alert.

'We can't risk putting out Ward's name and description. We have no idea who else might be working with him,' said Suzanne. 'As far as he knows, we're not on to him and with any luck, he'll be going about his business, unaware that the net is closing in.'

The trouble was that none of us knew what that business might be, so we had to search the entire building.

'Are we even sure he's here?' I asked as we tramped along yet another corridor.

'As sure as we can be,' responded Dan. 'We know he hasn't passed through any of the checkpoints in and out.'

'Wait.' I placed a hand on his arm. 'That man over there. It's Harry King.'

We were passing through what had once been a hotel lounge area, its expanse now dotted with makeshift desks and chairs. At the far end stood King, pretending to read a document, his eyes scoping the room beyond.

'What's in there?' I murmured.

'That room? It leads to the entrance to the bunker.'

'Come on,' I said, pulling my pistol from my belt.

At that moment, King turned and spotted us. A second later and he was running, sprinting towards the room that led to the bunker, all pretence thrown aside along with the documents he'd been holding. We raced after him, darting between the desks, zigzagging as we ran. King turned and fired as he reached the doorway.

'Get down!' I yelled.

The staff who'd been sitting quietly at their desks hit the floor under them. I reached the doorway and, keeping my back to the lintel, poked my pistol around it first, sweeping it in arcs as I followed, my eyes searching for King.

The room was empty save for dining tables and chairs neatly stacked to one side.

I raced on through to a small antechamber where the door to the basement was swinging open. He must have gone through it seconds before. I paused at the top of the stairs that led down, hearing Dan come up behind me.

'I'll go first,' he said. 'I know the way.'

The basement was well lit, a central corridor stretching before us with storerooms leading off it that mirrored the building above. We proceeded cautiously, listening out for any indication of King's location. Dan waved ahead, towards a thick stone door that stood ajar, signalling that this was our destination.

As we drew closer, a volley of shots spattered the corridor around us, ricocheting off the walls. We flattened ourselves against them, crouching low. He was firing blind, reaching around the stone door to let off another round of shots.

We began to zigzag, keeping to our combat crouch, my thighs screaming by the time we reached the door, staying low and to the hinged side of it.

King thrust his arm round again, firing wildly back down

the corridor. So he hadn't seen us. Good. That gave us more of a chance.

Dan held his finger up to his lips and I nodded. Then he motioned that he would shove the door open while I ran through. It was the only plan. He was far bigger and stronger than me but I was faster. I nodded again and he held up his fingers, counting down. Three... two... one...

We were off, the door slamming open, me hurtling through it, still keeping low, firing for all I was worth towards where I thought King was standing. The moment I actually got eyes on him, I stopped firing and stared, taking in the scene. There was yet another door in front of me, this one firmly shut. King had his arm around the throat of the soldier who'd been guarding it while another lay at his feet, presumably dead. He must have taken them by surprise. Or perhaps they still hadn't taken our warnings seriously enough.

As Dan came through the door after me, I heard him swear under his breath. 'Easy now. Let's not do anything stupid.'

King swung his gun, moving it from side to side, aiming first at Dan, then at me. The gun he'd apparently taken from the guard was stuck in his belt. A standard issue M1911. A Tommy gun lay on the floor, well out of reach. I had to hand it to King. He was good.

'You two,' he said, 'are a pain in the arse. I should finish you off here and now, but I have better things to do.'

'Like what?' I sniped. 'Killing General Eisenhower?'

'Actually, that's my job.'

Dick Ward stepped through the heavy stone door, looking as suave as he had the last time I'd seen him. He was holding another sub-machine gun. When he saw me looking at it, he smiled.

'Do excuse me,' he said. 'Very rude of me to point a gun at a lady, but needs must. I'm sure you understand.'

'Oh I understand all right,' I said, my mind racing, trying to think this through. *Keep him talking. Gain some time. Try to work out what the hell Dan is thinking.* 'You're a traitor, the same as him.'

Ward raised an eyebrow. 'A little harsh.'

'But true.'

'In any case, enough chit-chat. Time to say goodbye.'

'Just a second,' said Dan. 'What are you going to do when the bunker blows?'

Ward looked at him, trying to cover his surprise.

'You do know the bunker is primed to blow unless you open it with the right combination?'

His eyes darted to the door and back to Dan. 'Nice try.'

'I'm not trying anything. It's a fact. Just ask the guardsman here. Or try your luck. I'll wait.'

He was utterly relaxed, or at least so it appeared, that easy smile in place as he met Ward head-on. Ward glanced at the door, taking in the combination lock and the wires that led from it. Dan wasn't bluffing.

Ward smiled. 'Let me guess. You know the combination?'

'Of course. I set it.'

I stared straight ahead. Either this was yet another skill he hadn't bothered to mention or he really was bluffing this time.

'In that case, you'll have to tell me what it is or regrettably your lady friend here will die.'

'I don't think so,' said Dan, turning his pistol up so that he was pressing the barrel into his chin. 'You see, if that happens then, regrettably, I will die too and so will that combination you need.'

Checkmate.

Ward narrowed his eyes, evidently thinking it through. 'Very well then,' he said at length. 'You open the door and you both live.'

It was Dan's turn to smile. 'You're going to have to put down your weapons first. As a sign of good faith.'

'No way,' said King. 'Shall I take this one out?' He jabbed the guard with his gun.

'Calm down, King,' said Ward. 'Let's not do anything hasty here.'

He's under orders too, I thought. *He's acting for Skorzeny and therefore Hitler. If he gets this wrong, he'll die one way or another.*

'Let's compromise,' Ward went on. 'I throw this down and Harry keeps hold of the guard. That way, we all have some leverage.'

'Afraid not,' said Dan. 'Besides, you'll just pull that pistol you have tucked under your jacket.'

'Touché. So what do we do?'

'We? What I'm going to do is walk on out of here along with my "lady friend". Then you two clowns can work out how to explain to your SS buddies that you screwed up the biggest mission they ever gave you.'

A beat. It felt as if we were waiting for a thunderstorm to break, all the air suddenly sucked from that dank, cold, underground room which was little more than a cave.

Ward looked at King. 'Shoot them both,' he snapped.

FIFTY-SEVEN

I caught the flick of Dan's eyes in the millisecond before he moved, whipping round on Ward to jerk his gun arm up as he slammed into his chest with his elbow and followed up with a kick to his knees to bring him down. Before King had even registered what was going on, the guard threw his head back, contacting King's nose with a loud crack. As King's hands moved to his face reflexively, I grabbed his wrist and twisted it up and back hard, at the same time yanking on his little finger until I heard that snap. A kick to his balls and he was down too, scrabbling at his belt for his second gun. I fired into the back of his head. He fell forward without another sound.

'Stay where you are.'

Ward had somehow managed to pull his other weapon and was training it on Dan. The guard grabbed King's gun off him and fired, missing Ward by a whisker. I could see his finger on the trigger, squeezing, the barrel aimed directly at Dan's chest.

'No!'

Everything moved in slow motion, the world suspended for a heartbeat, no longer spinning on its axis but centred right here, right now, where everything, including my heart and soul, were focused. I held my breath, knowing that if I missed, even by a hair's breadth, Dan was done for, my finger squeezing too, a faction faster than his, my gun kicking back, the bullet flying from it too fast to even see, the blood bursting between Ward's eyes like a rose exploding into bloom. It was a perfect, clean kill.

'Attagirl,' breathed Dan, checking both bodies over to make sure they were really dead. He handed their weapons to the guard. 'Put these somewhere safe. We'll need them later.'

'Yessir.'

'At ease, soldier. You did a good job. Now stand back while I get this door open.'

I watched as his fingers worked the combination lock with precision, remembering Marianne's tales of lessons from a safecracker. Maybe Dan could show me when all this was over. Stupid thought. When this was over, so were we, at least like that. My work was over too. I had more important things to take care of, like my children. My mother. Although it appeared she could well and truly look after herself.

'Gotcha.'

The door to the bunker was safely open. I straightened my shoulders, preparing to meet the Supreme Allied Commander at last. But Eisenhower wasn't there. No one was there. The bunker was entirely empty, a plain table set in the centre of the space, chairs tucked neatly round it. There was a stack of files at one end of the table, but that was all. It was as if they'd never been here.

'Where are they?' I asked.

Dan gestured towards the back of the bunker. I could just about make out another door set deep into the wall, painted the exact same colour so that it blended in, only its combination lock marking it out. Dan proceeded to unlock that too, opening the door into another passageway beyond, one that smelled of earth and fresh air rather than dust and paint.

'Along there,' he said, 'is a concealed exit that opens into an enclosed wooded area. We keep a vehicle there at all times in case it's needed for a quick getaway.'

'So where has the general gone?'

'I'm not exactly sure. One of several places. As soon as we give the signal, he'll return. He's not too far away.'

'What are we going to do about Ward and King?'

'The clean-up boys will be along soon. Before they are, I want to find out their true identities, or at least Ward's. The real Dick Ward is apparently missing.'

'Was he ever here? The real Dick Ward?'

'According to London, he got as far as Paris, where he was met by one of his agents. That agent put him in a cab here, but he never made it. The man who arrived claiming to be Ward is the one I killed.'

'Do we know who he really is, the man who posed as Ward?'

'We believe he's an officer called Baron Stephan von Gruning who served with the Abwehr before they merged with the SS. Highly educated and spoke impeccable English, as we saw.'

'So we still have an MI5 agent somewhere out there?'

'Apparently so.'

'Alive or dead?'

'No idea.'
'Then we had better find out.'

FIFTY-EIGHT

'So long, buddy. You behave yourself now.'

Dan saluted his old friend. 'Why break the habit of a lifetime? You take care out there.'

'Don't you worry. We're going to kick their butts and then some. Those Germans are going to wish they'd stayed in bed by the time we finish with them.'

The two men looked at one another.

'Goodbye, Dan.'

'See you around, Andy.'

Another salute and Andy was marching back to his men, ready to pull out and head for the Ardennes.

'Do you think he'll be OK?' I asked.

'Andy? He's always OK.' Dan flashed me a smile that wasn't entirely convincing.

Steed emerged from the building and made his way over to us. 'Are you heading back to the city now?'

'We have a lot of loose ends to clear up,' I said.

'So do we. Not least how the hell someone like Ward, or

whoever he was, got past all of us, if you'll pardon my French, ma'am.'

'It's not so much your French as your accent when you speak it that troubles me.'

It took him a moment to realise I was joking.

He held out his hand and shook both of ours. 'If there's anything you need, don't hesitate to get in touch. We owe you a debt of gratitude.'

'You owe us nothing,' said Dan. 'It's our job and, besides, the general was never in any real danger.'

'All thanks to you. If you hadn't alerted us and then shown up, I dread to think what might have happened.'

'Well, now you can listen to the general's thoughts on being forced into a bunker when the Germans had just mounted a surprise attack on his troops in the Ardennes.'

Steed rolled his eyes. 'Can't wait.'

Dan was still grinning as we got in the car.

'I think I know where he might be,' I said as we drove away from Versailles, back towards Paris. 'The real Dick Ward. In that house on the Avenue Frochot, there was a room I didn't check. The one beside Philippe's. They could easily have him locked in there.'

Dan looked sceptical. 'Wouldn't he have made a noise when he heard us?'

'You're assuming he could hear us. Christine and Suzanne use knock-out drugs all the time on people. What's to say they haven't done that to him? It makes sense, if you think about it. Keeps him quiet and compliant.'

'That's if they even kept him alive. What's the incentive when everyone at Versailles believes the man they met was the real Dick Ward?'

'A senior MI5 officer like that is very valuable to the Germans. I have no doubt Philippe intended to hand him over as a prize.'

'You could be right, but our boys are there now, cleaning up. I can't believe they'd miss an MI5 officer.'

'They would if they weren't looking for one.'

'You know what? You have a good point. Let's head straight there. I'll call ahead, alert them to check that room and anywhere else they might have missed.'

'Now you're talking.'

He shot me a sideways look. 'You wouldn't be mocking my Americanisms by any chance, would you?'

'Who me? Never.'

'You're a wicked woman.'

'On the contrary, I am a very good woman.'

'Now on that we agree.'

His hand reached for mine and I let him hold it for a moment, relishing the warmth of it. Outside, it was bitterly cold, the windows frosting up even as we drove, but in here, with him, I felt as if we were cocooned.

Be careful, Juliette. Such feelings are dangerous. I knew that and yet I couldn't stop. How can you stop yourself feeling when it comes from somewhere within you that is your very essence? People talked of soulmates. He was mine. Heart and soul, bound together forever as if by an invisible cord. And yet it was a cord I must cut once more if I was to remain true to myself.

No more adventuring. No more running around trying to save the world, or at least my country. I'd seen what could happen when I didn't take care of my own. Now I really was the only one they had. It was all down to me.

'A penny for your thoughts.'

'You owe me a lot of pennies by now.'

He threw me a look. 'How do you say that in French?'

'We don't. We would just ask someone what they're thinking.'

He roared with laughter. 'You French have this reputation for being wild romantics when, in fact, you're a bunch of pragmatists.'

I laughed too. 'True. Although it's also true we're a nation of lovers. We love wine and cheese and...'

'You. I love you.'

The tears caught me unawares, seizing the back of my throat so I couldn't speak without giving myself away.

'It's OK,' he added. 'You don't have to say anything. I know it's hard for you right now, but I want you to know I love you anyway. Always have since that first moment I saw you. Always will.'

I stared dumbly through the windscreen, watching the raindrops begin to patter, turning to sleet. *Like my heart*, I thought. I had to let it frost over once more. The trouble was that warmth or rather the heat that surged between us. This wasn't just some storybook romance. I wanted him body and soul.

'Stop the car,' I commanded.

'What, here?'

'Yes. See that turning up ahead? Take it.'

He glanced at me but obeyed, turning off the road and up a farm track that led to a ruined barn, its roof collapsed so that it offered no shelter.

I looked around. We were invisible from the road thanks to the one remaining intact wall. I reached for him, my fingers working at his belt, his surprise turning to comprehension and then lust. He started tearing at my clothes too, his fingers clumsy in their eagerness, pulling my sweater over my head, pushing aside my brassiere straps, taking one nipple in his mouth and then the other while I teased and stroked the length of him.

His hands were inside my knickers now, working their way inside the silk, feeling something even silkier as I writhed under his touch.

I tore off my trousers and straddled him, pulling my knickers to one side as I eased him inside of me, throwing my head back and letting out a groan as that heat began to mount, suffusing both of us as we moved, together now, in tandem.

I could feel him holding back, waiting for me, but I wanted to be the one in control and so I moved even faster. He was holding my hips, thrusting up into me, unable to stop as I pushed first him and then me over the edge, crying out my name, burying his face in my neck as he half-sobbed it aloud.

'I love you too,' I said, dropping butterfly kisses all over his face, his brow. 'I love you. I wish I didn't, but I do.'

His hands stroked the length of my back, holding me by the hips, helping me off him. He reached for his handkerchief to gently wipe himself from me, holding me close again as I curled into his side, sated.

'You're shivering,' he said. 'Here, put this on.'

He pulled his coat from the floor of the car where it lay and wrapped it round me.

'I wish we could stay like this,' I said. 'Not go back. Forget our responsibilities.'

'You could never do that. It's one of the things I love about you. Your integrity and your sense of honour. Of duty.'

I looked at him sadly. 'It's the very thing that might tear us apart.'

He took my hand and kissed it. 'I know.'

There was nothing more to be said. He knew and I knew. There was only love and duty and pain, all mixed up together.

FIFTY-NINE

He wasn't there. They searched the entire house from top to bottom. So did we. No sign of the real Dick Ward, and anyone who might have been able to point us in the right direction was dead.

'MI5 are breathing down our necks,' said Suzanne. 'I don't want them to start interfering in our operations, but we need to maintain good relations.'

'So what do we do?' asked Marianne.

We were gathered in Dan's office in the Hotel Scribe, all of us together, refreshed after a few hours' sleep although I had spent most of the night huddled up next to my children in one bed while my mother slept in the other. I looked at the faces around the table. My friends as well as my colleagues.

'What about your cousin?' asked Dan. 'He and his friends were following Philippe. We might have missed something he saw. There's also his mother. I think it's about time we talked to her. Find out how much she knows.'

'I will talk to Guillaume. There's no point my questioning his mother. The woman hates me and always has, so she won't tell me anything.'

'I'll do it,' said Dan. 'I guess you guys are leaving today?'

'We have to,' said Suzanne. 'Churchill is demanding a thorough debrief, and we have loose ends in London to tie up before we can do that.'

'Eisenhower is also insisting on a debrief,' said Dan. 'This very afternoon, in case we can provide him with any intelligence on Skorzeny that will help him direct battle operations.'

'What news from the Ardennes?'

'The fighting continues to be very heavy, and the weather means our planes are grounded. The good news is that the Germans haven't broken through our lines. They're still holding, although Skorzeny's operation has caused a lot of trouble behind them.'

'All the more reason you make sure there are no loose ends.'

Suzanne looked at me. 'Your mother and children will be coming on the plane with us back to England. That way we can make sure they are absolutely safe.'

I met her gaze, feeling my heart contract. I would see this through. One last operation. Then it was time to become a mother again, as well as a daughter.

'Thank you. I'd like to say goodbye to them.'

'Of course. You can go with them to the airfield.'

'I want to stay here in Paris too,' said Antoine. 'I'd like to help. I understand that de Gaulle has given over the Hotel Lutetia to receive displaced persons. We must question them to make sure there are no collaborators who are trying to hide among them. There is also the matter of rounding up the other remaining agents like Harry King. I can help with both. We need to ensure no one slips through the net.'

I stared at my hands, unable to look at Antoine. Here was I with my mother and children, safe and sound, while his family were still somewhere out there in a German camp, suffering God knows what. Was it so selfish of me to want to give it all up and simply take care of my family? Maybe. Probably. I had joined the Resistance to free my country of its German oppressors as well as to fight a war. The war was not yet won, certainly not for Antoine. How could I, in all conscience, give up on my comrade in arms when he had never given up on me?

'Would you mind if it was I who questioned your aunt?' he asked me. 'I already spoke with the concierge at her apartment building and I feel there is more there to learn too. She did not have a lot to say. She may remember a little more with the right persuasion.'

'Of course not,' I said. 'That's if Dan doesn't mind?'

'Be my guest,' said Dan. 'You'll probably get more out of her than I would.'

'Excellent. Then I will get started right away.'

Antoine gave us all a little bow as he left the room. '*Au revoir, mes amis.*'

'We must say our goodbyes too,' said Suzanne. 'Or rather, *au revoir*. Dan, are you coming to the airfield too?'

'If you don't mind, I'll say my *au revoir*s now and go find Guillaume. I guess he'll be at the Café de Flore?'

'Without a doubt,' I said.

'Then I'll meet the rest of you at the airfield,' said Suzanne. 'There's just one small thing I need to clear up.'

Or rather, one small person. I knew instantly that she meant Levesque. I didn't much rate his chances.

An image rose from the recesses of my mind. The painting behind Levesque's desk of a younger Suzanne. How and why it was there I had no idea, but I knew those two had history. And I was absolutely certain Suzanne would make sure she erased that along with him if she felt it necessary.

SIXTY

Snow was beginning to drift across the runway as we drew up in front of it. The children looked out of the car window and squealed with delight.

'Look, Maman, look... it's snowing again.'

I mustered a smile. 'Yes, it is. What fun. That means it's probably snowing in England too. You'll be able to have a snowball fight.'

I had no idea if it was or not, but I had to make sure they understood where they were going and why. I had held each of them in turn at the hotel, explaining that Maman would see them soon, that she had just a little more work to do in Paris. I knew from their faces that they didn't grasp what I was saying, not really.

Now Natalie looked at me with a frown creasing her perfect forehead. 'Aren't you coming with us?'

'No, my darling, I can't right now. I told you. I have some work to do here.'

'Yes, silly, she told you. Remember?' Nicolas always got cross when he was trying to be brave.

'Nicolas, look after your sister. I need you to be a big boy and look after your grandmother too.'

'I will, Maman.'

I could see him biting his lip, willing himself not to cry. He'd endured so much in the past few days. His papa was now dead, his world upended. No matter that the children hadn't seen Philippe for much of their lives, he was still their father.

'Come – everyone's waiting.'

I could see them gathered by the plane steps. Marianne and Jack. Christine, swaddled in the most fabulous coat. Of course. No sign of Suzanne yet. I bundled them all out of the car, helping my mother out of her front seat.

'Will you be all right?' I asked as I enfolded her in my arms.

'Shouldn't I be asking you that?' she retorted.

'Probably.'

She held me at arm's length, giving me her sternest look. 'He's a good man, Juliette, and he loves you. Don't do anything stupid.'

I gaped at her, dumbfounded.

'You thought I hadn't noticed?' she went on. 'I have eyes. I saw the way he looked at you and the way you look back at him. You two were made for one another. Don't worry about me and the children. We'll still be here, waiting for you. Go and do what you must, Juliette. You deserve to be happy.'

I could see the tears clinging like diamonds to her face, the air so cold now that they froze even as they trickled from her eyes.

'Let's get you into the plane. It's perishing out here.'

The pilot had the engine running, keen to get away before the snow stopped him taking off. Still no Suzanne.

A slap of something cold in my ear.

'Ha ha! Got you, Maman.'

Nicolas shouting in glee, scraping up more snow from the ground to make another ball. This one hit Jack on the shoulder. He turned, scooping snow off the plane steps to throw one back.

I looked at my watch. Where the hell was she?

Suddenly, a car roared down the runway towards us and skidded to a halt beside the plane.

'Are we all ready?' Suzanne emerged unflustered from it, suitcase in hand.

A flurry of hugs and they were all safely on board. I stood alone, waving them off, smiling as brightly as I could while my own tears mingled with the snowflakes falling on my face. I held my breath as the plane started down the runway, picking up speed and then soaring into the sky.

'Be safe,' I whispered as I watched it rise and then turn, heading north, to England.

I watched it until it became a tiny dot, shrinking to nothing as it disappeared over the horizon. Then and only then did I get back in the car, my limbs stiff with the cold that seemed to have permeated only as far as the edges of my heart. My heart itself was aching with the kind of white-hot, searing pain you only feel when separated from those you love the most. It was a pain I knew too well. One I had endured for the years I spent alone, fighting with the Resistance. Each time, it grew sharper, rather than dulling. I suspected it would be sharpest of all when it came to Dan.

'I need to go somewhere before you take me back to the hotel,' I said to the driver.

'Very good, ma'am.'

I gave him Levesque's office address. I had a hunch that

was where they would have had their little chat, in front of her picture. Another loose end sewn up perhaps. Or a story coming full circle.

SIXTY-ONE

He was still upright in the big chair behind his desk, the neat bullet wound the only sign that Suzanne had been here. *At least she spared him the indignity of arrest and trial*, I thought, glancing at her portrait. There was nothing on the desk to indicate any struggle. No disarray, no papers flung everywhere. It was a Sunday, which meant there was no one else in the building. No staff tapping on their typewriters outside his office door. Just Levesque. And Suzanne.

'What was your secret?' I murmured as I gazed at the painting.

She stared back at me, enigmatic as ever. *Wouldn't you like to know?* her eyes seemed to say.

'Yes, I would,' I said out loud, and I had a feeling the answers lay in that picture.

I moved around the desk, careful not to disturb Leveque, and lifted it down from the wall. On the rear of the portrait, there was the usual backing paper. I ran my hand over it, feeling a slight bulge at the bottom-right corner.

Taking the paperknife from Levesque's desk, I laid the

picture down and slit the backing paper open. There was an envelope in there, tucked into the frame. I eased it out with my fingers and studied it. It looked as if it had been there since the picture was framed.

It was a small, square, ordinary envelope but, as I held it, I had the sense it could change the course of everything. Did I even want to see what was inside, let alone rock all of our worlds with a revelation? It felt that seismic, that potentially explosive. But then, had I ever shied away from the truth, especially one that could mean so much?

Without another thought, I slit the envelope open too.

Inside was a birth certificate that proclaimed one Suzanne Marie Charlotte to be the daughter of Jean Levesque while her mother was a woman named Mary Buckingham.

I stared at it, uncomprehending, for a second and then it all started to make sense. The portrait of the young, innocent Suzanne. Her perfect French. The link to Paris that had brought her back here to set up a brothel that was, in fact, a front for the Resistance and SOE, one she had transferred to Lyon to carry on the good work there. She knew who her father was and yet she chose the side of good, of the righteous. Or maybe that was why she did. She probably black-mailed him into changing sides to try to save his soul. I suspected Jean Levesque would have been proud of his daughter even as she shot him dead.

SIXTY-TWO

I smiled at the concierge. 'Do you remember me?'

'Of course I do,' she said. 'I expect you want to ask more questions.'

She looked pointedly at Antoine, standing alongside me. We had agreed I would do the talking, along with the bribing.

'If you don't mind,' I said. 'I brought you a little gift as it's almost Christmas.'

I held out the box of patisserie, cold meats and cheeses we'd purloined from the hotel, a wad of notes tucked discreetly within. She lifted the lid, eyeing the goodies and then spotted the money too.

'Come in,' she said, all smiles now. 'Can I offer you some coffee?'

'That would be wonderful. It's bitter outside today. I understand you've already met my friend here?'

She nodded at Antoine. 'Yes, yes I have. He didn't say he was a friend of yours.'

'I see. Well, he's not just a friend. He's a valued

colleague. We worked for the Resistance together in the south.'

She looked at him more closely now, her birdlike gaze softening a fraction. 'That is commendable. Now, how can I help you?'

I took the coffee she was proffering and sipped at it. 'Delicious. Thank you. You mentioned a friend of yours who works for someone who owns a mansion. You also said certain people hold soirées there which are really meetings. Can you give me the address?'

She wrinkled her nose. 'I don't want my friend to get in any trouble.'

'I can assure you that is the last thing that will happen. In fact, we will reward your friend as we have you.'

My implication was clear. The old woman was no fool.

'Very well then. This is the address.'

She scrawled it down on a piece of paper and handed it to me. It was just a few streets away, still in the 16th. The street name rang a bell.

'Thank you. You may just have saved a man's life.'

She looked at me, startled. 'Really?'

For a second I saw the young girl she must have been, eager and brave. Somehow life had bashed that out of her, as it has a way of doing. Mercifully, it hadn't yet managed to do that to me or my colleagues.

'Absolutely.'

'Just one more question,' said Antoine. 'Has there been any unusual activity in Juliette's aunt's apartment? Any comings and goings?'

'Now that you ask, there were a lot of people coming and going the past few days, until yesterday. Then nothing. They were all men. Didn't recognise any of them.'

'You didn't think to mention this to me before?'

'You didn't ask in the right way.'

She gave him a wily look, and I had to suppress a snort of laughter. This was how Parisians had survived this war, with a combination of guile and guts. I had to hand it to her – she was one gutsy woman, forging an existence alone in a city gone wild, where people fought over scraps like the pigeons in the streets and squares.

'Well,' I said, 'that fits. We can deal with my aunt later. Right now, we should really take a look at this mansion.'

The minute we turned into the street, I recognised the place. It was the art nouveau mansion where Levesque had taken me to that soirée what felt like a lifetime ago but was, in fact, only eight days. Just over a week and all our lives had changed irrevocably in that time. All except Antoine. His life was still torn apart by the absence of his family.

'I know this place,' I said. 'I killed its owner back at the other house.'

'The man who tried to rape you?'

'Yes. Louis. A fascist and a collaborator who was a good friend of Philippe's as well as the Nazis.'

Antoine spat on the ground in front of the house.

'Shall we knock on the door?'

It was opened by an elderly housekeeper who looked flustered on seeing us.

'Is your master in?' I asked, knowing full well he wasn't.

'He is not,' she said, casting us suspicious looks.

'It was your friend who gave us this address,' I said, holding out the piece of paper so she could scrutinise the handwriting. 'May we come in?'

'Well, I don't—'

We were already pushing past her, entering the hall

where I remembered the magnificent chandelier, going on through to the grand salon.

'The soirée was in here,' I said. 'It's where I first saw Philippe again.'

The housekeeper followed us, wringing her hands. 'I'm not sure you should be in here.'

'It's all right,' I said. 'We're with the US Army.'

A small lie but it would do. The Parisians looked on the US Army as their saviours.

'You don't look as if you're with the army.'

I pulled out my pistol. 'Do we now?'

She backed away, hands raised, lips working. 'Please. Do anything you like. My employer is not here anyway.'

'He won't be coming back either,' I said.

Her eyes grew rounder as she gaped at me.

'He's dead,' I added. 'As of yesterday. But we'll make sure you get paid until you can find another post.'

She crossed herself. 'Holy mother.'

'I doubt that will help where he's gone. Now, can you tell me if there are any guests in this house? Any visitors that you know of?'

Her face shut down, her expression growing sly.

'Ah silly me,' I said. 'I nearly forgot.'

I handed her another wad of notes.

'An early Christmas gift from the US Army. Perhaps you could show us where this guest is staying?'

'Nicely done,' murmured Antoine as we ascended the stairs behind her capacious rear. With every step, it swayed a little more. The thing had a vocabulary all of its own.

'In here,' she said, pointing at a door three flights up, under the eaves. 'But the gentleman in there is very poorly. He may not even be awake. He sleeps all the time, mostly, so

I simply leave his food tray for him and come back to get it at the end of the day.'

One meal a day. That was hardly looking after a guest. I pursed my lips but said nothing.

'The door is locked,' Antoine said. 'Do you have the key? You must have if you've been bringing him food.'

She was about to demur but thought better of it, glancing at the pistol still in my grip. With a tiny sigh, she retrieved a bunch of keys from her apron and inserted one in the lock.

'There you go but don't go telling anyone it was I who let you in. The master told me he is a very important person and is not to be disturbed.'

Ignoring her, we entered the room, where a figure lay under a pile of blankets, his mouth slightly open, his head lolling on the pillow. I looked back at the housekeeper still hovering by the door.

'Did you add anything to his food?' I asked.

Her gaze slid away from mine. 'I might have. It was the master who told me to. Said it was his medication. Two spoonfuls a day to be added to his food. It's mostly soup and stews so it's easy to mix it in.'

I stared at her for another moment. There was no way she was that stupid.

'Is there a telephone here?'

'Of course.'

'Show me where it is.'

Five minutes later, we had an ambulance on its way, along with a couple of soldiers to accompany him to the American military hospital.

The next call I put in was to Edward.

'You might want to send someone over,' I said. 'To collect a parcel.'

I could hear crackling on the line and then Suzanne spoke.

'You found him?'

'We did.'

'Good work. Everyone here is safe and well.'

'That's good to hear. *A bientôt*, Suzanne.'

We would talk about the portrait when I saw her, if we ever did. Some things were best left unsaid. Then there were other things you had to say. Things like 'I love you. I will always love you'. And 'goodbye'.

Things I was dreading.

SIXTY-THREE

23 DECEMBER 1944, PARIS

'I have a favour to ask,' said Guillaume.

He seemed older, so much more self-assured than he had just a couple of weeks back. His friends were at their customary table in the Café de Flore and I had made sure to buy them all a drink. Guillaume kept casting shy glances at the girl with them, the same one who'd accompanied him on his surveillance mission.

'Anything for you.'

'I want you to spare my mother.'

It was the last thing I'd expected to hear. She'd made his life a misery for so long and yet here he was, asking me to let her off the hook.

'You did say anything,' he added.

I could see the lost little boy still in there, somewhere, but it was a grown man who was speaking to me now, a man with enough guts to ask for mercy.

'I did, but, Guillaume, it's not that simple. She harboured known collaborators and criminals. She also colluded with them.'

'I know. I also know she is a lonely, unhappy woman who will not be here forever. Some days I think she would be happy to be dead now. If you spare her then maybe I can get her to think differently. She might even join the Communist Party.'

'Now that would be a miracle. Seriously, Guillaume, it's out of my hands now. It's up to the local authorities to decide whether or not to prosecute.'

'Yes, but you do have some influence.'

He looked up as Dan arrived, looking happier than he had for days.

'The tide is turning in the battle,' he said. 'The weather has improved enough for our air attacks to recommence. We executed three of Skorzeny's men yesterday and put three more on trial. At this rate, and with any luck, we'll be home for Christmas.'

Home. Wherever that was now.

'Wonderful,' I said. 'Let's drink to that.'

I had no idea if I could influence anyone over my aunt's arrest. Or even if I wanted to. Except that Guillaume had done so much to help and she was all he had, apart from me. I thought of my Nicolas, of how he would feel if it were me.

I patted his arm. 'I'll do my best.'

'Thank you.'

'I also have an invitation for you, from our colleague Antoine. He wondered if you would like to work with him as our, if you like, representatives in Paris. He's going to be carrying on his work hunting down collaborators and helping the dispossessed.'

Guillaume's face lit up. 'I would love that.'

I saw a cloud of doubt douse the sunshine almost as soon as it appeared.

'Antoine may be able to help with that matter we just discussed,' I added. 'Just don't start ranting communist propaganda at him. He prefers people to politics, especially as his family are still being held in a German camp.'

'You have my word,' said Guillaume. 'I'm so sorry to hear that.'

He really had grown up, I thought, feeling another surge of pride in him.

'So I guess this may be goodbye, Guillaume, at least for now,' said Dan. 'I'm trying to get us on a plane back to London tomorrow. Then you can spend Christmas with your kids, Juliette.'

'That would be wonderful.' I smiled at him, all kinds of thoughts whirling, like the snowflakes that had danced in the air the day the children and my mother left. I hadn't spent Christmas with them in four years. To see their faces as they opened the presents I'd already bought them would be the best Christmas gift I could ever have.

Dan reached into his pocket and placed something in my palm. A shiny penny. I turned it over in my hand.

'My thoughts will cost you more than a penny,' I said.

'How about dinner at the Ritz tonight?'

'It's a deal.'

I glanced around the Café de Flore, drinking it all in. England was home right now. My mother and children were there. But France, and in particular Paris, was where I belonged. As for my heart – that belonged right here, right now, with this man, while I could still give it to him. Or at least lend it. The moment we landed in England, I would have to take it back, although, inevitably, I would leave some pieces behind. Large, broken pieces. Unless some kind of miracle happened and I managed to have it all.

I held the penny tight in my palm, curling my fingers around it to keep it safe.

Maybe, just maybe, it would prove my lucky charm.

SIXTY-FOUR

'Madame, monsieur, so good to see you. The usual?'

I smiled up at Meier. 'Yes please.'

'I'll miss his martinis,' I said to Dan.

'I'll miss you.'

Straight for the gut. No messing around. That was my Dan.

I swallowed, looking around, trying to distract myself. The bar was buzzing as usual, every other face looking familiar. All around us, life carried on even as my heart splintered once more. I'd been so determined to stay strong, to carry this off with grace.

'Don't, Dan,' I whispered.

'Why not? It's the truth.'

Our cocktails arrived, his a whisky sour.

'To us,' he said, touching his glass to mine.

'To us.'

I couldn't look at him. Wouldn't look at him. If I did, all was well and truly lost. Instead, I gazed into the middle distance, somewhere beyond pain and impossible choices.

'Look at me,' he pleaded.

I opened my purse and pulled out his penny.

'Here you go,' I said. 'I prefer to keep my thoughts to myself.'

'No you don't. They're written all over your face.'

'Oh yes?'

'Yes. Along with your feelings. You're wondering how the hell you can walk away when we have something so good. You're also killing yourself with guilt over your kids and that bastard Philippe. You look at me and think that I could never fit into your little family, that it would be impossible to combine mine with yours, so why even try? Then there's the job you love, the one you're so good at, the one that you're going to leave.'

'I'm that transparent?'

'Yes.'

'Then I'm probably not as good at my job as I thought.'

It was meant to sound light-hearted, but I choked on the words. He was right about all of it. All except one thing. I could absolutely see him as part of my little family and us as part of his. That was the thing that hurt the most.

'The thing is, Juliette, you don't have to do this.'

'Yes I do.'

He put his finger to my lips. 'Don't say another word. Just look at me. Look at me, Juliette.'

I couldn't help it. I had to look at him. His eyes pulled at mine, as did his heart and soul. I was lost. I had always been lost when it came to Dan. I just didn't know it because I chose not to see it. Now I was seeing it and seeing him as if for the first time.

'I'm not hungry,' I said. 'At least, not for food.'

'I was hoping you might say that, which is why I arranged a little surprise.'

He signalled to Meier, so discreetly I might not even have noticed if I hadn't known him as well as I did.

Within seconds, Meier was at our table. 'I will arrange for your drinks to be sent up,' he said, a bellboy magically appearing to lead us to a lift, different from the one we'd taken the last time.

'Not the Imperial Suite?' I murmured as we ascended.

'No, madame, the Chopin Suite,' said the bellboy as he opened the door for us. Our cocktails were somehow already set out on a table along with an ice bucket in which sat a bottle of Dom Perignon. In one corner, there was a grand piano.

'I asked for this suite,' said Dan, 'because I want to play you something.'

He handed me a glass of champagne. Bemused, I perched on the sofa and took a sip. And then he began to play, and everything else went out of my mind as I sat, enraptured by the music he conjured from those piano keys.

Chopin's Nocturnes. I'd heard them so many times but never like this, the notes rippling through me, seeming to die off and then rising once more, flying into the air like those snowflakes, skittering as if they danced across some magical frozen lake. I was consumed, entranced, unable to tear my eyes from him as he played not just with his hands but with his entire body.

When, at last, the notes faded into nothing, leaving an echo that hung in the air, I placed my glass down and walked over to the piano. I held out my hand, taking his and leading him to the canopied bed, where I slid my clothes from my body as he watched, rapt as I had been, only ripping off his own clothes when I was naked, vulnerable under his gaze.

'You are so beautiful,' he whispered as he traced my curves and angles with one hand, the other pulling me to him in a fierce embrace.

Together, we sank onto the silken sheets, his hands playing me as he had the piano, my body singing out in response, beginning to move in rhythm together, feeling it engulf me as the music had, ripples rising, running through me, crying out in a crescendo that no composer could ever match.

Afterwards, we lay murmuring words of love and misery and hope all mingled with the song of silence into which we drifted, now and then stirring to reach for one another, to make love once more, lazily, while half asleep, curling up so that his arm became mine, limbs entangled, hearts tangled even more tightly. I prayed that the dawn would never come, just as another Juliette had, but, inevitably, it did.

I turned my head to look at him. 'Let's get up and walk through Paris one last time.'

I saw his eyelids flutter. Knew he was awake. 'What, now?'

'Yes. Then we can see the dawn break.'

'You're crazy.'

'I know.'

'I think it's what I love about you the most.'

'That and many other things.'

I felt his arm around me tighten. 'Maybe we should just stay here instead.'

I wriggled out of his embrace, laughing. 'You're incorrigible. Plenty of time for that later.'

He sat up, topaz eyes heavy with desire. 'I hope so.'

My heart juddered, missed a beat. 'Come on. I want us to see the sun rise together.'

Outside, the streets were deserted, the city still slumbering. Pavements glittered, icy and treacherous under our feet, but we kept one another steady. Our breath formed plumes of white smoke as we talked, lapsing into a companionable silence now and then to stop and stare at the lightening sky, marine blue tinged with the faintest hint of apricot, the rooftops bathed in the same peachy glow. It was going to be a fine day. A good day for flying. I threw off the thought. We were still here, together.

We wandered through the Jardin des Tuileries, marvelling at the frost-tipped branches and twigs catching the rising sun.

'Prettier than diamonds,' I said.

Dan broke off a twig, fashioning it into a circlet, then dropped to one knee, ignoring the slush and the frozen ground. 'Marry me.'

'You know I can't.'

'Do it anyway.'

'Get up. You'll freeze to death.'

'Not until you say yes.'

He took my hand, pushing the circlet over my ring finger.

'If only it was that simple.'

'It is.'

He got to his feet and led me over to the octagonal pond.

'Look in there,' he commanded. 'What do you see?'

I could see our reflections silhouetted against the sky, the dawn lending us golden halos.

He smiled. 'See, even the sun approves.'

Another lingering kiss. When I opened my eyes again to

stare into his, I could see flecks of gold in them too, glistening with love and something else – regret maybe.

'I have to go back home,' he said. 'To see Gracie. I can't get back there for Christmas so I need to spend some time with her. I've been given indefinite leave.'

'Of course. You must be with your daughter. She needs you. Just as my children need me. I'll be resigning after Christmas so I won't be in London, but I'll let you know where we end up.'

He looked at me, a long, searching look, then dropped a kiss on my forehead. 'Merry Christmas, Juliette.'

'Merry Christmas, Dan.'

I smiled to hide the unbearable ache in my heart.

SIXTY-FIVE

25 DECEMBER 1944, ENGLAND

Christmas Day dawned bright and clear. The children were up with the lark, scampering downstairs to see what Père Nöel had left in their shoes. I could hear their excited cries and then the sound of my mother soothing them. I threw on the ancient bathrobe that hung behind the door of my room, a relic of some former occupant, and went to join in the fun.

'Look, Maman, a doll!' Natalie held up the cloth doll I'd found for her in a little shop near the Ritz. She'd cost a large portion of my meagre salary, but it was worth it to see my little girl's face.

'And I have a train set,' announced Nicolas, already assembling it.

'I wouldn't be surprised if he became an engineer,' I said to my mother, who was unwrapping the parcel I'd left for her, exclaiming as she saw the exquisite shawl that was exactly the right shade of blue, not too bright and yet not too pastel. I liked it because it was elegant and yet warm, just like my mother.

She smiled. 'It's perfect. Here, this is for you.'

I took the box she handed me. 'You didn't have to get me anything.'

'I've been wanting to give this to you for a long time,' she responded. 'Go on. Open it.'

Curious now, I ripped off the wrapping paper and lifted the lid of the box. Inside there was a gold necklace set with amethysts, peridots and pearls.

'It was mine,' said my mother, 'given to me by your grandmother, who was one of the first to join the French Union for Women's Suffrage. De Gaulle finally granted us women the vote this year so I think it's time you had it.'

I waited as she fastened the clasp around my neck and then took a look in the mirror in the hall. A woman stared back at me who I scarcely recognised, me and yet not me. Had I really changed that much? My eyes were older and, I hoped, wiser, although the corners of my mouth were sloping down. I forced them into a smile.

'Thank you,' I said. 'It's an honour, and I'll treasure this. I had no idea I came from a line of such strong women.'

'You should have guessed. Where do you think you got it from?'

'True.'

She handed me a coffee. 'Drink up. You look as if you need it.'

At that moment, there was a knock at the door.

'Could you get that please, Juliette? I need to attend to the cooking. It's probably one of the villagers needing something.'

I opened the door, ready to greet a stranger, caught my breath and clutched the robe a little tighter around me.

'Merry Christmas. May I come in?' asked Dan.

I ushered him into the drawing room, too stunned to

speak. The children looked up and gave him shy smiles that grew broader when he produced a pile of brightly wrapped packages from behind his back.

'An elf gave me these on the way here,' he said. 'Apparently Father Christmas dropped them by mistake when he meant to leave them for you.'

'Thank you.' Nicolas took his with an expression that was half scepticism and half hope. *He's growing up*, I thought. What the hell was Dan doing here?

'How did you find us?' I asked.

'I bribed Suzanne,' he deadpanned, looking me up and down. 'Nice robe,' he added.

I looked down at the worn woollen garment that was designed for a man much bigger than me, the unflattering beige set off by a black and red tartan pattern.

'I'll just go and get dressed,' I muttered. 'Maybe you could offer Dan a coffee?'

Maman was already fussing round him as I ran upstairs. *She knew*, I thought. *She knew he was coming*. Were they all in on it? This was a set-up. A conspiracy.

I tore a brush through my hair, splashed water on my face and attacked my teeth with another brush. A dab of lipstick, another of rouge and I was done, my hair twisted now into a chignon. Along with one of the dresses I'd brought back with me from Paris, a dove-grey Lanvin, I was wearing the necklace my mother had just given me, matching pearls at my ears. A hint of perfume completed the ensemble. I may have been ambushed, but I was dressed for battle.

Dan's eyes lit up when he saw me enter the drawing room, turning that warm honey gold I knew so well.

'You look wonderful,' he said.

'You're very pretty, Maman,' piped up Natalie in agreement.

My mother handed me a glass of champagne. 'Dan brought us this.'

'Oh did he?'

'I brought this for you,' he said, handing me a package. 'Go ahead – open it.'

I could feel all their eyes upon me as I ripped off the wrapping paper to reveal a Manila envelope. Inside, there was a bundle of airmail letters. I pulled one out, looking at the address on the envelope and then at Dan.

'Long story,' he said. 'You might want to read those later.'

I could feel the tears, treacherous, clotting in my throat. 'Thank you,' I whispered.

'I also took the liberty of bringing a turkey as your mother here was kind enough to invite me for lunch.'

I stared at him. 'A turkey?'

'It's traditional, right?'

'Where exactly did you get a turkey on Christmas morning? Come to that, when exactly did my mother invite you to lunch?'

'I acquired it from a farmer.'

He kept a completely straight face.

'I see. And the invitation?'

'We need some more wood for the fire,' said Maman. 'Why don't you two go and get some from the shed?'

I knew when I was being set up. I also knew when my mother was doing her best to divert attention from a tricky question.

'Come on then,' I said, throwing my coat over my dress and sticking my feet in a pair of boots.

'Can we come?' asked Nicolas.

'Yes, can we come?' echoed Natalie.

I helped them on with their coats, Dan bending to do up Natalie's buttons.

She beamed at him. 'I like you.'

'I like you too.'

Great. Now my own children were getting in on the act.

I stomped out the door, stopping short at the snowstorm that greeted us. Forget whirling, this was the real thing, falling thick and fast. The children charged into it with cries of delight, scooping up the snow in their mittened hands and flinging it at one another.

'The shed's here,' I said, tugging the door open to reveal neatly stacked logs, which I began to pile into the basket I'd brought.

Dan pulled the door to behind him so that we were inches apart, the smell of wood mingling with the warm, musky scent of him.

'You didn't just get that turkey this morning, did you?'

'I may have prearranged it.'

'When exactly did my mother invite you for Christmas?'

'She told me before they left Paris that I was welcome to join you if we made it back in time.'

'The thing is...' I began, but he placed that finger on my lips again.

'The thing is that I love you, Juliette, and you love me, so we should be together. That's all we need to know. Apart from the other thing, which is that you love what you do, you're brilliant at it and you should keep on doing it.'

The shed was smaller than it looked. Or maybe it was his proximity. All of a sudden, I felt trapped, as if there was nowhere to run.

'That's the final thing,' he said. 'You don't need to run

anymore. You're safe now, Juliette, so why not be safe with me?'

'Will you stop reading my mind?'

'Only if you stop being so easy to read.'

It would be so simple to close the gap between us. Just a matter of taking a single step.

I heard a giggle from outside.

'Wait a minute.'

I flung open the door to see my children running away, peals of laughter ringing from them as they ran. I scooped up a ball of snow in my hand and flung it after them, hitting Nicolas between his shoulder blades. He wheeled round, still laughing, and threw a snowball at me in turn. Within minutes, we were one giant snowball fight, Natalie darting around shrieking with joy, Nicolas ducking the snowballs that Dan hurled his way, me doing my best to duck them too until finally, breathless, I called a halt.

'Come on, children,' I said. 'Time to go back in and help your grandmother.'

'I want to stay out here with you,' wailed Natalie.

'We're coming in too,' said Dan.

Nicolas looked at him, his expression serious once more. 'Are you staying?'

'For lunch? Yes.'

'No, I mean forever.'

For once, Dan looked lost for words. Then Nicolas turned to me. 'What about you, Maman? Are you staying?'

'Here with you? Yes, of course.'

'No, I mean in your job. Because you should. I can take care of Grandmère and Natalie. I've done all right so far.'

Then he walked over to us, took my hand and Dan's and held them together.

'There now,' he said. 'Fixed that too.'

I looked down at him, at my little engineer, and then at Dan. 'I suppose you have. It looks like you'll be getting another sister too. One called Gracie.'

'Are you ever coming in?' called my mother. 'It's freezing out there.'

I held out my other hand to Nicolas who, in turn, took Natalie's. Together we walked, all four of us, into the embrace of the cottage, feeling the warmth from the fire, the sense of coming home.

Dan was right. It was time to stop running. I was here right now with the people I loved most in the world. All the people. They would still be here, waiting, while I was out there saving the world, Dan alongside me.

Outside, the snow kept falling faster and faster, but in here I could feel myself slowing, the demons that had driven me for so long receding into the distance, driven out by the love that flowed around and between us, a love that bound us together as one family. My family. My loves. My Dan.

A LETTER FROM AMANDA

Dear reader,

I want to say a huge thank you for choosing to read *Paris at First Light*. If you did enjoy it, and want to keep up to date with all my latest releases, just sign up at the following link. Your email address will never be shared and you can unsubscribe at any time.

www.bookouture.com/amanda-lees

The characters in this book, and the others in the series, are based on people who actually lived, loved, fought and died for our freedom as well as their own. I deliberately haven't given their real names out of respect for their privacy and that of their families as I have, of course, imagined much of what happened too.

What is certain is that their courage, daring and resourcefulness were astounding, as were many of their feats. The events that unfold in this story are all based on fact, with a touch of poetic licence here and there, because there is no need to invent the often unbelievable stories that emerge from war.

It's a time of extremes, of people falling in love at first sight because there may never be another chance, of making decisions knowing that death could be one unlucky step away and that, above all, life is for living. Many peoples' lives were cruelly cut short in the Second World War and I wanted to acknowledge them and their suffering too.

I wrote this book, as I did the first in the series, at a very strange time in my own life when I had enormous battles of my own to fight and win. What kept me going was thinking of the extraordinary people I got to know as real-life characters and then as my fictionalised versions. They truly did live by Churchill's maxim to 'never give in'. They were undaunted in the face of overwhelming odds, loyal to their friends and comrades in arms as well as their countries, and, above all, were true heroes and heroines in the most noble sense.

I think we need heroes and heroines now more than ever. We've been through a global pandemic, and many are facing great hardships, financial and otherwise. Knowing that others have gone before us and made it through unimaginable situations while remaining resolute can be a great help. It certainly is for me.

Beyond that, I wanted to show the way love blossomed even in the midst of these circumstances. So many great love stories started in wartime, not least because all pretence was stripped away and people realised they could lose it all, including one another, at any moment. Love really is what makes the world go round, even when that world is ripped apart. Perhaps even more so then.

My characters live with me every day, as does the world they inhabited. I've spent so long delving into their real lives, looking at photographs of who they were and what they wore and walking the streets of Paris in 1944 in my mind, then a very different city to the one I know now. I feel a real duty to tell their stories because they reflect the stories of so many who lived and died with the same bravery and passion for what was right, including members of my own family and, I'm sure, yours.

I hope you love them as much as I do and gain a glimpse into a world which, while rich in history and nostalgia, I pray none of us ever see again. There are many more adventures ahead for my four women and their cohorts. It would be wonderful to have you with us for those as well as for this one. Above all, we must never forget the real people behind these stories, what they sacrificed as well as what they gave us. It's a generation that have nearly all gone now. Let's keep them in our hearts and pass on the tales of what they did.

I hope you loved *Paris at First Light* and if you did, I would be very grateful if you could write a review. I'd love to hear what you think, and it makes such a difference helping new readers to discover one of my books for the first time.

I love hearing from my readers – you can get in touch on my Facebook page, through Twitter, Goodreads or my website.

Thanks,

Amanda

amandalees.com

facebook.com/AmandaLeesAuthor

twitter.com/amandalees

ACKNOWLEDGEMENTS

Writing and publishing a book is like raising a child – it takes a village. A very talented one. First, there is my agent and friend, Lisa, who knows what she wants and, more importantly, what other people want. To be a successful agent you need to be part literary witch and part hustler, with side helpings of exquisite taste and gut instinct. She has the lot. As well as an amazing posse in Patrick, Zoe, Jamie and Elena.

Then there is my brilliant editor, Susannah, and the team at Bookouture, who not only get my books out into the world but make sure they have gorgeous covers, are superbly produced and come in all kinds of formats, including audio. Behind the scenes, they crunch data, perform wizardry and weave marketing magic. Peta, Saidah, Kim, Noelle, Sarah, Jess, Jenny, Isobel, Alba, Alex, Ruth, Richard, Lauren, Marina and so many others including Laura, my copy-editor, you're all fabulous and if I've left anyone out, it's only because this is getting like a wedding speech.

I'm lucky enough to also have my fellow author buddies – Karin, Vanessa, Anne, Victoria, Lisa, Martyn, Susi, Anna, Diane, Vicky, Sam and, again, too many more to mention who have been endlessly supportive. As ever, there is my constant inspiration, my daughter. I love you, and I am so proud of you. Next, the friends and family who have been there for me through times dark and light – Julia and Phil, Andrew, Josa, Guy, Nina, Barb, Christian, Jackie and Sam,

Marianne and Margaret, Claire and, finally, John, who taught me something I needed to learn. Some of those you may also recognise among the names of the main characters.

Above all, thanks to the women and men who served, and gave their lives in service for, their countries and our freedom. We will never forget you.